James Paterson, William Dunbar

The Life and Poems of William Dunbar

James Paterson, William Dunbar

The Life and Poems of William Dunbar

ISBN/EAN: 9783337408510

Printed in Europe, USA, Canada, Australia, Japan

Cover: Foto ©Raphael Reischuk / pixelio.de

More available books at **www.hansebooks.com**

THE
LIFE AND POEMS

OF

WILLIAM DUNBAR.

BY

JAMES PATERSON,

AUTHOR OF "WALLACE AND HIS TIMES," "THE SEMPILLS OF BELTREES,"
ETC.

"The excellent poet, unrivalled by any which Scotland
has produced."—SCOTT.

EDINBURGH:
WILLIAM P. NIMMO, 2 ST DAVID STREET.
LONDON: SIMPKIN, MARSHALL, AND CO.
1860.

PREFACE.

LITTLE by way of preface, and still less of apology, is necessary in presenting such a work as this to the public. It has long been a desideratum. Hardly, since the days of "The Evergreen," has any portion of the poems of Dunbar found their way through the press in a style which the public could appreciate. Throughout broad Scotland scarcely a vestige of his works is to be found, unless in the libraries of the wealthy who have a taste for antiquarian literature. Even the very "chap" press seems to have been afraid of grappling with the antiquated dress in which the beauties of the poet were hidden; and thus he has been shut out of those famous resting-places, the "boles" of the farmer's and peasant's ingles, where, in days gone by, selections from the writings of our best authors might often be consulted. As illustrative of this, it may be stated that BURNS—certainly the most intelligent and greatest of Scotland's peasant-born—had not, apparently, an opportunity of making himself acquainted with the works of Dunbar. *Ramsay* and *Fergusson* he knew and studied; but in his day " The Evergreen " had become so rare as to be limited to a class, so that he was not aware of THE GIANT, as Crabbe styled our poet, that had gone before him. The name of Dunbar, no doubt, is extensively known, but his poems are not; and it is with the view of rendering them accessible to all, both as to price and intelligibility, that the present publication has been undertaken.

Probably our greatest risk of censure lies in the medium course adopted as to the orthography of the poems. Those who stickle for the original dress will declaim against any deviation from it, while the popular reader will possibly be equally dissatisfied that we have not gone far enough in wholly discarding the old garb. We have attempted, perhaps, what is impossible—to please, in so far, all parties. A complete modernisation of Dunbar could not be accomplished without rendering it a paraphrase; and as all attempts of this kind, as in the Minstrel's " Wallace," and Ramsay's " Gentle Shepherd," have deservedly proved failures, such a mutilation never once occurred to us. What we have done is simply to modernise such words as are generally understood by ordinary readers, but

rendered obscure in consequence of their antiquated
spelling, and so to smooth the way to persons not
in the habit of perusing the works of old authors.
There was no necessity, for example, for continu-
ing to spell common words like *when* in the old
form of *quhen;* but there were others, such as
culroun, which could not be altered unless by sub-
stituting words of similar import.   Now, this is
what we have not done, and never intended doing,
because we would thereby have robbed the author
of that peculiar idiom which constitutes one of the
most interesting features of the olden poets. What
we have done is simply to render ordinary words
more intelligible, and explain such as have become
obsolete.

It may be necessary to remark, further, that in
Dunbar's time there seems to have been no fixed
standard of pronunciation. Words were frequently
lengthened or contracted, according to the measure
and rhythm. The rule we have followed in circumstances of this kind is very simple, as one or two
illustrations will explain :—

> " Quhen that I schawe to him your markis,
> He turnis to me again, and barkis."

These lines we print thus :—

> " When that I shaw to him your marks,
> He turns to me again, and barks."

We omit the *i* in *markis, turnis,* and *barkis,* because the measure does not require it, and these words could not have been so pronounced in the days of Dunbar. But there are other cases, again, in which the measure absolutely demands an additional syllable, and then the *i* is retained, as, for example :—

> " The street*is* were all hung with tapestrie ;"

Or as—

> " When March had with variand wind*is* past,
>   And April had, with her silver shours."

In the first of these lines the *i* is not only necessary in wind*is*, but the word *variand* must be pronounced with three syllables, *va-ri-and,* distinctly enunciated. So in the second line the *i* is not necessary in *shouris,* because the word April was pronounced *Aperil.*

But it is needless to load the memory with rules. The intelligent reader will easily understand why the same words are sometimes printed differently, and with more syllables in one case than another ; while the measure and rhythm will guide him generally where no special rule is indicated.

*_** *It has not been considered necessary to append a* GLOSSARY *to this volume, the more difficult words and obscure passages being amply explained in foot-notes.*

CONTENTS.

————

CONTENTS. ix

THE FLYTING OF DUNBAR AND KENNEDY.

LIFE AND POEMS

OF

WILLIAM DUNBAR.

DUNBAR, the Poet-laureate, it may be said, of the Court of James the Fourth, is admitted by the best authorities, both English and Scotch, to have been a poet of extraordinary merit, and that too at a period when there were many able followers of the Muse. He has been compared with Chaucer, less pathetic, but richer in the variety and quality of his imagination, humour, and powers of description. His pieces are not so lengthy as those of Chaucer; but it is generally allowed that a portion only of his writings has been preserved—the smaller and more epigrammatic.

The history of Dunbar and his works is, in short, a melancholy illustration of the havoc to which the literature of Scotland has been subjected, in consequence of the invasions, burnings, and destruction committed by "our auld enemies of England," and the civil broils arising out of our own feuds. The Reformation, too, however much it tended to the

national advancement otherwise, must have swept
away much of the early writings of the country.
With the down-pulling of the monasteries—those
rookeries, as Knox expressed it, where the rooks
found shelter—must have perished numerous evi-
dences of the culture which shed a lustre on the
close of the fifteenth and beginning of the sixteenth
centuries. The devouring flames, kindled by an
infuriated mob, destroyed in a few days the work
of ages, which would have been now the delight
and glory of the land. That the cartularies of the
larger religious houses did not wholly disappear,
we owe in some measure to the cupidity of the
neighbouring barons, who failed not to procure a
long lease or assignation of the best of the Church
lands, upon easy terms, from the despairing monks
prior to the final overturning. In this manner,
and by Crown grants, the monastical charters
frequently found their way to the charter-chests of
the barons, and many of them have fortunately
been preserved.*

Of the numerous poets of the reign of James
the Fourth, with the exception of Dunbar, Walter
Kennedy, and Gawin Douglas, scarcely anything
is known beyond the fact that they existed, and

* Some years ago, for example, the Earl of Panmure presented
the charters of the monastery of Arbroath to the authorities, to
be preserved in the town's archives. They are beautifully written, on fine vellum, and bound in three volumes octavo. They
have been since printed, adding another to the number of our
club books.

scarcely a line of their inditing has been preserved. But for the MS. collections of Bannatyne, Maitland, Reidpath, and Asloane, to whose gratuitous labour and love of letters Scotland can never be too grateful, the greater portions of even the works of Dunbar would have been lost. No doubt, "The Thrissill and the Rois," "The Goldyn Targe," "The Flyting" of Dunbar and Kennedy, and "The Lament for the Makaris," were printed in the time of the authors, by Chepman and Myllar, the first printers in Scotland, and might have had a chance of survival in some obscure corner; but such was the effect of the religious furor into which the nation was thrown by the first and second Reformations, not to speak of the Puritan war under Cromwell, that the very name of Dunbar and his contemporaries, as well as most of the profane writers and their writings, had been studiously set aside and forgotten. It was even attempted to wed favourite airs to "godly sangs," so that no vestige of the popular lyrical muse of Scotland should remain.

Until the time of Allan Ramsay, no attempt had been made to evoke the spirit of Scottish poesy from her unwholesome slumber. Ramsay was not only a poet himself, but did much to revive the taste of the people for the ancient muse. This was chiefly done through the medium of "The Evergreen," a collection of Scots poems written before 1600, published in 1724. The Bannatyne

MS. was the source from whence Ramsay drew his stores; but he had not sufficient experience in deciphering the antiquated hand in which it is written, and took considerable liberties with the original. Still, by his exertions, the names of Dunbar, and other poets of the olden time, were partially restored to popular favour, and the taste revived for what was national in poetry, in place of the cold, classical phantasies in which the learned indulged towards the close of the seventeenth and beginning of the eighteenth centuries. To this revival by Allan Ramsay, besides his own inimitable "Gentle Shepherd," we probably owe in a great measure the national outpouring of a Ferguson, a Burns, and a Scott.

Lord Hailes was the next to follow in the wake of Ramsay, in 1770, by a volume entitled "Ancient Scottish Poems. Published from the MS. of George Bannatyne, 1568." He was more critical, and no doubt better learned than his predecessor, whose liberties, or errors, he fails not to expose, though he himself falls into mistakes, rather surprising in one apparently so wary. Notwithstanding, Lord Hailes generally exhibits both good taste and judgment in his renderings of obscure phrases, and the admirers of ancient Scottish literature are, in no small degree, indebted to him. His glossary served as a good aid to Dr Jamieson, while labouring at his truly national work, the "Dictionary of the Scottish Language;" and his example stimulated other labourers, such as Pinkerton, in the same field. It remained, however, for Mr David Laing, of the Signet Library, to collect and publish not only all the poems known to have been written by Dunbar, but such as are ascribed to him. In the performance of this task, which he accomplished in 1834, he admits the obligation he owes to Lord Hailes, and says,—" It has afforded me much satisfaction in having been thus enabled to follow the footsteps of an editor, who, for learning, research, and judgment, was one of the brightest ornaments of our country during the last century."

Those who preceded Mr Laing only ventured to give *selections* from the poems. By printing the whole he, no doubt, conferred a boon on the curious; but some of them are so deeply tinged with the proverbially " high-kilted " manners of the age, that they might well have been spared, more espe cially as those so defiled are by no means remarkable as emanations of genius. The reverse, in fact, is the case. " The Tua Maryit Wemen and the Wedo," so gross as to place it outside the pale of all respectable homes, is chiefly remarkable, because it is composed in alliterative blank verse, a style not known to have been used in Scotland at the time; and because of the extreme immorality of certain ladies who birl at the wine very freely under the greenwood tree. Occasionally the author shews his inherent powers of description, but, as a whole, it has no pretensions to high poetical merit. By

way of illustration, we may here quote a few passages. It begins, and we give it in the original
spelling—

" Upon the midsumer evin, mirriest of nichtis,
I muvit furth allane, neir as midnicht wes past,
Besyde ane gudlie grene garth,* full of gay flouris,
Hegeit, of ane huge hicht, with hawthorne treis ;
Quhairon ane bird, on ane branche, so birst out his
    notis
That never ane blythfullar bird was on the beuche
    harde :
Quhat through the sugarat sound of his sang glaid,
And through the savour sanative of the sueit flouris,
I drew in derne to the dyk to dirkin efter myrthis ; †
The dew donkit ‡ the daill, and dynarit the foulis.§
" I hard, under ane holyn ‖ hevinlie green heuit,
Ane hie speiche, at my hand, with hautand ¶ wourdis ;
With that in haist to the hege so hard I inthrang
That I was heildit ** with hawthorne and with heynd ††
    leivis :

---

* Garden.

† To grope in darkness after mirth.   ‡ Wet.

§ Mr Laing explains this to mean that " the birds made a
cheerful din or noise ;" but this can hardly be the interpretation,
since it was past midnight, when all birds are mute, save, perhaps, the nightingale. Nor does Jamieson's " Dictionary" help
us to a meaning. *Dynarit* seems to mean *silenced*. " The dew
wet the dale, and *silenced* the birds.

‖ The holly grows to a great height and thickness. A fine
specimen of the growth of such trees may be seen at Niddrie-
Merschell, near Craigmillar.

¶ Haughty.   ** Covered.

†† Perhaps hindberry leaves.

Throw pykis of the plet thorne I presandlie luikit,
Gif ony persoun wald approche within that plesand
    garding.
 "I saw three gay ladeis sit in ane grene arbeir,
All grathit in to garlandis of fresche gudelie flouris ;
So glitterit as the gold wer thair glorius gilt tressis,
Quhill all the gressis did gleme of the glaid hewis ;
Kemmit was thair cleir hair, and curiouslie sched
Attour thair schulderis doun schyre, schyning full
    bricht ;
With curches, cassin thame abone, of kirsp cleir and
    thin :
Thair mantillis grein war as the gress that grew in May
    sessoun ;
Fetrit with thair quhyt fingaris about thair sydis :
Off ferliful fyne favour was thair faceis meik,
All full of flurist fairheid, as flouris in June ;
Quhyt, seimlie, and soft, as the sweit lillies ;
New up spred upon spray, as new spynist* rose,
Arrayit ryallie about with mony rich wardour,
That Nature, full nobillie, annamalit fine with flouris
Off alkin hewis under hevin, that ony heynd knew ;
Fragrant, all full of fresche odour, fynest of smell,
Ane marbre tabill coverit wes befoir thai three ladeis,
With ryale cowpis upon rawis full of ryche wynis :
And of thir fair wlonkes,† with tua that weddit war
    with lordis,
Ane wes ane wedow, I wist, wantoun of laitis.
And, as thai talket at the tabill of mony taill funde,

---

* Full blown.   † Women of rank.

> They wauchtit at the wicht wyne, and warit out wourdis;
> And syne thai spak more spedelie, and sparit no
> materis."

The scene here, past midnight at midsummer, when no more than a hazy darkness prevails, is beautifully described. The picture is complete; and fancy at once portrays the group, " wauchting at the wicht wyne." From this specimen the reader will easily comprehend what the alliterative style is. Take the fourth line—

> " Quhairon ane *bird* on ane *bransche,* so *birst* out his
> notis."

Birst, as applied to the singing of a bird, strikes the ear as somewhat harsh. It is used for the sake of alliteration; yet it is perfectly correct. The bird so *pressed* out his notes.

The widow starts the conversation—

> " Bewrie, said the wedo, ye weddit wemen ying,
> Quhat mirth ye fand in maryage, sen ye war menis
> wyffis;
> Reveill gif ye rewit that rakles conditioun?
> Or gif that ever ye loffit leyd upone lyf mair
> Nor thame that ye your fayth hes festint for ever?
> Or gif ye think, had ye chois, that ye wald cheis better?
> Think yet it nocht ane blist band that bindis so fast
> That none unto it adew may say bot the deithe alane?"

Then the ladies, one after the other, relate their experiences. The first is sick of her old " wallidrag."

" God gif matrimony were made to mell for ane yeir !
    It war bot monstrous to be mair, but gif our myndis
        plesit :
    It is agane the law of luif, of kynd, and of nature,
    Togiddir hartis to strene,* that stryveis with uther :
    Birdis hes ane better law na bernis be meikill,†
    That ilk yeir, with new joy, joyis ane maik."‡

The second married lady follows up in a still
more fierce denunciation of her husband, whom she
describes as young, but wasted by a debauched life—

    " He is for ladyis in luf a richt lusty schadow ;"

and blames her friends for casting her away on
" sic a craudoune."

" Anone quhen this amyable had endit hir speche,
    Loudly lauchand the laif allowit hir mekle :
    Thir gay wiffis maid game amang the grene leiffis ;
    Thai drank, and did away dule, under derne bewis ;
    Thai swapit of the sueit wyne, thai swan quit of hewis,
    Bot all the pertlyar in plane thai put out thair vocis."

The widow then took up the tale, by admitting
that she was a shrew from the beginning, but full of
dissimulation, so that people thought her a saint—

" I schaw you, sisters in schrift,§ I wes a schrew evir,
    Bot I wes schene in my schrowd, an schew me innocent ;
    And thought I dour wes, and dane, dispitois, and bald,
    I wes dissymblit suttelly in a sanctis liknes :

---

* Strengthen.   † Bernis that are meikle-men.
‡ Mate.   § Confession.

I semyt sober, and sueit, and sempill without fraud,
Bot I couth sexty dissaif that suttillar wer haldin."

Her story is a very depraved one. She had been twice married, and both husbands loved her, so well did she manage her part. The first was "ane hair* hogeart:"

"Weil couth I claw his cruke bak, and keme his cowit noddill."

Her second husband was "a merchand myghti of gudis," but of middle age, and of less noble blood than herself, upon which she rung the changes so as to bring him thoroughly under her rule—

"Quhen I the cur had all clene, and him our cummyn haill,
I crew abone that cradone, as cok that were victoir."

Still she modified her dislike, until she had "gottin his biggingis to [her] barne, and his burrow landis;" and "quhen he had warit all on [her] his welth, and his substance," then she let loose her long bottled-up dislike, dressing her own children "like barronis sonnis, and maid bot fulis of the fry of his first wyf," at the same time banishing from her "boundis his brether ilk ane." And now, having *erded* him also, she is on the look-out for a third husband. The two married wives thanked her for "her soverane teching."

* Hoary.

" Than culit thai thair mouthis with confortable drinkis ;
And carpit full cummerlik, with cop going round."

The poet then describes the breaking up of the
company in the same glowing spirit displayed in
the introduction—

" Thus draif thai our that deir night, with danceis full
noble,
Quhill that the day did up daw, and dew donkit the
flouris ;
The morow myld wes and meik, the mavis did sing,
And all remuffit the myst, and the meid smellit ;
Silver schouris doune schuke, as the schene cristall,
And birdis schoutit in schaw, with thair schill notis ;
The goldin glitter and gleme so gladit thair hertis,
Thai maid a glorious glee amang the grene bewis.
The soft souch of the swyr,* and soune of the stremys,
The sueit savour of the sward, and singing of foulis,
Myght comfort ony creatur of the kyn of Adam ;
And kindill agane his curage thocht it were cold sloknyt.
" Than rais thir ryall roisis, in thair riche wedis,
And rakit hame to thair nest, through the rise † blumys ;
And I all prevely past to a plesand arber,
And with my pen did report thair pastance most mery."

With much archness the poet concludes—

" Of thir three wantoun wiffiis, that I haif writtin heir,
Quhilk wald ye waill to your wif, gif ye suld wed one ?"

In printing the poems of Dunbar as full as he
found them, Mr Laing has shewn great research, if

---

* The neck or opening to a valley.   † Brushwood.

not equal accuracy, and no doubt he has his reward in the approval and thanks of the more rigidly
antiquarian world.

We do not, however, mean to follow his footsteps. Having carefully selected our material, and
collated the doubtful passages with the Bannatyne
MS., we have excluded the more indelicate pieces,
and so riddled the explanatory annotations of
Hailes and others as to bring the work within
something like its natural dimensions. At the
same time, we by no means wish it to be understood that Dunbar was immoral. On the contrary,
there is every reason to believe that he was comparatively an amiable person. His looseness of
language, and, it may be, of conduct in some
instances, was the fault of the age, and by that
standard it is but right that he should be judged.
But there is no reason why the blemishes of bygone
times should be repeated in the present; and still less
that, because of these objectionable poems—only
one or two in number—the remainder should be
shut out from that popularity to which their high
merit entitles them. In this spirit the present
work has been undertaken, so as at once to supply
a moderately-priced, intelligible, and accurate edition of the poems of one of the greatest of our
olden poets—the BURNS, as he may be styled, of
the fifteenth and sixteenth centuries.

And that they may the more readily find their
way to public favour, we have been at much pains

so to modernise the orthography, that the reader
may have little more difficulty in their perusal than
he would experience with almost any of our modern Scottish poets. And this, we flatter ourselves,
has been accomplished without in any way marring
the peculiarities in language or style of the author.
Where the words are obsolete, the old spelling has
been adhered to, with explanatory notes. We know
that the mere literary antiquary will declaim against
this liberty, but it is no reason why, because of his
humour, the beauties of our ancient poets should
be locked up from the masses. As well might
there be no translations from the dead languages,
that all might be compelled to read in the original,
or remain without a knowledge of ancient literature. It is surely sufficient for the student of history, of language, or of literature, that such writings
do exist in their original form, and may be consulted at convenience, without compelling all to
follow his example, or be deprived of one of the
greatest pleasures of which an intelligent mind can
be susceptible—a knowledge of what the genius of
his country has provided for his instruction and
gratification.

The research of all the annotators and biogra-
phers of WILLIAM DUNBAR, it may well be remarked, has done very little to penetrate the
obscurity in which the wars, the feuds, and the
Calvinism of the past have involved his memory.
Beyond the fact, for which Mr Laing must get

credit, that his name occurs in the old register of the University of St Andrews as one of the *determinantes*, or Bachelors of Arts, in St Salvator's College, in 1477, and again in 1479, as having taken his degree of Arts, scarcely a single iota has been added beyond what his own pen and that of his poetical contemporary, Kennedy, supplies. As it required three years' attendance at college before a student was entitled to rank among the *determinantes*, Mr Laing concludes, on the calculation as in our own times, that Dunbar must then have "had at least attained fifteen or sixteen years of age," thus dating his birth about 1460. But the nature of his remonstrances with James IV., his royal patron in after life, if they are to be viewed in any other light than tolerated exaggerations, would lead us to believe that he had been born several years earlier.

From what Dunbar says, in "The Flyting" with Kennedy, as to his making "fairar Inglis" with his *Lothian* hips than he could "blabbar with his Carrik lippis," it may be inferred that he was born in Lothian; and the supposition has been carried so far as to connect him with the *Dunbars of Beill*, almost the only branch of the Earls of March who survived the attainder of that family by James I. "Magistro Willielmo de Dunbar," son of "Patrick of Dunbar of Bele," appears in a deed dated 3d July 1440. This *Maister William* was too old to be the poet himself, and too young to be his father,

though he may have been his uncle, or some near
relation. But whether he was of the Bele family
or not, Kennedy, in " The Flyting," is careful to
shew that, while a descendant of Cospatrick of
Dunbar, who had betrayed Scotland, he had no
immediate connexion with the Dunbars of Westfield :—

" Deulbeir hes nocht ado with ane Dunbar,
    The Erle of Murray bure that surname rycht,
  That evir trew and constant to the kingis grace war,
    And of that kin cam *Dunbar of Westfield*, knycht ;
    That successioun is hardy, wyse, and wicht,
  And hes na thing ado now with thee, devill ;
  But Deulbeir is thy kin, and kennis thee weith,
    And hes in hell for thee ane chalmer dycht."

Thus there was no other branch of the Dunbars
of any note, save that of *Beill*, from whom the
poet could be descended, and possibly he *was*
descended from them ; but if Kennedy is good as
an authority in one way, he must be equally so in
another. Elsewhere, in reference to Dunbar's birth,
he says :—

" Wanthriven *funling*, that Natour made ane *yrle*."

Yrle means a dwarf ; so we are to understand that
the poet was not only of doubtful parentage, but
personally of dwarfish stature. At all events, we
may conclude that, whatever branch of the Dunbars
he sprang from, they had by no means escaped the
ruin which so richly befell the traitorous house of

Dunbar. Although " The Flyting " is to be considered as a mere trial of rhyming skill in banter, without enmity on either side, yet it is evident that unless the statements of the parties were based on something like reality, they would have fallen pointless.

Of the educational progress of Dunbar, nothing is known beyond the fact that he studied at St Andrews, and took the degree of Master of Arts in 1479. That, early in life, he became a friar of the order of St Francis, or Grey Friars, a branch of whom, the *Observantines*, was established in Edinburgh by James I.,* we know from his own statement, in " The Visitation of St Francis : "—

> " Gif evir my fortoun wes to be a freir
>   The dait thairof is past full mony a yeir ;
>   For in to every lusty toun and place,
>   Off all Yngland, from Berwick to Kalice,
>   I haif in to thy habeit maid gud cheir.

> " In freiris weid full fairly haif I fleichit,
>   In it haif I in pulpet gone and preichit
>   In Derntoun kirk, and eik in Canterberry
>   In it I past at Dover oure the ferry,
>   Throw Piccardy, and thair the peple teichit."

Dunbar had evidently no relish for the life of a friar, having long before abandoned the garb which his tempter, the devil, in the form of St Francis, urged him to resume. With arch humour he says :

* The present Greyfriars' Church still keeps in memory the order of St Francis.

> " In haly legendis haif I herd allevin,
> Ma sanctis of bischoppis, nor freiris, be sic sevin ;
> Off full few freiris that hes bene sanctis I reid ;
> Quhairfoir ga bring to me ane bischoppis weid,
> Gife evir thow wald my saule yeid unto hevin."

It is no doubt to this period in the poet's life that Kennedy alludes in " The Flyting : "—

> " Fra Attrik Forrest furth ward to Dumfreiss
> Thow beggit with ane pardoun in all kirkis."

The fact of his having acted in the capacity of a pardoner is all but admitted by Dunbar, and the circumstance, although he had not himself so frequently alluded in his poems to the poverty of his position, sufficiently indicates the want of family patrimony. And yet he says, in one of his remonstrances to the king :—

> " I wes in yowth on nureiss knee
> Dandely ! bischop, dandely !
> And quehn that age now dois me greif,
> Ane sempill vicar I can nocht be ;"

which would imply that the prospects of his childhood were such as to warrant the expectation of promotion in the Church. The birth and parentage of Dunbar are thus involved in much mystery.

It is not known for a certainty when he came to be employed by the king. He is supposed to have been in the embassy to France, which sailed, under the Earl of Bothwell, from Berwick in 1491. An item in the treasurer's accounts, dated 16th July of that year, is believed to refer to the poet :—" Item, till a prest that wrayt the instrumentis and oderis letteris, that past with the imbassitouris in France, 36s." It is very probable that Dunbar was the priest referred to. Indeed, he could hardly have entered the royal service at an earlier period, as James only ascended the throne in 1488, and would, in 1491, be nineteen years of age. The name of the ship in which the embassy sailed was, as stated in the treasurer's accounts, the *Katryn*, and Kennedy, in " The Flyting," in allusion to Dunbar's going abroad, says—

" Into the *Katherene* thow maid ane fowll Kahute ;"

a strong coincidence in proof of the fact that the poet actually was attached to the embassy which sailed in that vessel.

It is of some importance that this point should be understood, because upon it turns most of the few known incidents in the life of Dunbar. It would appear that, when " The Flyting " was written, or at least a portion of it, he was abroad. He says to Kennedy :—

" Or thow durst move thy mind malitius
    Thow saw the saill abone my heid updraw ;
But Eolus full woid, and Neptunus,
    Mirk and moneless, wes met with wind and waw,
    And mony hundreth myle hyne cowd us blaw
By Holland, Seland, Zetland, and Northway coist,

> In desert place quhair we wer famist aw ;
> Yet come I hame, fals baird, to lay thy boist."

Upon the strength of these statements—not thoroughly understood apparently—but chiefly on the coincidence of the name of the vessel, Laing at first concluded that " The Flyting " must have been written "a few years after 1491," and to render this possible, he made Dunbar remain in Paris after the return of the Scottish embassy, that he might fulfil the commissions with which he supposed him to have been intrusted, not only to the court of France, but to other crowned heads. It is clear from Kennedy that his opponent *was* abroad at the time he wrote his last reply :—

> " Thow hes ane tome purss, I haif steidis and takkis,
>   Thow tynt culter, I haif culter and pleuch ;
> For substance and geir thow hes a widdy teuch
>   On Mont Falcone,* about thy craig to rax.
> And yit Mont Falcone gallowis is our fair,
>   For to be fylit with sic ane frutless face ;
> *Cum hame,* and hing on our gallowis of Air.

*　*　*　*　*　*

> " Because that Scotland of thy begging irkis,
> Thow schainis in France to be a knycht of the feild ;

*　*　*　*　*　*

> " Thow may nocht pass Mont Bernard for wyld beistis,
>   Nor win throw Mont Scarpy for the snaw ;

---

* In Paris, where criminals used to be hung.

> Mont Nicholace, Mont Godard thee arrestis,
>   Sic beis of brigand blindis thame with ane blaw.
> In Paris with thy maister, Burreaw,
> Abyd." . . . .

In France Dunbar evidently was when Kennedy wrote this, but that Dunbar's last voyage to the Continent occurred in 1491 is out of the question.

It is known that the Earl of Bothwell's embassy, which sailed in July 1491, returned in the end of November following. Laing presumed that Dunbar was left in Paris, " for the purpose of crossing the Alps in the further prosecution of ' the erandis' of his royal master;" but it is not likely that one so little known at court as to be designated "a prest that wrayt the instrumentis and oderis letteris," should be so hastily intrusted with the king's ambassadorial business. Indeed, there was hardly time, from the sailing of the *Katryn* in July 1491 till her return in November of the same year, to have experienced so much peril and fatigue, and in July the weather is seldom so " mirk and moneless " as Dunbar describes. According to his own statement, he must have been abroad many times on the " kingis erandis." In his " Complaint to the King " he says :—

> " Gif I be ane of thay my sell,
>   Throw all regiounes hes tein hard tell,
>   Of quhilk my wryting witness beiris."

And in another address to his majesty, on the often

reiterated subject of his "small reward," he gives us some notion of the various countries he had visited :—

> "Nocht I say this, by this countrie,
> France, Ingland, Ireland, Almanie,
> Bot als be Italie and Spaine,
> Quhilk to consider is ane paine."

That "The Flyting" was written at several periods, with considerable intervals between, seems beyond question. In reply to Kennedy's first assault, Dunbar, alluding, as we have seen, to his having been cast away on the northern coasts, says—

> "Yet *come* I hame, fals baird, to lay thy boist."

At whatever time this voyage had taken place, he had come home, and wrote his reply while in Scotland; but before Kennedy had again buckled on his armour for another tilt, Dunbar had gone to France upon some new mission, and was there, as already shewn, when the contest was brought to a close.

For these and other reasons we think "The Flyting" could not be written so early as "a few years after 1491." Kennedy speaks of Dunbar's sailing in the *Katryn* as having occurred twenty years before their poetical feud :—

> "The dirt cleivis till hir towis this twenty yeir ;"

a passage which Mr Laing found necessary to

explain away as meaning twenty years *to come.*
But although necessary to coincide with his then
theory, this is not the true reading. Were we to
view it in its literal sense, however, and taking it
for granted that the voyage referred to by Kennedy
actually occurred in 1491, it would bring the composition of " The Flyting " down to 1511, which
we know could not be, as it was printed in 1508 ;
but suppose the verses to have been published soon
after they were finished, and their popularity seems
to indicate that this was the case, there would be
little impropriety in speaking, in 1506 or 1507, of
a thing having lasted " this twenty yeir " which
originated in 1491, at least fifteen years before ;
and it is evident that in passing from the previous
topics, as to Dunbar's shaping " in France to be a
knycht of the field," he drops the present for something that is past.

Mr James Chalmers, nephew of the author of
" Caledonia," to both of whom Mr Laing expresses
his obligations, was of opinion that " The Flyting "
was " not composed till between 17th March
1503-4, when Dunbar said his *first mass* in the
king's presence, and the summer of 1505, when
Stobo is supposed to have died." Mr Chalmers
proceeded on the idea that Dunbar had not been a
priest for any length of time before he said his first
mass, and therefore the question of Kennedy—

" Ane benefice quha wald gif sic ane beist?"
would have been inappropriate prior to the 17th

March 1503-4. Mr Laing, however, met this by stating that he must have been in holy orders when he travelled as a mendicant friar, because Dunbar himself says he then preached both in England and France, and that " the terms of the grant of his pension, in August 1500, shew equally clearly that he was qualified to accept, and that he expected some benefice." This is, to some extent, true; but if " The Flyting " was written during the absence of Dunbar, when on his voyage in the *Katryn*, the question could not have been put with so much pungency as after his pension from the crown, which was to continue until his promotion to a benefice.

In the notes to " The Flyting," Mr Laing extends the supposed period of its composition to between 1492 and 1497, without assigning any reason for this change of opinion. It can hardly be surmised that Dunbar remained abroad from the sailing of the *Katryn*, in July 1491 to 1497, which one would require to do in order to give Mr Laing's argument any weight. Again, in an additional note, referring to Mr Chalmers's suggestion, he says, " Whether Dunbar's admission to the highest order of priesthood in the Romish Church was immediately preceding the date of his performing mass in the king's presence, cannot be ascertained; . . . but this at least qualified him to officiate as king's chaplain, when attending James in his occasional visits to different parts of the country." In other words, Mr Laing admits that " admission to the highest order of priesthood " was a necessary qualification before being presented to a benefice, and the probability is, that Dunbar was not so qualified any length of time before the 17th March 1504–5.

But we are not left altogether to surmise in this matter. Dunbar, after having *come home* to lay his false boast, says of Kennedy :—

> " *In till ane glen* thow hes, owt of repair,
> Ane laithly luge that wes the lippir mennis."

Now, *Walter Kennedy*, the poet, was the sixth son of Gilbert, first Baron Kennedy, and the ancestor of the *Kennedies* of GLENTIG, in Carrick, which property he acquired from John Wallace of Glentig, and had a charter of the lands 8th December 1504. There can be no doubt that the above lines refer sarcastically to GLENTIG, the newly-acquired laird-ship of Kennedy, otherwise there would have been no point in the sarcasm ; and if so, it shews that even Dunbar's principal part of " The Flyting " must have been written after December 1504. It is true that the pension granted to Dunbar was paid very regularly twice a year, from 1500 down-wards, during the reign of James IV. ; but there was ample time for him to have visited not only France, but other foreign countries during the in-termediate periods. Nor can it be supposed that all the services to the king, for which he prayed so frequently for guerdon, were performed before 1500, when his small pension of £10 Scots was first obtained.

Nor are we to suppose that Dunbar was so far advanced in years between 1504 and 1508, when "The Flyting" was printed, as to be incapable of the spirit it displays. Lord Hailes spoke in ignorance of facts in his remarks on the "Lament for the Makaris," written at the latest in 1507–8, for the poem was printed in 1508. "We see the once gay Dunbar," say his lordship, "now advanced in years, deprived of his joyous companions, and probably jostled out of court by other wits younger and more fashionable. This 'Lament' has not the spirit of some of his earlier compositions. The solemn burden, '*Timor mortis conturbat me*,' seems to shew under what impressions the aged poet composed this general elegy. It may serve as a proper introduction to his religious poems." The spirited and beautiful poem, "The Thrissill and the Rois," was written in 1503. Dunbar could hardly have been so much depressed by age in 1507—only four years afterwards—as to be capable of only indulging in such poems as the "Lament." If born in 1460, as supposed by Mr Laing, he would be no more than forty-seven in 1507, and therefore by no means an aged person. His genius, however, was capable of almost every range of feeling—the pathetic, the lively, and the humorous; and if he was solemn in the "Lament," it was because the subject was solemn, and he himself in bad health at the time :—

> " I that in heill wes and glaidness,
>   Am trublit now with gret seikness."

There can be no doubt that many of his most humorous court ditties were written after this, and his frequent allusions to his age and services, as in his " Petition of the Grey Horse, Auld Dunbar," must be taken with a caution—poetical, but not strictly true.

It would be impossible to arrange the poems of Dunbar in anything like chronological order. They may, however, with some degree of propriety, be classed under two different periods—the period before and after his retention at court. Though no doubt frequently employed in the capacity of secretary to the Scottish embassies before 1500, he was not recognised as a familiar attendant in the royal household until that time. Much of the poetry of Dunbar—at least what of it has been preserved—has reference to the court, and that portion, of course, can easily be identified as belonging to the second period into which we propose to divide his writings. All such pieces as cannot be so identified, we shall place in the first. It is very clear that he had early imbibed a love for the muses. He himself says, in his " Thrissill and the Rois," written in 1503 :—

> " Yit nocht incressis thy curage to indyt,
>   Quhois hairt sum tyme hes glaid and blisfull bene,
>   Sangis to mak undir the levis grene."

Chaucer, the father of the English language, as well as of English poetry, had been studied with much devotion by Dunbar. In his " Goldyn Targe " he describes him as " rose of rhetoris all." And in some of his earlier pieces, such as " The Tua Maryit Wemen and the Wedo," there are evident traces of imitation. But in playfulness and flexibility of genius, the scholar is admitted, by good judges, to have surpassed the master. In pathos he alone is deficient—at least there is no evidence of his having tried his powers in assailing the heart. Reason and humour were the chief supports upon which he leaned.

There are a number of pieces, anonymous in all the MS. collections, which have been ascribed to Dunbar. Amongst these the longest is " The Freiris of Berwik," preserved in the Bannatyne and Maitland MSS.; an edition of it was also printed at Aberdeen in 1622; in all of which it is given as anonymous. Pinkerton, who printed it from the Maitland MS. in 1786, was the first to ascribe it to Dunbar; and not a few have since coincided in his opinion. With all Pinkerton's ability, however, we have no great faith in his *dictum*. He was too impatient and impulsive to form a calm and correct judgment. The tale, as Mr Laing observes, must have been written before the suppression of the greater monasteries by Henry VIII. in 1539, thus bringing it near the time of Dunbar. It is, besides, a well told, excellent tale, illustrative of the loose morality of the Romish ecclesiastics; but we must be pardoned when we say that it has scarcely a single characteristic of his composition. It has none of those descriptive passages in which his muse loved to revel, and the language in which it is clothed is by no means from the same mint. When neither Bannatyne nor Maitland were aware of so popular a poem ever having been attributed to Dunbar, it is presumptuous in any writer, however eminent, to parade his opinion in opposition even to their *negative* authority. Errors are often perpetrated in this manner, and in all cases of anonymous writings, we hold it best to leave them rather without paternity than run the hazard of assigning them to a wrong party. Many gross blunders have been committed in this way, for it is not enough that an author, so many centuries ago, was capable of composing certain anonymous poems, nor even that they resemble his style. There were several writers in the time of Dunbar, as his " Lament for the Makaris " shews, capable of writing such a tale as " The Freiris of Berwik." Indeed, it may be questioned whether he, a priest himself, in daily expectation of a benefice, and possibly in possession of a bishopric before his death, would have so far played into the hands of the Reformation party by penning such a talc. Indeed, amongst the pieces attributed to Dunbar, there are only one or two so characteristic of his muse as to deserve a place amongst his works.

In arranging the poems which may be supposed to have been written before the poet's connexion with the court, at least, such as have no manifest reference to that period, we pretend to no guide save what consideration may suggest. Much the greater portion of the MSS. that have been preserved, belong to that period when he had become a pensioner of the king—a circumstance which confirms us the more in the opinion that " The Flyting " with Kennedy did not take place till after 1504, when his fame as a " makar " was established.   We shall give precedence to

" The Golden Targe,"

a poem which, from its being so purely allegorical, may savour more of the scholastic days of the poet than his later productions :—

> Bright as the stern * of day begoud to shine,
> When gone to bed were Vesper and Lucine†
>   I raise, and by a rosary did me rest ;
> Up sprang the golden candle matutine,
> With clear depurit‡ beams crystalline,
>   Gladd'ning the merry fowlis in their nest ;

---

* Star.   † The goddess *Lucina.*   ‡ Purified.

Ere Phœbus was in purple cape revest *
Up raise the lark, the heaven's minstrel fine
　In May, in till a morrow mirthfullest.

Full angel-like thir birdis sang their hours †
Within their curtains green, in to their bours,
　Apparelled white and red, with blooms sweet ;
Enamelled was the field with all colours,
The pearly droppis shook in silver shours ;
　　While all in balm did branch and leavis fleet
　　To part fra Phœbus, did Aurora greet ;
Her crystal tears I saw hing on the flours,
　Whilk he for love all drank up with his heat.

For mirth of May, with skippis and with hops,
The birdis sang upon the tender crops,
　With curious notes, as Venus' chapel clerks :
The roses young, new spreading of their knops,‡
Were powderit bricht with heavenly beriall§ drops,
　　Through beams red, burning as ruby sparks ;
　　The skies rang for shouting of the larks,
The purple heaven oure scal't in silver slops
　Ouregilt the trees, branches, leaves, and barks.

Doun through the ryce‖ a river ran with streams
So lustily again they likand ¶ lemes,
　That all the lake as lamp did leme ** of licht,
Whilk shadowit all about with twinkling gleams ;
That bowis bathit were in fecund beams
　Through the reflex of Phœbus' visage bricht ;

---

* Attired.　　† Orisons.　　‡ Buds.　　§ Shining.
‖ Twigs or bushes.　　¶ Pleased.　　** Gleam.

On every side the hedges raise on hicht,
The bank was green, the brook was full of bremes,*
   The stanneris clear† as stern in frosty nicht.

The crystal air, the saphyr firmament,
The ruby skies of the orient,
   Cast beriall beams on emerant‡ bowis green ;
The rosy garth§ depaint and redolent
With purple, azure, gold, and goulis‖ gent
   Arrayed¶ was, by Dame Flora the queen,
   So nobilly, that joy was for to seen ;
The rock again the river resplendent
   As low enluminit** all the leaves sheen.

What through the merry foulis harmony,
And through the river's soun that ran me by,
   On Flora's mantle I sleepit as I lay,
Where soon in to my dream's fantasy
I saw approach again the orient sky
   A sail, as white as blossom upon spray,
   With merse†† of gold, bricht as the stern of day;
Whilk tendit to the land full lustily,
   As falcon swift desirous of her prey.

And hard on burd‡‡ unto the bloomit meads,
   Among the green rispis§§ and the reeds,

---

* Rapids.   † Pebbles.   ‡ Emerald.
§ Garden.   ‖ Gules, red—a term in heraldry.
¶ "Gent-arrayed," genteely arrayed.   ** Illuminated.
†† Merse usually means land that had once been under water.
Here it signifies a mast—"with mast of gold."
‡‡ None of the annotators or editors of Dunbar explain the
meaning of *burd*, as here used. It must mean, "And hard on
bore unto," &c.   §§ Coarse, jaggy grass.

Arrivit she, where fro anon there lands
Ane hundreth ladies, lusty in to weeds,
As fresh as flouris that in May up spreads,
  In kirtles green, withouten kell* or bands
  Their bricht hairs hang glittering on the strands
In tresses clear, wyppit † with golden threads
  With pappis white, and middles small as wands.

Descrive ‡ I would, but who could weel indite,
How all the fields with their lilies white
  Depaint were bricht, whilk to the heaven did glcte : §
Nocht thou, Homer, as fair as thou could write,
For all thine ornate styles so perfite ;
  Nor yet thou, Tullius, whose lips sweet
  Of rhethoric did in till terms flete : ||
Your aureate ¶ tongues both been all too lyte, **
  For to compile that paradise complete.

There saw I Nature, and als †† dame Venus queen,
The fresh Aurora, and lady Flora sheen,
  Juno, Latona,‡‡ and Proserpina,
Diana, the goddess chaste of woods green,
My lady Clio, that help of makaris §§ been,
  Thetes, Pallas, and prudent Minerva,
  Fair feynit |||| Fortune, and lemand ¶¶ Lucina,
Thir michty queens in crounis micht be seen,
  With beamis blithe, bricht as Lucifera.

---

* Dress for a woman's head.   † Bound.

‡ Describe.   § Glitter. || Flow.

¶ Golden.   ** Little.   †† Also.

‡‡ Apollo in the MS., which must be an oversight, as they were all ladies.

§§ Poets. |||| Feigned, deceiving.   ¶¶ Gleaming.

There saw I May, of mirthful monethis queen,
Betuix April and June, her sister sheen,
  Within the garden walking up and doun,
Wham of the foulis gladdeth all bedene ;*
She was full tender in her yearis green.
    There saw I Nature present her a goun
    Rich to behold, and noble of renoun,
Of every hue under the heaven that been
    Depaint, and braid be gude proportioun.

Full lustily thir ladies all in fere †
Enterit within this park of most plesere,‡
  Where that I lay oure helit§ with leaves rank ;
The merry foulis, blissfullest of cheer,
Salust‖ Nature, me thocht, on their manere,¶
    And every bloom on branche, and eke on bank,
    Openit and spread their balmy leaves dank,
Full low enclining to their queen so clear,
    Wham of their noble nourishing they thank.

Syne to dame Flora, on the samin wise,
They saluse,** and they thank a thousand syse ;††
    And to dame Venus, love's michty queen,
They sang ballads in love, as was the gyse,‡‡
With amorous notes, lusty to devise,
    As they that had love in their heartis green ;

---

* Quickly.   † Together.
‡ Pronounced as the French *plaisir*.   § Concealed.
‖ Saluted.   ¶ *Manière*, French.   ** Salute.
†† Times.   ‡‡ Mode, fashion.

C

Their honey throats, openit fro the splene,*
With warbles sweet did pierce the heavenly skies,
    While loud resownit the firmament serene.

Ane other court there saw I consequent,
Cupid the king, with bow in hand ybent,
    And dreadful arrows grundin sharp and square;
There saw I Mars, the god armypotent,
Awful and stern, strong and corpolent;
    There saw I crabbit Saturn, auld and haire,†
    His look was like for to perturb the aire;
There was Mercurius, wise and eloquent,
    Of rhetoric that fand the flouris faire.

There was the god of gardens, Priapus;
There was the god of wilderness, Phanus;
    And Janus, god of entry delightable;
There was the god of floods, Neptunus;
There was the god of windis, Eolus,
    With variand look, richt like a lord unstable;
    There was Bacchus, the gladdir‡ of the table;
There was Pluto, the elrich incubus,
    In cloak of green; this court usit no sable.

And every one of thir in green arrayit,
On harp or lute full merrily they playit,
    And sang ballads with michty notis clear:
Ladies to dance full soberly essayit,
Endlang the lusty river so they may it:§

---

* The heart, a common expression with Dunbar, and other
old poets.   † Hoary.
    ‡ One who makes glad.   § May, a maid—maided it.

Their observance richt heavenly was to hear;
Then crap I through the leavis, and drew near,
Where that I was richt suddenly affrayit,
All through a look, whilk I have bocht full dear.

And shortly for to speak, be lovis queen
I was espyit: she bad her archers keen
Go me arrest; and they no time delayit;
Than ladies fair let fall their mantlis green,
With bowis big in tressit* hairis sheen,
All suddenly they had a field arrayit;
And yet richt greatly was I nocht affrayit,
The party was so pleasant for to seen
A wonder lusty bicker me essayit.

And first of all, with bow in hand ybrent,
Came dame Beauty, richt as she would me schent;†
Syne followit all her damsels yfere,
With mony diverse awful instrument,
Unto the press, Fair Having with her went,
Fine Portraiture, Pleasance, and lusty Cheer.
Than come Reason, with shield of gold so clear,
In plate and mail, as Mars armypotent,
Defendit me this noble chevalier.

Syne tender Youth came with her virgins ying,
Green Innocence, and shameful Abasing,
And quaking Dread, with humble Obedience;
The *Golden Targe* harmit they nothing;
Courage in them was nocht begun to spring;
Full sore they dread to done a violence:

---

* Tressed.   † Destroy.

Sweet Womanhood I saw cum in presence,
Of artilye* a warld she did in bring,
  Servit with ladies full of reverence.

She led with her Nurture and Lowliness,
Continence, Patience, Gude Fame, and Steadfastness,
  Discretion, Gentrise,† and Considerance,
Levefell‡ Company, and honest Business,
  Benign Look, mild Cheer, and Soberness :
  All thir bore ganyeis§ to do me grievance;
But Reason bore the *Targe* with sik constance,
Their sharp essayes micht do no duress‖
  To me, for all their awful ordinance.

Unto the press pursuit Hie Degree,
Her followit aye Estate and Dignitie,
  Comparison, Honour, and Noble Array,
Will, Wantonness, Renoun, and Libertie,
Riches, Freedom, and eik Nobilitie :
  Wit ye they did their banner hie display;
  A cloud of arrows as hail-shour lousit they,
And shot, while wastit was their artilye,
  Syne went aback reboytit¶ of their prey.

When Venus had perceivit this rebute,
Dissimulance she bad go mak pursuit,
  At all power to pierce the *Golden Targe* :
And she that was of doubleness the ruit
Askit her choice of archers in refute.
  Venus the best bad her go wale at large ;

---

* Artilye—artillery.   † Gentleness.   ‡ Leiffull—lawful.
§ Javelins.   ‖ Injury.   ¶ Repulsed.

She took Presence, plicht*. anchors of the barge,
And Fair Calling, that weel a flayn† could shoot,
  And Cherishing for to complete her charge.

Dame Homeliness she took in company,
That hardy was, and handy in archery,
  And brocht dame Beauty to the field again;
With all the choice of Venus' chivalry
They come, and bickerit unabasitly;
  The shour of arrows rappit on as rain;
  Perilous Presence, that mony sire has slain,
The battle brocht ane bordour‡ hard us by,
  The salt was all the sarer suth to sayn.§

Thick was the shot of grundin‖ dartis keen;
But Reason with the Shield of Gold so sheen,
  Warily defendit whosoever essayit;
The awful stoure he manly did sustene,
While Presence cast a powder in his een,
  And then, as drunken man, he all forwayit:¶
When he was blind, the fule with him they playit;
And banist him amang the bowis green;
  That sorry sicht me suddenly affrayit.

Than was I woundit to the death weel near,
And yoldyn** as a woful prisonnere††
  To lady Beauty, in a moment space;
Me thocht she seemit lustier of cheer,

---

* Pledged.   † Arrow.   ‡ Jester.
§ The jester's jokes were all the sorer, because it was truth he spoke.
‖ Sharpened.   ¶ Went astray.   ** Holden.
†† French, *prisonnier.*

Efter that Reason tynt had his een clear,
 Than of before, and lustier of face :
 Why was thou blindit, Reason ? why, alace !
And gert ane hell my paradise appear,
 And mercy seem, where that I fand no grace.

Dissimulance was besy me to sile,*
And Fair Calling did oft upon me smile,
 And Cherishing me fed with wordis fair ;
New Acquaintance embracit me a while,
And favourit me, while men micht go a mile,
 Syne took her leave, I saw her never mair :
 Than saw I Danger toward me repair,
I could eschew her presence be no wyle,
 On side she lookit with ane fremyt fare. †

And at the last departing could her dress,
And me deliverit unto Heaviness
 For to remain, and she in cure me took ;
Be this the Lord of Windis, with wodness,
Good Eolus, his bugle blew, I guess ;
 That with the blast the leavis all to shook,
 And suddenly, in the space of a look,
All was hyne‡ went, there was but wilderness,
 There was no more but birdis, bank, and brook.

In twinkling of ane eye to ship they went,
And swith up sail unto the top they stent,
 And with swift course atour the flood they frak ;§
They firit gunnis with powder violent,

---

* Circumvent.

† Fremyt fare—strange countenance.

‡ Hence.

§ Hurried.

Till that the reik raise to the firmament,
  The rockis all resounit with the rak,
  For reird* it seemit that the rainbow brak;
With spirit afraid upon my feet I sprent,†
  Amang the clewis,‡ so careful was the crak.

And as I did awake of my sueving,§
The joyful birdis merrily did sing
  For mirth of Phœbus' tender beams sheen;
Sweet were the vapours, soft the morrowing,
Halesum the vale, depaint with flouris ying;
  The air attemperit, sober and amene;‖
  In white and red was all the field beseen,
Through Nature's fresh enamelling,
  In mirthful May, of every moneth queen.

O reverend Chaucer! rose of rhetoris all;
As in our tongue ane flower imperial,
  That raise in Britain ever, who reads richt,
Thou bears of makars the triumph riall;¶
Thy fresh enamellit terms celical**
  This matter could illuminit have full bricht:
  Was thou nocht of our English all the licht,
Surmounting every tongue terrestrial,
  Als far as May's morrow does midnicht.

O moral Gower, and Lydgate laureate,
Your suggarit lips and tonguis aureate,
  Been to our earis cause of great delite;
Your angel mouthis most mellifluate,

---

* Noise.   † Sprung.   ‡ Cliffs.
§ Sueving—dreaming.   ‖ Pleasant.   ¶ Royal.
** Heavenly.

Our rude language has clear illuminate,
　　And fair oure gilt our speech, that imperfite
　　Stood, or your golden pennis schupe* to write;
This isle before was bare, and desolate
　　Of rhetoric, or lusty, fresh indite.

Thou little quair,† be ever obedient,
Humble, subject, and simple of intent,
　　Before the face of every cunning wicht:
I know what thou of rhetoric has spent;
Of all her lusty roses redolent
　　Is none into thy garland set on hicht,
　　Ashame there of, and draw thee out of sicht!
Rude is thy weed, disteynit,‡ bare, and rent,
　　Weel ocht thou be afferit of the licht.

That this beautiful allegory was amongst the
earlier of Dunbar's productions is presumable not
only from the subject, but the mode in which it is
handled. His address to Chaucer at the close, in
which he loses sight of his own claims to merit, in
admiration of the " rose of rhetoris all," and of the
writings of " moral Gower, and Lydgate laureate,"
indicate that he had been fresh from the reading
of these authors, which, one would suppose, must
have occurred early in life. It is not to be won-
dered, therefore, as Warton remarks, that " the
discerning reader will observe that the cast of this
poem is tinctured with the morality and imagery
of the ' Romaunt of the Rose,' and the ' Floure and

* Shaped.　　　† Book.　　　‡ Distended.

Leafe,' of Chaucer." Hailes was of opinion that Dunbar, believing himself to be of Anglo-Saxon origin, " was too apt to despise those who were born *without the English pale."* The fact is, that education in England and Scotland, then as now, was essentially similar, hence the contempt entertained for the common language of the people, and especially whatever was of *Erschery*—Irish or Gaelic. Yet Dunbar, notwithstanding his devotion to Chaucer, has innumerable phrases entirely Scottish, of which the great English poet never could be " the lycht." At the same time, his genius shines all the more brilliantly that he spares not his encomiums on that of others.

There never was penned by Chaucer, or any one else, so gorgeous a description of a May morning as we have in " The Golden Targe," while the allegory is not more beautifully conceived than powerfully sustained. The moral sought to be inculcated, as the reader will perceive, is, that Reason is the Golden Targe in love, as well, it may be said, as in all other matters. The poem was printed by Chepman and Myllar in 1508, no doubt with the sanction and revisal of the author. It became exceedingly popular.

TO A LADY.

Sweet rose of virtue and of gentleness,
Delightsome lilie of every lustiness,
   Richest in bounty, and in beauty clear,
   And every virtue that is most dear,
Except only that ye are merciless.

In to your garth* this day I did pursue,
There saw I floweris that fresh were of hue ;
   Baith white and red most lusty were to seen,
   And hailsome herbis upon stalkis green ;
Yet leaf nor flow'r find could I nane of rue.

I doubt that March, with his cauld blastis keen,
Has slain this gentle herb, that I of mean ;
   Whose piteous death does to my heart sic pain
   That I would mak to plant his root again.
So comfortand his leaves unto me been.

Pinkerton, who was the first to publish these love verses, from the Maitland Collection, in 1786, is warm in their praise, and no doubt they are couched in a fine strain. Dunbar complains of the fair one's cruelty, and, while in her garden were to be found both flowers and herbs, beautiful and wholesome, he could discover none of *rue*, which, in the language of love, signifies pity, grief, or lamentation—a plant so gentle, that the cold winds of March may have destroyed it. But to suppose that the poet himself was actually in love at the

* Garden.

time he penned this address is perhaps taking poetical sentiment too literally; and to suggest, as Dr Irving and others have done, that "Maestress Musgraeffe," an English lady of the court, was the object of his passion, is allowing conjecture an unbridled sweep. His adoration of Mistress Musgrave was of too mature a character to inspire so fine a poetical conceit, and we think the verses are more likely to have been written "in life's early morning, when fancy was young," before he became so intimately acquainted with the life and pastimes of the royal household.

THE MERLE AND THE NICHTINGALE.

In May, as that Aurora did up spring,
  With crystal ene chasing the cluds sable,
I hard a merle, with merry notes, sing
  A sang of love, with voice richt comfortable,
  Again the orient beams amiable,
Upon a blissful branch of lauryr* green ;
  This was her sentence sweet and delectable,
A lusty life in lovis service been.

Under this branch ran doun a river bricht,
  Of balmy liquor, crystalline of hue,
Again the heavenly azure skies licht ;
  Where did, upon the tother side, pursue

* Laurel.

A nichtingale, with suggarit notes new,
Whose angel feathers as the peacock shone :
  This was her song, and of a sentence true—
All love is lost but upon God alone.

With notes glad, and glorious harmony,
  This joyful merle so salust* she the day,
While rung the woodis of her melody,
  Saying, Awauk, ye lovers of this May ;
  Lo, fresh Flora has flourish'd every spray,
As nature has her taucht, the noble queen,
  The field been clothit in a new array :
A lusty life in lovis service been.

Never sweeter noise was heard with livin' man
  Nor made this merry, gentle nichtingale ;
Her sound went with the river as it ran
  Out throw the fresh and flourish'd lusty vale :
  O Merle ! quoth she, O fule ! stint of thy tail,
For in thy song gude sentence is there none,
  For both is tint, the time and the travail
Of every love but upon God alone.

Cease, quoth the Merle, thy preaching, Nichtingale :
  Sall folk their youth spend in to holiness ?
Of young sancts growis auld feinds but fabel.†
  Fy ! Hypocrite, in yearis tenderness,
  Again the law of kind thou goes express,
That crookit age makes one with youth serene,
  Whom Nature of conditions made diverse :
A lusty life in lovis service been.

---

* Saluted.   † Without fable.

The Nichtingale said, Fule, remember thee,
  That both in youth and eild, and every hour,
The love of God most dear to man sould be;
  That him, of nocht, wrocht like His ain figour,
  And deit Himself fro deid him to succour;
O whether was kythit * there true love or none?
  He is most true and steadfast paramour,
And love is lost but upon Him alone.

The Merle said, Why put God so great beauty
  In ladies, with sic womanly having,
But gif He would that they sould lovit be?
  To love eik Nature gave them inclining;
  And He of Nature that worker was and king,
Would nothing frustir † put, nor let be seen,
  In to his creature of his ain making:
A lusty life in lovis service been.

The Nichtingale said, Not to that behoof
  Put God sic beauty in a lady's face,
That she sould have the thank therefor, or luve,
  But He the worker, that put in her sic grace;
  Of beauty, bountie, riches, time, or space.
And every gudeness that been to come or gone,
  The thank redounds to Him in every place:
All love is lost but upon God alone.

O Nichtingale! it was a story nice
  That love sould not depend on charitie;
And gif that virtue contrair be to vice,
  Than love maun be a virtue, as thinks me;

---

* Produced, manifested.   † Contrary.

For aye to love envy maun contrair be:
God bad eik love thy nichtbour fro the splene,*
　And who than ladies sweeter nichtbours be?
A lusty life in lovis service been.

The Nichtingale said, Bird, why does thou rave?
　Man may tak in his lady sic delight,
Him to forget that her sic virtue gave,
　And for his heaven receive her colour white:
　Her golden tressit† hairis redomyt‡
Like to Apollo's beamis though they shone,
　Sould not him blind from love that is perfyte,
All love is lost but upon God alone.

The Merle said, Love is cause of honour aye,
　Love makis cowards manhood to purchase,
Love makis knichtis hardy at assay,
　Love makis wretchis full of largeness,
　Love makis swear folkis full of business,
Love makis sluggardis fresh and weil bessen,
　Love changes Vice in Virtue's nobleness;
A lusty life in lovis service been.

The Nichtingale said, True is the contrary;
　Sic frustir love it blindis men so far,
In to their minds it maks thame to vary;
　In false, vain glory they so drunken are,
　Thair wit is went, of woe they are not 'ware,
While that all worship away be fro them gone,
　Fame, guids, and strength: wherefor weil say I dare,
And love is lost but upon God alone.

---

* Heart.　　　　† Bound.　　　　‡ Decked.

Then said the Merle, Mine error I confess ;
  This frustir love all is but vanitie ;
Blind Ignorance me gave sic hardiness,
  To argue so again the veritie.
  Wherefor I counsel every man, that he
With love not in the fiendis net be tone,
  But love the love that did for his love die ;
All love is lost but upon God alone.

Than sang they both with voices loud and clear :
  The Merle sang, Man, love God that has thee wrocht.
The Nichtingale sang, Man, love the Lord most dear,
  That thee and all this warld made of nocht.
  The Merle said, Love Him that thy love has socht,
Fra heaven to erd,* and here took flesh and bone.
  The Nichtingale sang, and with His dead thee bocht.
All love is lost but upon Him alone.

Then flew thir birdis oure the bowis sheen,
  Singing of love amang the leavis small ;
Whose ythand † plead yet made my thochtis green,
  Both sleeping, wauking, in rest, and in travail :
  Me to recomfort most it does avail
Again for love, when love I can find none,
  To think how sang this merle and nichtingale,
All love is lost but upon God alone.

This poem called in Asloane's MS. " The Disputation between the Merle and Nichtingale," may
also be presumed to be one of the poet's early productions, quite in keeping with his character as an

* Earth.   † Diligent.

ecclesiastic.   The moral of the disputation is good, though the arguments are rather stiff and unnatural; yet there is something pretty in the idea of love to God being the burden of two of our finest singing birds, the merle and the nightingale.

BEST TO BE BLYTHE.

Full oft I muse, and has in thocht,
How this false warld is aye on flocht,*
  Where nothing firm is nor digest ;
And when I have my mind all socht,
  For to be blythe I think it best.

This warld ever does flicht and vary,
Fortune so fast her wheel does carry ;
  Na time but† turning can tak rest,
For whose false change sould none be sary ;‡
  For to be blythe me think it best.

Would men consider in mind richt weil,
Ere fortune on him turn her wheel,
  That erdly honour may not lest,
His fall less painful he sould feel ;
  For to be blythe me think it best.

Wha with this world does warsle and strive ;
And does his dayis in dolour drive,
  Though he in lordship be possest,
He livis but ane wretchit life :
  For to be blythe me think it best.

----

* Flight.   † Without.   ‡ Sorry.

Of warldis gude and great riches,
What fruit has man but meriness ?
  Though he this warld had east and west,
All were povertie but gladness :
  For to be blythe me think it best.

Who would for tinsall * droup or die,
For thing that is bot vanitie ;
  Sen to the life that ever does lest,
Here is but twinkling of an e'e :
  For to be blythe me think it best.

Had I for warldis unkindness
In heart tane my heaviness,
  Or fro my pleasans† been opprest,
I had been dead lang syne doubtless :
  For to be blythe me think it best.

How ever this warld may change and vary,
Let us in heart never more be sary ;
  But ever be ready and addrest,
To pass out of this frayful fary :
  For to be blythe me think it best.

The muse of Dunbar was frequently of a philosophical cast, and while we have had him instilling,
as in " The Golden Targe," the necessity of keeping reason awake, and that there is nothing lovable
but the Author of all good, we have him here
tendering his advice to be merry under all circumstances. But he was a man of very various moods
—joyous, sad, and humorous by turns.

* Loss.   † Pleasure.

OF CONTENT.

Who thinks he has sufficience,[*]
And of gudes has no indigence ;
　Though he have nowther land nor rent,
Great micht, nor hie magnificence,
　He has enough that is content.

Who had the riches into Ynd,[†]
And were not satisfied in mind,
　With poverty I hold him schent ;[‡]
Off covatyce[§] sic is the kind :
　He has eneuch that is content.

Therefore I pray you, breither dear,
Not to delight in dainties seir ;[||]
　Thank God if it is to thee sent,
And if it gladly mak gude cheer :
　He has eneuch that is content.

Defy the warld, fenyeit[¶] and false,
With gall in heart, and hunyit[**] halse :
　Wha maist it serves sall soonest repent :
Of whose subjects sour is the salse : [††]
　He has eneuch that is content.

Gif thou has micht, be gentle and free ;
And gif thou stands in povertie,
　Of thine ain will to it consent ;
And riches sall return to thee :
　He has eneuch that is content.

---

[*] Suffic-i-ence.　　[†] India.　　[‡] Overpowered.
[§] Covetousness.　　[||] Strange.　　[¶] Feigned.
[**] Honeyed.　　[††] Sauce.

And ye and I, my breither all,
That in this life has lordship small,
  Let languor not in us imprent;
Gif we not climb we tak no fall:
  He has eneuch that is content.

For who in warld most covetous is,
In warld is puirest man, I wis,
  And most needy of his intent;
For of all gudes no thing is his,
  That of no thing can be content.

"A most excellent moral poem," says Pinkerton, "written with great neatness and brevity." There is a series of pieces, in the same moral strain, which cannot be identified with any particular time and circumstance, and may as well follow each other.

———

NO TREASURE AVAILS WITHOUT GLADNESS.

Be merry, man, and tak not sair in mind
  The wavering of this wretchit warld of sorrow;
To God be humble, and to thy friend be kind,
  And with thy nichtbours gladly lend and borrow;
  His chance to nicht, it may be thine to-morrow;
Be blythe in heart for ony aventure,
  For oft with wise men it has been said aforrow,*
Without gladness avails no treasure.

Mak thee gude cheer of it that God thee sends,
  For warld's wrak but† weelfare nocht availis;

———
* Before.   † Without.

Nae gude is thine, save only that thou spends,
　Remenant all thou bruiks but with bailis :*
　Seek to solace when sadness thee assailis ;
In dolour lang thy life may not indure,
　Wherefore of comfort set up all thy sailis ;
Without gladness avails no treasure.

Follow on pity, flee trouble and debate,
　With famous folkis aye hald thy company ;
Be charitable and humble in thine estate,
　For wardly honour lastis but a cry ;
　For trouble in erd tak no melancholy ;
Be rich in patience, gif thou in gudis be puir,
　Who lives merry he lives michtily ;
Without gladness avails no treasure.

Thou sees thir wretches set with sorrow and care,
　To gather gudis in all their lives' space ;
And when their bags are full their selves are bare,
　And of their riches but the keeping has :
　While others come to spend it that has grace,
Whilk of thy winning no labour had nor cure,†
　Tak thou example, and spend with merriness ;
Without gladness avails no treasure.

Though all the wark that ever had living wicht
　Were only thine, no more thy part does fall,
But meat, drink, clais, and of the lave a sicht,
　Yet to the judge thou sall give compt of all ;
　Ane reckoning richt comes of ane ragment‡ small :

---

* Sorrow.   † Charge.   ‡ A scroll.

Be just and joyous, and do to none injure,
  And truth sall mak thee strong as ony wall ;
Without gladness avails no treasure.

Lord Hailes was of opinion that the moral of this poem would "not be admired; but there is *one* expression in it which ought to be remembered, as containing more good sense than some systems of ethics.

  'No more thy pairt dois fall,
Bot meit, drink, clais, *and of the laif a sicht.*'

In modern language Dunbar would have expressed himself thus—

'What riches give us, let us then explore ;
  Meat, drink, and clothes ; what else ? *a sight of more!* '"

This is a curious specimen of the critic's poetical talents. Most readers will prefer the lines of Dunbar to that of Hailes, as the best poetry, and most grammatically expressed. Dunbar's advice may not sound well in the ears of those whose delight lies "in gathering geir," yet his philosophy is strictly true in a sense : "When their bags are full their selves are bare," and of their wealth have but the keeping. Another follows in the same strain.

ADVICE TO SPEND ANE'S AIN GUDE.

Man, sen thy life is aye in weir,
And deid is ever drawing near,
Thy time unsicker and the place,
    Thine ain gude spend while thou has space.

Gif it be thine, thy self it uses,
Gif it be not, thee it refuses ;
Ane other of it the profit hes ;
    Thine ain gude spend while thou has space.

Thou may to-day have gude to spend,
And hastily to-morn fra it wend,
And leave ane other thy bags to brais ;*
    Thine ain gude spend while thou has space.

While thou has space, see thou dispone,
That for thy geir, when thou art gone,
No wicht ane other slay nor chace;
    Thine ain gude spend while thou has space.

Some all his days drives oure in vain,
Aye gathering geir with sorrow and pain,
And never is glad at Yule nor Pace ;
    Thine ain gude spend while thou has space.

---

* Jamieson, followed by Laing, gives the meaning of this word, *to embrace*. It would rather seem to be another form of the word *brus* or *brusch*, to *force open*, or the common English word *bruise, to crush ;* and the line might be read thus—" And leave ane other thy bags to *empty*."

Sine comes ane other glad of his sorrow,
That for him prayit nowther even nor morrow ;
And fangs it all with merriness ;
    Thine ain gude spend while thou has space.

Some great gude gathers, and aye it spares,
And after him there comes young heirs,
That his auld thrift sets on an ace ;*
    Thine ain gude spend while thou has space.

It is all thine that thou here spends,
And not all that on thee depends,
But his to spend it that has grace ;
    Thine ane gude spend while thou has space.

Trust not ane other will do thee to,
It that thyself would never do ;
For gif thou does, strange is thy case ;
    Thine ain gude spend while thou has space.

Look how the bairn does to the mother,
And tak example be nane other,
That it not after be thy case ;
    Thine ain gude spend while thou has space.

---

* "This age," says Hailes, "is not to be told what 'settis on an ace' implies. It may be more necessary to explain the phrase 'auld thrift.' It is wealth accumulated by the successive frugality of his ancestors." Nevertheless, most readers will be at a loss to comprehend what *ace* means. Jamieson tells us that in Orkney the word *ace* signifies the smallest division of anything, a single particle, a unit—hence the *ace* in cards does not render the words of Dunbar very intelligible. To be set on the smallest *division* of his auld thrift may be the poet's meaning; but it seems somewhat doubtful. Neither Sibbald nor Laing attempts to give any explanation.

Those whose good fortune it is to live upon the "auld thrift" will hardly be willing to join in the sentiment of Dunbar, seeing that, if their ancestors had lived by his rule, they would have been compelled to be the "authors of their own fortune." Lord Hailes was puzzled with the two last verses. "The sense," he says, "is probably this: Do not expect that another will do for you that which you would never do for yourself. The child draws milk from its mother's breast, but gives nothing in return." Sibbald was of a different opinion: "The meaning seems rather to be—as an infant subsists entirely upon the milk which it draws from its mother's breast, so your heir will probably spend all the wealth which you leave to him, before he thinks of any other means of subsistence. It will then be impossible for him to make you enjoy after death that which you could not enjoy while you was in life." Still Sibbald does not mend the matter. Whether the heir spent all the wealth left to him or not, it would have been equally impossible for him to make a dead man enjoy that which he would not, or could not, while in life!

NONE MAY ASSURE IN THIS WARLD.

Whom to sall I complene my wo,
And kyth* my caris ane or mo?

----

* Expose.

I knaw not amang rich or puir,
Wha is my freind, wha is my foe ;
  For in this warld may none assure.

Lord ! how sall I my days dispone,
For lang service reward is none ;
  And short my life may here endure ;
And losit is my time bygone :
  In to this world may none assure.

Oft Falsett * ridis with ane rout,
When Truth goes on his foot about,
  And lak of spending does him spur ; †
Thus what to do I am in doubt :
  In to this warld may none assure.

Nane here but rich men has renoun,
And but puir men are pluckit doun ;
  And nane but just men tholes injure,
Sa Wit is blindit and Ressoun :
  In to this warld may none assure.

Virtue the Court has done despyiss ; ‡
Ane rebel to renoun does ryiss,
  And carles of nobles § has the cure,
And bumbards‖ bruiks the benfyiss :
  In to this warld may none assure.

All Gentrice ¶ and Nobilitie
Are passit out of hie degree ;

---

* Falsehood.   † Spure or spur—scrape.
‡ Despite.   § Clowns of nobles.   ‖ Drivellers.
¶ Honourable birth.

On Freedom* is laid foirfaltour ;†
In Princes is there no pity ;
   For in this warld may none assure.

Is none so armit in to plate,
That can fra trouble him debait ;‡
   May no man lang in wealth endure,
For wo that ever lies at the wait :
   In to this warld may none assure.

Flattery wears ane furrit goun,
And Falsett with the Lords does roun ;
   And Truth stands barrit at the dure ;
And Honour exile is of the toun :
   In to this warld may none assure.

Fra everilk mouth fair words proceeds,
In every heart deception breeds,
   Fra everilk e'e goes look demure,
But fra the hands goes few gude deeds .
   In to this warld may none assure.

Tongues now are made of white whale-bone
And hearts are made of hard flint stone ;
   And e'en of amiable, blythe azure,
And hands of adamant, laith to dispone :§
   Into this world may none assure.

Yet heart, with hand and body, all
Maun answer Death when he does call,

---

* Freedom seems here spoken of in the sense of liberality.
† Forfeiture.   ‡ Protect himself.   § Give away.

To compt before the Judge future ;
Sen all are deid, or than die sall,
  Wha sould in to this warld assure ?

No thing but Death this shortly craves,
Where Fortune ever as foe dissaves,
  With freindly smilings of ane hure,
Whose false behests, as wind hind waves :
  In to this warld may none assure.

Oh ! wha sall wield the wrang possession,
Or the gold gatherit with oppression,
  When the angel blaws his bugle sture ?
Whilk unrestorit helps no confession :
  In to this warld may none assure.

What help is there in lordships seven,
When na house is but hell and heaven,
  Palace of light, or pit obscure,
Whair youls are heard with horrible stevin ?*
  In to this warld may none assure.

Ubi ardentes animæ,
Semper dicentes væ ! væ !
  Sall cry, alas ! that women them bure ;
O quantæ sunt istæ tenebræ !
  In to this warld may none assure.

Than who sall work for warld's wrak,
When flood and fire sall oure it frak, †
  And freely frustir‡ field and fure,§
With tempest keen and hideous crak ?
  In to this warld may none assure.

---

* Noise.   † Rage.   ‡ Destroy.   § Furrow.

> Lord ! sen in time so soon to come,
> De terra surrecterus sum,
>   Reward me with none erdly cure,
> But me receive in regnum tuum :
>   In to this warld may none assure.

This is an admirable homily on the vanity of all things—poetically, but strongly put. It would be idle to indulge in suggestions as to the time of its composition. It suits all times; yet we could hardly suppose it so applicable to the reign of James IV. as to that of his less energetic father, whom his rebellious subjects slew at the battle of Sauchy Burn, in 1488. If so, it must be a very early production of the poet : or, referring to the Queen's Regency, after Flodden, it may be one of more mature age. The mingling of sentences of the " Breviary," as Hailes remarks, was common both in Dunbar's time and later.

ERDLY JOY RETURNS IN PAIN.

> Of Lentren* in the first morning,
> Early as did the day upspring,
> Thus sang ane bird with voice up plain,†
> All Erdly joy returns in pain.

> O man ! have mind that thou maun pass;
> Remember that thou are but ass, ‡
> And sall in ass return again :
> All Erdly joy returns in pain.

----

* Lent.   † High and unpolished.   ‡ Ashes.

Have mind that eild aye follows youth,
Death follows life with gaping mouth,
Devouring fruit and flouring grain:
All Erdly joy returns in pain.

Wealth, worldly gloir,* and rich array,
Are all but thorns laid in thy way,
Cover'd with flowers laid in ane train:
All Erdly joy returns in pain.

Come never yet May so fresh and green,
But Januar come as wud and keen;
Was never sic drouth but anis† come rain:
All Erdly joy returns in pain.

Evermair unto this warld's joy,
As nearest heir succeeds noy,‡
Therefore when joy may not remain,
His very§ heir succcedis pain.

Here health returns in seikness;
And mirth returns in heaviness;
Toun in desert, forest in plain:
All Erdly joy returns in pain.

Freedom‖ returns in wretchedness,
And truth returns in doubleness,
With fenyeit words to mak men fain:
All Erdly joy returns in pain.

Virtue returnis into vice,
And honour into avarice;

---

* Glory. † At once. ‡ Annoyance.
§ True. ‖ Liberality.

With covetice is conscience slain :
All Erdly joy returns in pain.

Sen Erdly joy abidis never,
Work for the joy that lasts ever ;
For other joy is all but vain :
All Erdly joy returns in pain.

OF THE WARLD'S VANITY.

O wretch! be ware! this warld will wend thee fro,*
  Whilk has beguilit mony great estate ;
Turn to thy freind, believe not in thy foe,
  Sen thou maun go, be graithing † to thy gait ;
  Remeid in time, and rue not all too late ;
Provide thy place, for thou away maun pass
  Out of this vale of trouble and deceit :
Vanitas Vanitatum, et omnia Vanitas.

Walk forth, Pilgrim, while thou has dayis licht,
  Dress fro desert, draw to thy dwelling-place ;
Speed home, for why? anon comis the nicht
  Whilk does thee with ane ythand ‡ chase !
  Bend up thy sail, and win thy port of grace ;
For and the Death ouretak thee in trespass,
  Then thou may say thir wordis with alace !
Vanitas Vanitatum, et omnia Vanitas.

Here nocht abides, here stands no thing stable,
  For this false warld aye flittis to and fro ;
Now day up bricht, now nicht as black as sable,

---

* Will lead astray.　　　　† Preparing.　　　　‡ Eager.

Now ebb, now flood, now freind, now cruel foe ;
Now glad, now sad, now weel, now into wo ;
Now clad in gold, dissolvit now in ass ; *
So does this warld ay transitory go :
Vanitas Vanitatum, et omnia Vanitas.

Little may be said of the foregoing verses, save
that they are only preserved in the Maitland MS.,
and are worthy of Dunbar's moral and didactic
muse. We shall follow them by a still more ex-
quisite chime on the same subject.

OF THE CHANGES OF LIFE.

I seek about this warld unstable,
To find ane sentence conveniable ;
  But I can not, in all my wit,
  Sae true ane sentence find of it,
As say it is deceivable.

For yesterday, I did declare
How that the time was saft and fair,
  Come in as fresh as peacock feddar ;
  This day it stangis like ane eddar,
Concluding all in my contrair.

Yesterday fair up sprang the flours,
This day they are all slain with shours ;
  And fouls in forest that sang clear,
  Now weepis with ane dreary cheer,
Full cauld are baith their beds and bours.

---

* Ashes.

> So next to Simmer, Winter beïn : *
> Next efter comfort, caris keen ;
>   Next efter dark nicht, the mirthful morrow ;
>   Next efter joy, aye comis sorrow :
> So is this warld, and aye has been.

Pinkerton justly remarks that "this is a piece of elegant morality," and proceeds to explain the simile of "as fresh as peacock feddar," which must be obvious to every one. He tells from Hoveden that, in 1186, "Urban III. sent Henry II. of England a crown of peacock's feathers, richly set in gold, as a mark of supreme favour. This sounds as odd in our ears as Dunbar's comparison." Pinkerton does not seem to have been aware of the old Scottish weather adage—

> "March comes in like a lion and goes out like a lamb :
> April comes in like *an adder* and goes out like a *peacock's tail;*"

hérbs and flowers being then in flourish. The fourth verse is particularly beautiful, especially the last line, in reference to the cheerless condition of the singing birds—

> "Full cauld are baith their beds and bours."

---

* Exists. The poet frequently uses the preterperfect of *be* in this sense.

OF MAN'S MORTALITY.

Memento, Homo, quod cinis is !
   Think, Man, thou art but erd and ass ; *
Lang hear to dwell na thing thou press,†
   For as thou come, so sall thou pass,
   Like as ane shadow in ane glass :
Syne glides all thy time that hear is ;
   Think, though thy body were of brass,
Quod tu in cinerem reverteris.

Worthy Hector, and Hercules,
   Forcye ‡ Achill, and strong Samson,
Alexander of great nobleness,
   Meek David, and fair Absolon,
   Has playit their pairts, and all are gone,
At will of God, that all thing steeris :
   Think, Man, exception there is none ;
Sed tu in cinerem reverteris.

Though now thou be maist of cheer,
   Fairest and pleasantest of port,
Yet may thou be, within ane year,
   Ane ugsum, ugly, foul tramort : §
   And sin thou knaws thy time is short,
And in all hours thy life in weir is,
   Think, Man, among all other sport,
Quod tu in cinerem reverteris.

---

* Ashes.   † Pursue eagerly.
‡ Forceful   § Corpse.

Thy lusty beauty, and thy youth,
  Shall fade as does the summer flouris,
Syne sall thee swallow with his mouth,
  The dragon Death, that all devours ;
  No castle sall thee keep, nor tours,
But he sall seek thee with thy feirs ;
  Therefore, remember at all hours,
Quod tu in cinerem reverteris.

Though all this warld thou did posseid,*
  Nocht after death thou sall possess,
Nor with thee tak, but thy guid deed,
  When thou does fro this warld thee dress :
  So speed thee, Man, and thee confess,
With humble heart and sober teiris,
  And sadly in thy heart impress,
Quod tu in cinerem reverteris.

Though thou be taklit never so sure,
  Thou sall in deathis port arrive,
Where nocht for tempest may endure,
  But fiercely all to speiris † drive ;
  Thy Ransomer, with woundis five,
Mak thy plicht-anchor,‡ and thy steiris,§
  To hald thy saul with him on live,
Cum tu in cinerem reverteris.

This ranks among the best of Dunbar's moral and religious pieces.

* Possess.   † Splinters.
‡ Sure anchor.   § Guides.

OF THE NATIVITY OF CHRIST.

Rorate Cœli desuper !
  Heavens distil your balmy show'rs,
For now is risen the bricht day-ster,
  Fro the Rose Mary, flow'r of flow'rs :
  The clear sun, whom no cloud devours,
Surmounting Phœbus in the east,
  Is coming of his heav'nly tow'rs ;
Et nobis Puer natus est.

Archangels, angels, and dompnationis,*
  Tronis, potestatis, and martyrs seer,
And all ye heavenly operationis,
  Star, planet, firmament, and sphere,
  Fire, erd, air, and water clear,
To Him give loving, most and lest,
  That come in to so meek maniere ;
Et nobis Puer natus est.

Sinners, be glad, and penance do,
  And thank your Makar heartfully ;
For He, that ye micht not come to,
  To you is coming full trimily,
  Your saulis with His bluid to by,
And lowse you of the Feind's arrest,
  And only of His awin mercy ;
Pro nobis Puer natus est.

All clergy do to Him incline,
  And bow unto that Bairn benyng,

* Condemned.

And do your observance divine,
   To Him that is of kingis King ;
   Incense His altar, read, and sing
In haly kirk, with mind digest,
   Him honouring attour all thing,
Qui nobis Puer natus est.

Celestial fowlis in the air,
   Sing with your notes upon hicht ;
In firthis * and in forests fair
   Be mirthful now, at all your micht,
   For passit is your dully† nicht ;
Aurora has the cluddis prest,
   The sun is risen with gladsome licht,
Et nobis Puer natus est.

Now spring up flouris from the root,
   Revert you upward naturally,
In honour of the blessed fruit,
   That raise up fro the Rose Mary ;
   Lay out your leavis lustily,
Fro deid tak life now at the lest,
   In worship of that Prince worthy,
Qui nobis Puer natus est.

Sing heaven imperial, most of hicht,
   Regions of air mak harmony ;
All Fish in flood, and Fowl of flicht,
   Be mirthful and mak melody :

---

* Inclosures.   † Dolly, or dowie—doleful.

All GLORIA IN EXCELSIS cry,
Heaven, Erd, Sea, Man, Bird, and Beast,
He that is crownit above the Sky,
Pro nobis Puer natus est.

These spirited and highly poetical verses may
have been written as a Christmas carol, which was
by no means unknown in Scotland at an early
period.

ANE BALLAD OF OUR LADY.

Haile, sterne superne !   Haile, in eterne,
In Godis sicht to schyne !
Lucerne in derne, for to discerne
Be glory and grace devyne ;
Hodiern, modern, sempitern,
Angelicall Regyne !
Our tern inferne for to dispern,
Helpe rialest rosyne.
Ave MARIA, gratia plena !
Haile, fresche flour femynyne !
Yerne us, guberne, Virgin matern,
Of reuth baith rute and ryne.

Haile, yyng, benyng, fresche flurising !
Haile, Alphais habitakle !
Thy dyng of spring maid us to syng
Before his tabernakle,
All thing maling we doune thring,
Be sicht of his signakle ;
Quhilk King us bring unto his ryng,
Fro dethis dirk umbrakle.

Ave MARIA, gratia plena !
  Haile Modir and Maid but makle !
Bricht sygn, gladyng our languissing,
  Be micht of the mirakle.

Haile, bricht, be sicht, in hevyn on hicht !
  Haile, day sterne orientale !
Our licht most richt, in clud of nycht,
  Our darkness for to scale :
Haile, wicht, in sicht, puttar to flicht
  Of fendis in battale !
Haile, plicht, but sicht ! Haile, mekle of mycht !
  Haile, glorious Virgine, haile !
    Ave MARIA, gratia plena !
  Haile, gentill nychtingale !
Way stricht, cler dicht, to wilsome wicht,
  That irke bene in travale.

Haile, Quene serene ! Haile, most amene !
  Haile, hevinlie hie Empryss !
Haile, schene, unseyne with carnale eyne !
  Haile, Rois of Paradyss ! '
Haile, clene, bedene, ay till conteyne !
  Haile, fair fresche flour-de-lyce !
Haile, grene daseyne ! Haile, fro the splene,
  Of Jhesu genetrice !
    Ave MARIA, gratia plena !
  Thow bair the Prince of Pryss ;
Our tryne to meyne, and go betweyne,
  As humile Oratrice.

Haile, more decore, than of before,
  And swetur be sic sevyne,

Our glore, for lore, for to restore,
  Sen thow art Quene of Hevyne!
Memore of sore, stern in Aurore,
  Louit with Angellis stevyne;
Implore, adore, thow indeflore,
  To mak our oddis evyne.
    Ave MARIA, gratia plena!
  With lovingis lowde ellevyn,
Quhill store and hore, my youth devore,
  Thy name I sall ay nevyne.

Empryre of pryse, Imperatrice,
  Brycht polist precious stane;
Victryce of vyce, hie genitrice
  Of Jhesu, Lord soverayne:
Our wyse pavyse fro encmyis,
  Agayne the feyndis trayne;
Oratrice, Mediatrice, Salvatrice,
  To God gret suffragane!
    Ave MARIA, gratia plena!
  Haile, sterne meridiane!
Spyce, flour-de-lice of Paradyse,
  That bair the gloryus grayne.

Imperial wall, place palestrall,
  Of peirless pulcritude;
Tryumphal hall, hie trone regall
  Of Godis celsitude;
Hospitall riall, the Lord of all
  Thy closset did include;
Bricht hall, cristall, rois virginall,
  Fulfillit of angell fude.

     Ave MARIA, gratia plena !
     Thy birth has with His blude,
     Fra fall mortall, originall,
     Us ransomid on the rude.

The peculiar versification and frequently-recurring rhyme of this poem, with its numerous obsolete words, render it next to impossible, even were it profitable, to attempt a modification of the spelling.

THE MANNER OF PASSING TO CONFESSION.

O sinful man, thir are the forty days
    That every man suld wilful penance dree ;
Our Lord Jesu, as haly writ says,
    Fastit Himself our example to be :
    Sin sic ane michty King and Lord as He,
To fast and pray was so obedient,
We sinful folk suld be more diligent.

I red thee, man, of thy transgression,
    With all thy heart, that thou be penitent ;
Thou shrive thee clean, and mak confession,
    And see thereto that thou be diligent,
    With all thy sins in to thy mind present,
That every sin be thy self beschawin,*
To thine confession it may be kend and knawin.

Upon the body gif thou has ane wound
    That causes thee great pains for to feel,

---

* Shewn.

There is no leech may mak thee haill and sound,
  While it be seen, and cleansit every deil ;
  Richt sa thy shrift, but it beschawin weel,
Thou art not able remission for to get,
Wittingly and thou suld ane sin foyet.*

Of twenty wounds, and ane he left unhealit,
  What avails the leeching of the lave ?
Richt sa thy shrift, and there be ocht concealit,
  It avails not thy silly saul to save ;
  Nor yet of God remission for to have :
Of sin gin thou wald have deliverance,
Thou suld it tell with all the circumstance.

Sa that thy Confessor be wise and discreet,
  Than can thee discharge of every doubt and weir,†
And power has of thy sins complete :
  Gif thou can not shew forth thy sins perqueir,‡
  And he be blind, and can not at thee speir,
Thou may richt weel in thy mind consider
That ane blind man is led forth be ane ither.

And sa I hald, that ye are baith beguiled ;
  He can not speir, nor thou can not him tell,
When, nor how, thy conscience thou has filed ;
  Therefore, I red that thou excuse thy sell,
  And ripe thy mind how every thing befel,
The time, the place, and how, and in what wise,
So that thy confession may thy sins price.§

---

* Forget.   † Weir, in this sense, means danger.
‡ Fully, or fairly.   § Purchase.

Advise thee weel, ere thou come to the Priest,
　Of all thy sins, and namely of the maist,
That they be ready printed in thy breast ;
　Thou suld not come to shrive thee in great haste,
　And syne sit doun abasit as ane beast :
With humble heart and sad contrition
Thou suld come to mak thine confession.

With thine awin mouth thy sins thou suld tell ;
　But sit and hear the Priest has nocht ado,
Wha kens thy sins better nor thy sell ?
　Therefore, I red thee, tak gude tent thereto ;
　Thou knaws best where binds thee thy shoe ;
Therefore, be wise afore ere thou there come,
That thou shaw forth thy sins all and sum.*

Where seldin† compt is tane, and has a heavy charge,
　And syne is reckless in his governance,
And on his conscience he taks all too large,
　And on the end has no rememberance,
　That man is abill‡ to fall ane great mischance,
The sinful man that all the year oure sets,
Fra Pasche to Pasche,§ richt mony a thing forgets.

I red thee, man, while thou art stark and young,
　With pith and strength into thy years green,
While thou art able baith in mind and tongue,
　Repent thee, man, and keep thy conscience clean ;
　Till bide till age has mony peril seen :
Small merit is of sins for to irk
When thou art auld, and may na wrangs wyrk.

---

* All and whole.　　　　† Seldom.
‡ Fit, liable.　　　　§ Easter.　　．

After the manner of the " Priest's Tale," in Chaucer, Dunbar here very forcibly urges the necessity of full and clear confession, if it is to have any useful effect. The next relates to the same much-abused sacrament of the Romish Church.

THE TABLE OF CONFESSION.

To Thee, O merciful Saviour, Jesus,
  My King, my Lord, and my Redeemer sweet,
Before Thy bloody figure dolorus,
  I schir * me clean, with humble heart contreit,
  That ever I did unto this hour compleit,
Baith in work, in word, and eik in intent ;
  Falling on face, full low before Thy feet
I cry Thee mercy, and lasar † to repent.

To Thee, my meek, sweet Saviour, I me shrive,
  And does me in Thy mercy maist excelling,
Of the wrang spending of my wittis Five,—
  In Hearing, Seeing, Gusting,‡ Twitching,§ and
    Smelling,
  Ganestanding,‖ grieving, offending, and rebelling,
Against my God and Lord Omnipotent ;
  With tears of sorrow from my ene distilling,
I cry Thee mercy, and lasar to repent.

----

* Shrive.   † Leisure.   ‡ Tasting.
§ Touching.   ‖ Opposition.

I, wretched sinner vile, and full of vice,
  Of the Seven Deidly Sins does me shrive,—
Of Pride, of Ire, Envy, and Covetice,
  Of Lechery, Gluttony, with Sloth aye till oure
    drive,
  Exercising vices ever in all my live,
For whilk, alace ! I servit to be schent :*
  Rue on me, Jesu, for Thy woundis five !
I cry Thee mercy, and lasar to repent.

I shrive me, Lord ! that I abusit have
  The Seven Deeds of Mercy Corporall,—
The hungry meat, nor thirsty drink I gave,
  Nor veseit† the seik, nor did redeem the thrall,‡
  Herbreit§ the wilsome, nor naked clad at all,
Nor yet the deid to bury took I tent :
  Thou, that put mercy above Thy works all,
I cry Thee mercy, and lasar to repent.

Lord ! I have done full little reverence
  Unto the Sacraments Seven of great renown,—
Thy Haly Supper for my sin recompence,
  Baptising, Penance, and Confirmation,
  Matrimony, Order, and Extreme Uncion ;
Hereof, as far as I was negligent,
  With heart contrite, and tearis falling doun,
I cry Thee mercy, and lasar to repent.

---

* Destroyed.   † Visited.
‡ Those in thraldom.
§ Harboured, from herbery, an hostelry.

Thy Ten Commands—a God for till honour,
  Not ta'en in vain His name, na slayer to be,
Father and mother to worship at all hour,
  To be no thief, the haly day to uphie,
  Nichtbours to love, false witness for to flee,
To leave adultry, to covet na man's rent ;
  In all thir, Lord ! culpable knaw I me ;
I cry Thee mercy, and lasar to repent.

I trow in to the blessed Haly Spreit,
  And in the Kirk, to do as it commands,
And to Thy dome that we sall rise compleit
  And tak our flesh again, baith feet and hands,
  All to be safe in state of grace that stands ;
Plain I revoke in thir where I miswent,
  Before the Judge and Lord of sea and lands,
I cry Thee mercy, and lasar to repent.

I sinnit, Lord ! that not being strong as wall,
  In Houp, in Faith, in fervent Charitie ;
Not with the Four Virtueis Cardinall,
  Againis vices sure enarming me,
  With Fortitude, Prudence, Temperance, thir three
With Justice ever in wark, word or intent ;
  To Thee, Christ Jesu, casting up mine e'e,
I cry Thee mercy, and lasar to repent.

The Seven Commands of the Kirk,—that is to say,
  Thy teind to pay, and cursing to eschew,
To keep the festuall* and the fasting day,
  The mess on Sunday, the parish Kirk pursue,

---

* Festival.

To proper Curate to mak confession true,
Anis in the year to tak the sacrament ;
   In thir points, where I offendit, sair I rue ;
1 cry Thee mercy, and lasar to repent.

Of sin also against the Haly Spreit,
   Of shrift postponit, of sin against nature,
Of incontrition, of confession indiscreet,
   Of ressait* sinful of Thee, my Salvatour,
   Of undone penance, and satisfaction sure,
Of the Seven Gifts the Haly Ghaist me sent,
   Of Paternoster, and seven Petitions pure ;
1 cry Thee mercy, and lasar to repent.

Not thanking Thee of gratitude nor grace,
   That thou me wrocht, and bocht me with Thy deed ;
Of this short life remembering not the space,
   The heaven's bliss, the hell's hideous feid,†
   But‡ more trespass, my sinnis to remeid,
Concluding never all through in mine intent ;
   O Thou, whose bluid on rude§ for men ran reid,
I cry Thee mercy, and lasar to repent.

I knaw me vicious, Lord, and richt culpable,
   In aiths swearing, leising,‖ and blaspheming,
Of frustrat speaking in court, in kirk, and table,
   In words vile, in vanities expreming,¶
   Praising my self, and evil my nichtbours deming,**
And so in idleness may days I have spent ;

Thou that was sent on rude for my redeming,
I cry Thee mercy, and lasar to repent.

I sinnit in conceiving thochts jolly,
  Up to the heaven extolling mine intention,
In hie exaltit arrogance, and folly,
  Proudness, derision, scorn, and vilipention,*
  Presumption, inobedience, and contemption,
In false vain gloir, and deidis negligent ;
  O Thou, that deit on rude for my redemption,
I cry Thee mercy, and lasar to repent.

I sinned also in reif,† and in oppression,
  In wrangous guids taking and posseding,‡
Contrar gude reason, conscience, and discretion,
  In prodigal spending, but rewth§ of puir folks needing,
  In foul deceptions, in false inventions breeding,
To conqueiss‖ honour, treasure, land, and rent,
  In fleshly lust above measure exceeding,
I cry Thee mercy, and lasar to repent.

Of mind dissymulat,¶ Lord ! I me confess,
  Of feud under ane friendly countenance,
Of partial judging, and perverse wilfulness,
  Of flattering words for finding of substance,
  Of false soliciting for wrang deliverance
At council, session, and at Parliament ;
  Of everilk guilt, and wicked governance,
I cry Thee mercy, and lasar to repent.

---

* Undervaluing. † Robbery—pillage. ‡ Possessing.
§ Plenty. ‖ Acquire.
¶ Given to dissemble.

I shrive me of all cursit company,
  In all time, witting and unwitting me,
Of criminal causes, of deed of felony,
  Of tyranny, and vengeful crueltie,
  Of hurt or slauchter, culpable gif I be,
In ony wise, deed, counsel, or consent ;
  O dear Jesu ! that for me deit on tree,
I cry Thee mercy, and lasar to repent.

Though I have not thy precious feet to kiss,
  As had the Magdalene, when she did mercy crave,
I sall as she, weep tearis for my miss,
  And every morrow seek Thee at Thy grave ;
  Therefore, forgive me, as Thou her forgave,
That sees my heart, as sinner penitent !
  Thy precious body, in breist I resaif ;
I cry Thee mercy, and lasar to repent.

Thou mak me, Jesu, on Thee to remember !
  I ask Thy passioun* in me so to abound,
While nocht of me unmanyeit† be a member,
  But fall in woe, with Thee, of every wound ;
  And every straik mak through my heart astound,
That ever did strain Thy fair flesh innocent ;
  Sa that no part of my body be sound,
But crying Thee mercy, and lasar to repent.

Of all thir sins that I did here expreme,
  And als forget to Thee, Lord ! I me shrive,
Appealing fra Thy Justice Court extreme,
  Unto Thy Court of Mercy exulyfe ;‡

---

* Suffering.   † Unmaimed.   ‡ As an exile.

Thou mak my ship in blessed port arrive,
That sailis here in stormis violent,
And save me, Jesu ! for Thy woundis five,
That cries Thee mercy, and lasar to repent.

Dunbar appears to have been a true Roman Catholic, and had a deep insight into the venality of the human heart. He calls the verses a " Table of Confession," from which any particular sinner may select the particular crimes he has been guilty of. As a friar he had, no doubt, experience in auricular confession.

OF THE PASSION OF CHRIST.

Amang thir Freirs, within a closter,
  I enterit in ane oratory,
And kneelit doun with ane Pater-noster,
  Before the michtie King of glory,
  Having His Passion in memory ;
Syne till His mother I did incline,
  Her halsing* with ane gaudee-floree ;†
And suddenly I sleepit syne.

Me thocht Judas, with mony a Jew,
  Took blessit Jesus, our Salvatour,
And shot Him furth, with mony a schew,‡
  With shameful words of dishonour ;

----

* Hailing.   † Festive song.   ‡ Shove.

And like ane thief or ane tratour,
They led that heavenly Prince most hie,
With menacing attour measour,
O mankind ! for the love of thee.

Falsely condemnit before ane Judge,
They spittit in His visage fair ;
And, as lions, with awful ruge,*
In ire they harl't Him here and there,
And gave Him mony buffets fair,
That it was sorrow for to see ;
And of His claiths they tirvit † Him bare ;
O mankind ! for the love of thee.

Thae tyrants to revenge their teyne,‡
For scorn they clad Him in to white ;
And hid His blissful, glorious eyne,
To see whom angels had delite ;
Dispituously syne did Him smite,
Saying, Gif Son of God thou be,
Wha straik Thee now, thou tell us tyte ?§
O mankind ! for the love of thee.

In teyne, they tirrit Him again,
And till ane pillar they Him band ;
While blood out bristit at every vain,
They scourgit Him baith foot and hand :
At every straik ran forth a strand,
Micht have ransomit warlds three ;
He baid in stound‖ while He micht stand,
O mankind ! for the love of thee.

---

* Roughness.   † Uncovered.   ‡ Spite.
§ Quickly.   ‖ Acute pain.

Next all in purpour* they Him clad,
   And syne with thornis sharp and keen,
His saikless bluid again they shed,
   Piercing His head with pikis green ;
   Uneis† with life He micht sustene
That Croun, on thrung‡ with crueltie,
   While flood of bluid blindit his eyne,
O mankind ! for the love of thee.

Ane cross that was baith great and lang,
   To bear they gave that blessit Lord ;
Syne furiously, as thief to hang,
   They harlit him forth with raip and cord ;
   With bluid and sweat was all deflored§
His face, the food of angels free ;
   His feet with stanes were riven and scored,
O mankind ! for the love of thee.

Again they tirvit Him back and side,
   As brym‖ as any baris wod ;¶
The claith that clave to His clear hide,
   They rave away with ruggis rude,
   While fiercely followit flesh and bluid,
That it was pity for to see ;
   Na kind of torment He gainstood,
O mankind ! for the love of thee.

Unto the cross of breadth and length,
   To gar His limbis larger wax,
They straightit Him with all their strength,
   While to the end they gart Him rax ;

---

* Purple.   † Scarcely.   ‡ Thrown on.
§ Disfigured.   ‖ Fierce.   ¶ Bears mad.

Syne tyt* Him up with great iron tax,†
And Him all nakit on a tree
　They raisit on loft, be houris sax,
O mankind! for the love of thee.

When He was bendit all on breid‡
　While all His veins brist and brak,
Till gar His cruel pain exceed,
　They let Him fall down with a swak,
　While cross and corps§ and all did crak ;
Again they raisit Him on hie,
　Ready mair torment for to tak,
O mankind! for the love of thee.

Betwix twa thieves the sp'rit He gave
　Unto His Father most of micht ;
The erd did tremble, the crags raive,
　The sun obscurit of his licht ;
　The day wox dark as ony nicht,
Deid bodies raise in the citie :
　God's dear Son all thus was dicht,‖
O mankind! for the love of thee.

In weir¶ that He was yet on life,
　They ran a rude spear in His side,
And did His precious body ryf,**
　While bluid and water did furth glide :

---

* Tightened, or fastened.　　† Nails.　　‡ Breadth.
§ Body.　　‖ Handled.
¶ In case—in doubt.　　** Wound

> Thus Jesus, with His wounds wide,
> As martyr sufferit for to die,
> And tholit to be crucified,
> O mankind! for the love of thee.

The above poem, descriptive of the sufferings of Christ under the hands of the Jews, was probably written when the author was himself a friar.

OF THE RESURRECTION OF CHRIST.

> Done is a battle on the Dragon black,
> Our Champion Christ confoundit has his force;
> The yetts of Hell are broken with a crack,
> The sign triumphal raist is of the Cross,
> The Devils tremmils with hideous voice,
> The sauls are borrowit,* and to the bliss can go,
> Christ with His blood our ransoms does indoce;†
> Surrexit Dominus de sepulchro.
>
> Dungin‡ is the deidly dragon Lucifer,
> The cruel serpent with the mortal stang;
> The auld keen tiger, with his teeth on char,§
> Whilk in a wait for us has lain so lang,
> Thinking to grip us in his clawis strang;
> The merciful Lord would not that it were so,
> He made him to felye‖ of that fang:
> Surrexit Dominus de sepulchro.

---

* Redeemed.   † Endorse.   ‡ Overthrown.
§ On edge.   ‖ Fail.

He for our sake that sufferit to be slain,
   And like a lamb in sacrifice was dicht,
Is like a lion risen up again,
   And as gyane * has raxit Him on hicht :
   Springin is Aurora radius and bricht,
On loft is gone the glorious Apollo,
   The blissful day departed fro the nicht ;
Surrexit Dominus de sepulchro.

The great Victor again is risen on hicht,
   That for our quarrel to the death was woundit ;
The sun that wox all pale now shinis bricht,
   And darkness clear't, our faith is now refoundit ;
   The knell of mercy fra the heaven is soundit ;
The Christians are deliverit of their wo,
   The Jewis and their error are confoundit :
Surrexit Dominus de sepulchro.

The foe is chas't, the battle is done ceiss,†
   The prison broken, the jevellours fleet and flemit ; ‡
The war is gone, confirmit is the peiss,
   The fetters loosit, and the dungeon temit,§
   The ransom maid, the prisoners redeemit ;
The field is won, oure comin is the fo,
   Dispulit‖ of the treasure that he yemit : ¶
Surrexit Dominus de sepulchro.

This and the following verses may be said to
complete the religious pieces of Dunbar.

---

* Returning.   † Is done and ceased.
‡ The jailers frightened and fled.   § Emptied.
‖ Despoiled.   ¶ Prized.

ANE ORISON.

Saviour, suppose my sensualitie,
   Subject to sin, has made my saul oft syis,*
Some spark of licht and spiritualitie,
   Waukens my wit, and reason bids me rise ;
   My corrupt conscience asks, clipis † and cries,
First grace, syne space, for to amend my myss ; ‡
   Substance with honour, doing nane suppryis,§
Friends' prosperity, here peace, syne heaven's bliss.

OF LYFE.

What is this lyfe but ane straucht way to deid,
   Whilk has a time to pass and nane to dwell ;
A sliding wheel us lent to seek remeid ;
   A free choice given to Paradise or Hell ;
   A prey to death, whom vain is to repell ;
A short torment for infinite glaidness,
As short ane joy for lasting heaviness.

Both of these little pieces are good, the last excellent. The conception of life, as a straight road to death, with only two choices, short enough for the one, and long enough for the other ultimatum, is not less ingenious than beautiful. It is given anonymously in the Maitland, but is ascribed to Dunbar in the Bannatyne MS., and there can be no doubt as to the author.

* Subject to doom.   † Divulges.
‡ Failure.   § Wrong or oppression.

GUID COUNSEL.

Be ye ane lover, think ye not ye suld
  Be weel advisit in your governing?
Be ye not sa, it will on you be tauld;
  Be ware therewith for dreid of mis-demying;*
  Be not a wreche,† nor scarce in your spending;
Be laith alway to do amiss or shame;
  Be rulit richt, and keep weel this doctring,
Be secret, true, increasing of your name.

Be ye ane liar, that is warst of all;
  Be ane tratlar,‡ that I hald as evil;
Be ye ane janglar,§ and ye fra virtue fall,
  Be never mair on to thir vice's thrall;
  Be now and aye the maister of your will;
Be never he that leising‖ sall proclaim;
  Be not of language where ye suld be still;
Be secret, true, increasing of your name.

Be not abasit ¶ for no wicked tongue;
  Be not sa set as I have said you heir;
Be not sa large unto thir sawis sung;**
  Be not oure proud, thinking ye have no peir,
  Be ye so wise that others at you leir;††
Be never he to slander nor defame;
  Be of your love no preacher as ane freir;‡‡
Be secret, true, increasing of your fame.

---

* Misjudging.   † Niggard.   ‡ Idle talker.
§ Wrangler.   ‖ Falsehood.   ¶ Abashed.
** Do not despise these sayings.   †† Learn.
‡‡ Be more honest as a lover than a friar as a preacher.

The counsel conveyed in these line is excellent, but the meaning of some of the lines is obscure.

OF MEN EVIL TO PLEASE.

Four manner of folks are evil to please,
Ane is that riches has and ease,
Gold, silver, corn, cattle, and ky,
And wald have part fra others by.*

Ane other is of land and rent
So great ane lord, and so potent,
That he may nouther it rule nor gy ;†
And yet wald have fra others by.

Ane is that has of noble bluid
Ane lusty lady, fair and gude,
Baith virtuous, wise, and womanly ;
And yet wald have ane other by.

Ane other does so dourly drink,
And ale and wine within him sink,
While in his wame no room be dry ;
And yet wald have fra others by.

In earth no wicht I can perceive,
Of guid so great abundance have,
Nor in this world so wealthful wy,‡
Yet he wald have from others by.

---

* Besides.　　　　† Guide.　　　　‡ Person.

> But yet of all this gold and guid,
> Or other cunyie,* to conclude,
> Wha ever it have, it is not I ;
> It goes from me to others by.
>
> And namely at this Christ's mess,
> Wherever Sir Gold made his regress,
> Of him I will no largess cry ;
> He gaed fra me till others by.

The custom of giving largess—a present or bounty—at festivals, and especially at Christmas, is well known. This poem is only attributed to Dunbar in Reidpeth's MS., but there can be no question as to the author. It is characteristic of the poet, both in composition and sentiment—

> " Quha evir it haif, it is nocht I ;
> It gois frome me to utheris by."

INCONSTANCY OF LOVE.

> Wha will behald of Love the chance,
> With sweet, deceiving countenance,
> In whaise fair dissimulance,†
>   May none assure.
>
> Whilk is begun with inconstance,
> And ends not but ‡ variance ;
> She halds with continuance,
>   No serviture.§

---

* Coin.   † Dissemblance.   ‡ Without.
§ Superiority.

Discretion and considerance
Are both out of her governance ;
Wherefore, of it the short pleasance,
    May not endure.

She is of new acquaintance,
The auld gaes fra remembrance ;
Thus I give oure the observans
    Of Love's cure.

It is ane point of ignorance
To love in sic distemperance,
Sen time mispendit may advance
    No creature.

In Love to keep allegiance,
It war as nice ane ordinance
As wha wald bid ane deid man dance,
    In sepulture.

These verses only occur in the Bannatyne MS.,
and though possessing less of the poetical vigour of
the author, still they are not altogether unworthy
of him.

ANE HIS AIN ENEMY.

He that has gold and great riches,
And may be into merriness,
  And does gladness fra him expel,
And lives in to wretchedness,
  He workis sorrow to him sell.

He that may be but * sturt or strife,
And live ane lusty pleasant life,
   And syne with marriage does him mell,†
And binds him with ane wicked wife,
   He workis sorrow to him selL

He that has for his ain genyie,‡
Ane pleasant prop, bot mank or menyie,§
   And shoots syne at ane unco shell,
And is forfain‖ with the fleis of Spenyie,¶
   He workis sorrow to him sell.

And he that with guid life and truth,
But varians ** or under sleuth,
   Does ever mair with ane maister dwell,
That never of him will have no rewth,
   He workis sorrow to him sell.

Now all this time let us be merry,
And set nocht by this warld a cherry:
   Now while there is guid wine to sell,
He that does on dry bread wirry,
   I give him to the Devil of Hell.

Here we have the muse of Dunbar in a playful humour, and certainly the concluding stanza is

---

* Without.   † Meddle.   ‡ Instrument of war.
§ A prop for the gun, without defect or injury.
‖ Jaded.
¶ *Cantharides.* "This circumstance," says Lord Hailes, "gives us an high idea of the elegance and refinement of our forefathers"!
** Without variance.

amusing enough. While there is good wine to sell, he that would choke upon dry bread is only fit for the lower regions, is a thoroughly Bacchanalian sentiment. In ancient times, from our intimate connexion with France, wine was abundant and cheap in Scotland, and great care was taken that it should not be adulterated. In 1482, it was enacted by parliament, that those who mixed or corrupted wine should be punished by death. Ale and wine were the chief drinks in old times. *Usquebagh*, or whisky, is never mentioned in any of the writings of the fifteenth and sixteenth centuries, at least in so far as we have seen. If distilled in the Highlands at that period, which is very doubtful, it must have been gradually brought into repute as the taxes on foreign liquors were increased; and yet we know that the making of corn brandy, a species of whisky, has been long practised by the Scandinavians.

THE TWA CUMMERS.*

Richt earlie on Ash Weddinsday,†
Drinking the wine sat cummers tway ;
  The tane couth ‡ to the tother complein ;
Siching and supping couth she say,
  This lang Lentren makes me lean.§

-----

* Gossips.   † First day of Lent.   ‡ Began.
§ Every one knows that flesh meat is forbidden by the Roman Catholic Church during Lent.

On couch, beside the fire, she sat,
God wait * gif she was great and fat,
  Yet to be feeble she 'did her fein ;
And aye she said, Let preif † of that :
  This lang Lentren makis me lean.

My fair, sweet Cummer, quoth the tother,
Ye tak that niggirtness of your mother ;
  All wine to taste she wad disdein
But Mavasy, ‡ she bad § nane other :
  This lang Lentren makis me lean.

Cummer, be glad, both even and morrow,
Though ye suld baith beg and borrow ;
  Fra our lang fasting see you refrein,
And let your husband dree the sorrow :
  This lang Lentren makis me lean.

Your counsel, Cummer, is guid, quoth scho,‖
All is to tene ¶ him that I do ;
  In bed he is not worth a bean ;
Fill the cup, Cummer, and drink me to :
  This lang Lentren makis me lean.

Of wine, out of ane choppin stoup,
They drank twa quartis, soup and soup :
  Sic drouth the cummers did constrein,**
Be than to mend they had guid houp,
  That Lentren suld not mak them lean.

---

* God wit.   † Let taste.   ‡ Malmsey wine.
§ She *bad* for no other—*desired* no other.
‖ She.   ¶ Anger.
** There are various readings of this line.

There is great humour and keen satire in these
verses, at the same time that, as Pinkerton says,
they afford "a curious picture, from the life, in the
style of Flemish paintings."

THE DEVIL'S INQUEST.

This nicht in my sleep I was aghast,
Me thocht the Devil was tempting fast,
  The people, with aiths of crueltie;*
Saying, as through the mercat he past,
  Renunce thy God, and cum to me.

Me thocht, as he went through the way,
Ane priest sweir't braid, be God, verey,†
  While at the altar received he.
Thou art my clerk, the Devil 'gan say,
  Renunce thy God, and cum to me.

Than swore ane courteour, meikle of pride,
Be Christis woundis bluidy and wide,
  And be His harms ‡ was rent on tree.
Than spak the Devil, hard him beside,
  Renunce thy God, and cum to me.

Ane merchant, his geir as he did sell,
Renuncit his pairt of heaven for hell.

---

* Grievous oaths.
† Very—pronounced *verray* in Aberdeenshire.
‡ *Who* is necessary here to bring out the meaning.

The Devil said, Welcome mot* thou be,
Thou sall be merchant for my sell,
　　Renunce thy God, and cum to me.

Ane goldsmith said, The gold is sa fine,
That all the workmanship I tine ;
　　The fiend receive me gif I lie.
Think on, quoth the Devil, that thou art mine,
　　Renunce thy God, and cum to me.

Ane tailyour said, In all this toun,
Be there ane better weel made goun,
　　I give me to the fiend all free.
Gramercy, tailyour, said Mahoun,
　　Renunce thy God, and cum to me.

Ane souter said, In guid effeck,
Nor I be hangit be the neck,
　　Gif better buits of leather may be.
Fy, quoth the fiend, thou sairis of blek,†
　　Gae cleanse thee clean, and cum to me.

Ane baxter said, I forsake God,
And all His warks, even and odd,
　　Gif fairer bread there needs to be.
The Devil leuch, and on him couth nod—
　　Renunce thy God, and cum to me.

Ane flesher swore be the sacrament,
And be Christ's bluid maist innocent,
　　Never fatter flesh saw man with e'e.
The Devil said, Hald on thy intent,
　　Renunce thy God, and cum to me.

---

* May.　　　　　　　　† Smells of blacking.

The maltman says, 1 God forsake,
And mot the devil of hell me take,
  Gif ony better malt may be,
And of this kill I have inlaik : *
  Renunce thy God, and cum to me.

Ane browstar swore the malt was ill,
Baith red and reekit on the kill,
  That it will be nae ale for me ;
Ane boll will not six gallons fill :
  Renunce thy God, and cum to me.

Be God's bluid, quoth the tavernnier,†
There is sic wine in my celleir,
  Has never come in this countrie.
Tut, quoth the Devil, thou sells oure dear :
  Renunce thy God, and cum to me.

The smith swore be rood and raip,
In till a gallows mot I gaip,
  Gif 1 ten days wan pennies three,
For with that craft I cannot thraip : ‡
  Renunce thy God, and cum to me.

Ane minstrel said, The fiend me ryfe, §
Gif I do ocht but drink and swyfe ;‖
  The Devil said, Than I counsel thee,
Exerse ¶ that craft in all thy life :
  Renunce thy God, and cum to me.

---

* Deficiency.   † Tavern-keeper.
‡ This word puzzled Lord Hailes ; but its obvious meaning is
thrive.
§ Rive.   ‖ Sing or play.   ¶ Exercise.

Ane dysour* said, with words of strife,
The devil mot stick him with a knife
　　But he cast up fair syisis† thrée ;
The Devil said, Endit is thy life :
　　Renunce thy God, and cum to me.

Ane thief said, God that ever I chaip,‡
Nor ane stark widdy gar me gaip,
　　But I in hell for geir wald be.
The Devil said, Welcome in a raip :
　　Renunce thy God, and cum to me.

The fishwives flett,§ and swore with granes,
And to the Fiend, saul, flesh, and banes,
　　They gave them, with ane shout on hie.
The Devil said, Welcome all at anis :‖
　　Renunce your God, and cum to me.

The rest of craftis great aiths swair,
Their wark and craft had nae compair,
　　Ilk ane into their qualitie.
The Devil said, than, withouten mair :
　　Renunce your God, and cum to me.

This is a curious and admirable satire on the
times. Should we suppose Edinburgh to have
been the scene of the poet's vision, we have only to
fancy what the High Street was at a much later
period, to appreciate the words, " as throw the
mercat he past." In that haunt of most of the
citizens of note were to be found all and more than

* Gamester.　　　　　† Sixes at dice.　　　　　‡ Escape.
§ Scolded.　　　　　‖ At once.

the devil held inquest upon. The satire is levelled not only against the vulgar practice of swearing, but against the roguery which prevailed amongst tradesmen then as well as now. Nor does he omit his own profession—the priesthood. Swearing was made the subject of acts of parliament in Mary's time, and subsequent reigns. In Sir David Lindsay's "Satyre of the Three Estates," the reader will find a pretty full sprinkling of the oaths then prevalent. Even King James VI. was accused by the Kirk of being "blottit with banning and sweiring." In fact, it was fashionable amongst the upper classes down to our own times, and this in the other portions of the kingdom as well as Scotland. Hailes, in his remarks on this poem, observes that Dunbar seems to have had "a strange antipathy at shoemakers." It would be difficult to account for this, but certainly his satire is unusually severe in reference to that craft—

> "Fy, quoth the Fiend, thou sairis of blek,
> Ga clense thee clene, and cum to me."

Nothing could be more cutting than this, that a shoemaker was too foul even for the Fiend. Lord Hailes, whom Laing copies without remark, had some trouble with the reading of the third last verse, beginning

> "Ane thief said, God that ever I chaip," &c.

Hailes printed this line, "*Ill* that evir I chaip,"

and, in a note, observed that " the MS., instead of *ill,* had God.   The word *chaip* is used for *escape.*   So that the sense is, ' I will not desist from my vocation till I be hanged.' "   But, with all due deference to Lord Hailes, if the reader goes over the verse carefully, he will read it in another sense : " God though I never escape, (that is, His vengeance,) nor the gallows, yet I would go to hell for the sake of money, and thereupon the devil welcomes him *even ' in a raip.' "*   By this, the true reading, the humour of the poet is brought thoroughly out.

BEAUTY AND THE PRISONER.

Sen that I am a Prisoneir
   Till her that fairest is and best,
I me commend, fra yeir to yeir,
   In till her bandoun* for to rest ;
   I govit† on that guidliest,
Sa lang to luk I took laseir ‡
   While I was ta'en withouten test,
And led forth as a Prisoneir.

Her Sweet Having, and Fresh Beautie,
   Has woundit me but§ sword or lance ;
With her to go commandit me,
   On till the Castle of Penance.

---

* Command.   † Gazed.   ‡ Leisure.   § Without.

I said, Is this your governance,
To tak men for their looking here ?
  Beauty sayis, Yea, sir, perchance
Ye be my Lady's Prisoneir.

They had me bundin to the yett,
  Where Strangeness had been porter aye ;
And in deliverit me thereat,
  And in thir termis 'gan they say :
  Do wait, and let him not away,
Quoth Beauty unto the porteir.
  On till my Lady, I dare say,
Ye be too puir a Prisoneir.

They cast me in a deep dungeon,
  And fetterit me but* lock or chain ;
The captain, hecht † Comparison,
  To look on me he thocht great deign :
  Though I was wo, I durst not plain,
For he had fetterit mony affeir ;‡
  With piteous voice thus couth I sene,§
Wo is a woful Prisoneir !

Languor was watch upon the wall,
  That never sleepit, but ever woke ;
And Scorn was bourdour‖ in the hall,
  And oft on me his babble shook ;
  Looking with many a dangerous look.
What is he yon, that methis ¶ us near ?

---

* Without.　　　　　† Called.　　　　‡ Many of the same.
§ Could I say.　　　　‖ Jester.
¶ Comes within our boundary.

He be too townage,* be this book,
To be my Lady's Prisoneir.

Guid Houp syne rounit † in my ear,
    And bad me baldlie brieve a bill ; ‡
With Lawliness he suld it bear,
    With Fair Service send it her till :
    I woke, and writ her all my will.
Fair Service fure § withouten fear,
    Saying till her, with words still,
Have pity on your Prisoneir.

Than Lawliness to Pity went,
    And said till her, in terms short,
Let we yon Prisoneir be schent,‖
    Will no one do to us support ?
    Gar lay ane siege unto yon fort,
Than Pity said, I sall appear.
    Thocht says, I hecht,¶ come I ourethort—
I houp to louse the Prisoneir.

Than to battle they were arrayit all,
    And aye the wawart ** keepit Thocht ;
Lust bear the banner to the wall,
    And Business the great gyn †† brocht.
    Scorn cries out, says, Wald ye ocht ?
Lust says, We wald have entry here.
    Comparison says, That is for nocht,
Ye will not win the Prisoneir.

---

* Townish—that is, too much of the burgher, and not enough
of the baron.   † Whispered.
    ‡ Write a letter.   § Went, or carried it.   ‖ Ruined.
    ¶ Promised.   ** The van.   †† Ordnance

They therein schup * for to defend,
    And they therefurth sailyeit † ane hour :
Than Business the great gyn bend,
    Struck doun the top of the fore tour.
    Comparison began to lour,
And cryit furth, I you requeir,
    Soft and fair, and do favour,
And tak to you the Prisoneir.

They fyrit the yetts deliverly,‡
    With faggots were great and huge ;
And Strangeness, where that he did lie,
    Was burnt into the porter lodge.
    Lustily they lackit but a judge,
Sic straiks and stychling § was on steir ;
    The seemliest was made assege,‖
To whom that he was Prisoneir.

Through Scorn's nose they put a prik,
    Thus he ¶ was banist and gat a blek ; **
Comparison was erdit quik,
    And Languor lap and brak his nek ;
    They sailyeit fast all the fek,††
Lust chasit my Lady's chalmerleir,‡‡
    Guid Fame was drounit in a sek ;
Thus ransomit they the Prisoneir.

---

* Shaped.   † Assailed.   ‡ Quickly.
§ Flying of hot embers.   ‖ A siege.
¶ Mr Laing says these words are a mistake for "Bissiness;"
but he forgets that *Bissiness* was one of the assailants.
** Was made black.   †† Rest.   ‡‡ Chancellor.

Fra Slander hard Lust had undone
   His enemies, him agains
Assemblit ane seemly sort full sone,
   And raise and rowttit * all the plains ;
   His cusing † in the Court remains,
But Jalouse folks and Geangleirs,‡
   And false Invy that no thing lanes,§
Blew out on Love's Prisoneir.

Syne Matrimony, that noble king,
   Was grievit, and gatherit ane great host,
And all enermit,‖ without leising,
   Chased Sklander to the west sea coast ;
   Than was he and his lineage lost,
And Matrimony, withouten weir,
   The band of friendship has indost
Betwix Beauty and her Prisoneir.

Be that of eild was Guid Fame's air,¶
   And coming to continuatioun,
And to the Court made his repair,
   Where Matrimony than wore the croun ;
   He gat ane confirmatioun,
All that his mother aucht but weir : **
   And baid still, as it was reason,
With Beauty and the Prisoneir.

This is another of Dunbar's allegorical pieces, written in his usual felicitous style ; but, as Mr

---

* Ranged.   † Accusing.   ‡ Wrangler.
§ Conceals.   ‖ Armed.
¶ By the time Good Fame's heir was of age.
** All that his mother possessed without contention or doubt.

Laing suggests, it may be merely a poetical version of one of the pageants common at the time. He fails, however, to shew any instance of this kind prior to 1512, when " Le Fortresse Dangerus" was exhibited before Henry VIII. Another pageant was performed at a banquet given by Cardinal Wolsey, in honour of the ambassadors from Charles V., in 1522, more akin to Dunbar's plot. Still these scenic representations, even the first mentioned, must have occurred many years after " Bewty and the Prisoneir " was written. At the same time, it is quite possible that the idea was suggested by some one or other of the masks which then formed the staple of courtly amusement. There is also considerable resemblance to Gawin Douglas's " King Hart," in the mode in which Dame Pleasaunce and her ladies assail his castle. But Douglas was contemporary with Dunbar, and both might probably be indebted to the same source. Be this as it may, no other poet of his age, in so far as we have the means of judging, could have handled the subject so well. " Lady, help your Prisoneir " is mentioned in the " Complaynt of Scotland," 1549, and no doubt the same poem is meant. It must thus have been popular, though it is not known to have been in print before produced by Mr Laing from the Bannatyne MS., in which there were mistakes which he was unable to correct. We have endeavoured to rectify these.

———

The foregoing poems may be considered as having been, for the most part, composed by Dunbar in his younger years, while a student or a wandering friar, or in the more exalted position of secretary to various embassies which James IV. is known to have sent to the continental courts. For his services in this way, and perhaps as much on account of his poetical reputation, the king granted him a pension of ten pounds yearly, in 1500. The gift is recorded in the Privy Seal Register, and is as follows:—" A Lettre maid to Maister* Williame Dunbar of the gift of ten li of pensioune, to be pait to him of our souerane Lordis cofferis, be the Thesaurare, for al the dais of his life, or quhil he be promovit be our souerane Lord to a benefice of xl li, or above;" dated August 15, 1500. From this period to the death of the king at Flodden, in 1513, Dunbar was intimately connected with the royal househeld, and his ballads and other verses on subjects incidental to the court, throw considerable light on the domestic occupations and pastimes of the sovereign.

Although James was elevated to the throne amidst rebellion and the assassination of his father, and although it is said the circumstance frequently preyed upon his mind in after-life, yet his court was perhaps one of the gayest that the Scottish monarchy can boast. He was himself of a sprightly

---

* Professional men, especially masters of art, were invariably styled " Maister."

and gallant disposition, too much devoted, no doubt, to pleasures of an unlicensed character, yet occasionally subjected to fits of melancholy and piety, which made him a frequent and liberal donor to the Church. He was, at the same time, a patron of literature, and also of the arts and sciences, so far as known in his day, and justice was so well administered, and treason so put down, that the country rose to a state of prosperity and an influence among the nations altogether unknown in former times. The navy of Scotland never assumed such importance as in his reign, and commerce flourished in an extraordinary degree. He built the Palace of Holyrood, and greatly enlarged those of Stirling and Falkland, as appears from the Treasurer's Accounts; and he was himself one of the best jousters at the numerous tournaments which he gave for the amusement of the court and the foreign ambassadors. He was, in every sense, one of the most accomplished knights of his day.

The bustle and enterprise occasioned by the measures of the king are thus happily described by Dunbar in one of his addresses to his majesty :—

> " Schir, ye have mony servitouris,
> And officiaris of dyvers curis ;
> Kirkmen, courtmen, and craftismen fyne ;
> Doctouris in jure, and medicyne,
> Divinouris, rethoris, and philosophouris,
> Astrologis, artistis, and oratouris ;

> Men of armes, and vailyeand knychtis,
> And mony uther gudlie wichtis ;
> Musicianis, menstralis, and mirrie singaris ;
> Chevalouris, callandaris, and Frensche flingaris ;
> Cunyouris, carvouris, and carpentaris,
> Beildaris of barkis, and ballingaris ;
> Masounis, lyand upon the land,
> And schip wrichtis hewand upone the strand ;
> Glasing wrichtis, goldsmythis, and lapidaris,
> Pryntouris, payntouris, and potingaris ;
> And all of thair craft cumming,
> And all at anis laboring,
> Quhilk pleisand ar and honorable ;
> And to your Hienes profitable ;
> And richt convenient for to be,
> With your hie regale Majestie."

That the first printing press in Scotland was established by James IV. is a great fact in attestation of his love of literature; and there are numerous proofs in the Treasurer's Accounts of his extreme fondness for music. In 1489, the year after he ascended the throne, a band of English pipers came to Edinburgh, and they played at the Castle gate, where his majesty heard them, and rewarded them with twelve *demyes*.* In 1491, three English pipers were heard by the king at Linlithgow, and paid seven unicorns.† In his nu-

---

* A gold coin, equal to twelve shillings Scots. The payment is dated 10th July 1489.

† A gold coin, struck in the reign of James III. ; but we are not informed of its precise value.

merous excursions throughout the country, James frequently carried instruments of music in his train. In 1494-5, an organ had been sent to Stirling; and in 1497, 9s. were paid for " tursing the Kingis organis betuix Strivelin and Edinburgh." In 1502, John Goldsmyth, in Inverness, was indemnified for his advances "for ane cais to turs the organis in," 7s. 8d.; and there was paid to " ij childer that bure the organis and thair bellysis ouir the month and agane, xxviijs." In 1506, John Goldsmyth was again employed in packing the organ in Eskdale, the opposite part of the kingdom. In 1498, 13s. were paid "for ane quhissil to the king." The person who played on the whistles was called " Quhissil Gibbon." His name first appears in the Treasurer's Accounts in 1497. In 1502, there was paid to William, the *tabronar*, " to by him quhissilis, by the kingis command," 14s.; and in 1503, " to the *cornut*, to by him quhisslis, be the kingis command," 43s. In the beginning of the sixteenth century, the names of various " quhissi-laris" appear in the Treasurer's books; and one of them, no doubt belonging to the court, had, in 1505, " Frenche tartane to be ane cote"* pro-vided for him. A " Frensch quhissilar " was at court about that time, and, in 1506, ten French crowns were given him " to pass his way." Among the " musicianis, menstralis, and mirrie singaris," mentioned by Dunbar, the Treasurer shews that

* The royal livery of James IV. was red and yellow.

there was one Nicholas Gray, who played "on the dron"—the drone bagpipe. In 1505, besides "Jamie Wederspune," the fiddler, there was "Jamie that playis on the drone." In 1506, the royal household had four Italian schawmeris,* who are sometimes styled "iiij childer chawmeris;" so that they had been young persons. In that year he was attended by them when landing in a boat at Blackness. Julian Drummond was player on the *tuba ductilis*† in the king's household, both in the reign of James IV. and James V. He is supposed to have been descended of a branch of the Hawthornden family, who had gone to Italy. The Treasurer's Accounts shew that harpers of various nations attended the court; and that something like competitions occasionally took place between the English, Irish, Highland, and Lowland harpers. Frequent gratuities are entered as having been given to the performers. Of the "oratouris," and "Frensche flingaris," of whom Dunbar speaks, many proofs could be adduced from the Treasurer's Accounts. By orators the poet, no doubt, means storytellers. Richard Wallace, a courier, or bearer of letters, was at times a teller of tales or "geists" to the king. There was also "Widderspune the foulare, that tald tales and brocht foulls to the king," together with "Watchod the tale tellare," all of whom occur between 1496 and 1497. "Hog

* Players on the cornet.
† An instrument, probably, of the nature of the trombone.

the jestour," and "Thomas the jestour" are frequently mentioned. "March 5, 1507–8. To the
Frenche menstrallis, that maid ane danss in the
Abbay,* be the kingis command, 12 French
crowns, £8, 8s." These were, possibly, the
"Frensche flingaris" referred to by Dunbar, though
they are styled minstrels. It is to be regretted that
there is nothing in the Treasurer's Accounts to
indicate whether the minstrels sung, like the trou-
badours, as well as played. The contrary, indeed,
may be inferred from the distinction made between
singers, musicians, and orators. But there were
other dancers beside the French flingers; in particular the morris-dancers, of whom he elsewhere
says :—

"Sum lait at evin bringis in the Moreis."

"Jan. 6, 1503–4. To Colin Campbell, and his
marrowis, that brocht in the moress daunss, for
thair expensis maid thairin, be the kingis command,
20 French crowns, equal to £14 Scots." "Franche
Maister John," (afterwards Abbot of Tungland)
"Thomas Boswel," (ancestor of the Boswells of
Auchinleck and Balmuto) "and Gwilliam Taw-
broner" frequently appear among the makers of
dances before the king. In 1512, (Dec. 5) Mon-
sieur La Mote, the French ambassador's servants,

* Is it to be supposed from this that Holyrood Palace was
not built, or finished, at this time? It is supposed to have been
built about the beginning of the sixteenth century.

received " 10 crowns, of wecht £9 " for dancing
" ane morris to the king."

His majesty was not unfrequently entertained
with theatrical performances, at least what were
called plays, especially in the earlier portion of his
reign.   " Patrick Johnston, and the playaris of
Lythguou that playt to the king " occur repeatedly
from 1488 to 1492.

Such were the pastimes and pastime-makers of
the court of James IV., the patron of Dunbar.
And in this motley throng it was the fortune of
the poet to mix as one of the royal contributors of
amusement, though in a higher capacity.   That he
wore the king's livery is apparent from more than
one entry in the Treasurer's books :—" 27th Jan.
1506-7 : Item, to Maister William Dunbar, be
the Kingis command, for caus he wantit his *goun*
at Yule, vli."   Again, " Jan. 23, 1511-12 : Item,
to Maister William Dunbar, for his yule leveray,
vj elnis ane quartar Parise blak to be hyme ane
gowne, price eln xls. summa xij ii. x s."   " Item,
allowit to the said Maister William, attour his
leveray was tane at yule in anno vcxj. [1511,] v.
quartaris scarlete, price iijli. ijs. vjd."   Thus we
have a pretty accurate idea of the position and
atmosphere in which moved one of the greatest
poets of his day.   He was an ecclesiastic besides,
and had said his first mass before the king on the
17th March 1503-4, for which he had a gratuity
of seven French crowns, or £4, 18s. Scots.   Un-

fortunately there is no portrait or figure of the bard of any kind; but we may conceive a person under the medium height, if we believe Kennedy, attired in the king's livery of red and yellow, over which was worn a black gown, when officiating in his character of chaplain.

We may fancy the character of the monarch who found recreation in such curious and varied forms: at one time listening to a new ballad by his poet-laureate anon to the tales of his courier or fowler, again delighted with the minstrels and merry singers, the jesters, and, late in the evening, with the morris-dancers. Again, we find him busily superintending his numerous public works, particularly his ship-building yards, perhaps pacing the unfinished deck of the " Great Michael ; " and next we see him riding over moor and fell, frequently a hundred miles at a stretch, to some distant "justice aire," to see that his judges were not napping. Now we may find him at the tilting ground, the most approved of men-at-arms, in the highest excitement and humour; and, ere the sound of revelry has passed from the royal apartments, at midnight he may be discovered a repentant recluse among the *Observant* Friars of Stirling. And yet, notwithstanding this somewhat capricious character of the sovereign, the reign of James IV. may be styled the "golden age" of poetry and music in Scotland. To this period we are in all likelihood indebted for many of those

fine old airs which still survive, and which the
puritanism of the sixteenth and seventeenth centuries could not sweep away, for they were en-
graven on the living memory, and handed down
in that way from age to age.

Nor was the art of painting neglected. In 1506
there occurs this entry in the Treasurer's Accounts :
"To David Prat, the payntour, in compleit payment of the *altar paynting*, as resting awand to
him, ij. li. ixs." This picture, now at Holyrood
Palace, was long at Hampton Court, and is supposed, on good grounds, as shewn by Mr Laing in
a paper read some time ago to the Antiquarian
Society, to have originally formed the altar-piece
of Trinity Church.

James, at the same time, was not above the
weakness of the age in matters of science. He
was a believer in astrology and alchymy, and spent
no small portion of his means in unattainable
results. His principal agent in attempting to con-
vert the baser metals into gold was an Italian from
Lombardy. He had practised medicine in France,
and became attached, in the capacity of leech or
doctor, to the Scottish court. His name frequently
appears in the Treasurer's Accounts as "Maister
John, the French medicinar." Bishop Lesley says,
"He causit the king believe that he, *be multiplyinge*,
and utheris his inventions, wold make fine golde of
uther mettall, quhilk science he callit the quint-
assence, whereupon the king made great cost; but

all in vain." Stirling appears to have been the seat of his secret operations. So early as 1501-2, March 3, "iiij hary nobles were sent *to the Leich to multiply*, summa £9." Though success did not attend these foregone efforts, yet they are understood to have led to the commencement of the gold mines at Crawford moor, which were not altogether unremunerative.

As an attendant at the court, Dunbar had ample leisure to "brief ballatis;" and it is to be supposed that only a small portion of the workings of his muse during so many years, notwithstanding the industry of Bannatyne and others, has come down to our time. Yet the probability is, that his position—living in almost daily expectation of a benefice, and feeling the irksomeness of depending upon favours which a breath might blow to the winds, while it was expected that, by the exercise of his muse, he should contribute to the amusement of the king—marred those higher flights which his active mind might have engaged in under different circumstances. That the small pension of ten pounds—which he enjoyed without augmentation from the crown till 1510, when a considerable addition was made to it—came to him through his own petitioning for favour, does not appear from his works. By the terms in which it was conveyed, it is evident that the king meant it as a temporary reward until a benefice should be given him; and thus he was kept in a continual state of "hope

deferred," the worst possible for a poetical temperament. There were several other literary persons, besides Dunbar, who enjoyed similar small
pensions. It must be admitted, at the same time,
that the poet had various gratuities conferred upon
him at intervals, which helped to eke out his yearly
allowance.

Amongst the first duties of importance that fell
to the lot of our poet-laureate was the auspicious
marriage of the king with the Princess Margaret of
England. It is very probable that Dunbar accompanied the embassy sent to England, in October
1501, to conclude the negotiations for the marriage; but that he remained, as Mr Laing surmises,
to witness the affiancing, which took place, with
much splendour, at St Paul's Cross, on the 25th
January 1502, is more than doubtful. The entry
in the Treasurer's Accounts, from which it is
known that he was in England at all at the time,
proves that he did not remain. It is dated " Dec.
20, (1501.) Item, to Maister William Dunbar,
quhilk was payit to him *efter he cam furth of Ing-
land, vli.*" It is evident from this that he had
been in England, but just as clear that he had returned to Scotland before or on the 20th December
1501; therefore he could not have *remained* in
England till the espousals, on the 25th January
1502. Mr Laing shews, from the privy purse expenses of Henry VIII., that " the Rhymer of Scotland received £6, 13s. 4d., in reward from Henry

VIII., on the 31st of December 1501, and a similar sum on the 7th of January following." Now, this "Rhymer of Scotland" could not be Dunbar, unless these gratuities were paid to some one of the embassy on his account; for it is clear he could not be in Edinburgh on the 20th December 1501, and again in London on the 7th January 1502. Travelling at that time was not so expeditious as now: a journey from Edinburgh then, and long afterwards, was seldom performed in less than three weeks.

Be this as it may, it became the pleasant duty of the bard to celebrate the marriage of the royal pair in verse. The Princess Margaret did not make her entrance into Edinburgh till the 7th August 1503, the progress from London having occupied fully a month. She was met by the king on the boundaries of his ancient dominion, and escorted to the capital with the utmost gallantry and chivalric display. The union was celebrated at Holyrood, the day after Margaret's arrival, and the Treasurer's Accounts attest the magnificence of the preparations made for the occasion. Dunbar was then, though perhaps past middle life, but a young courtier, full of expectation, and the epithalamium which he composed in honour of the auspicious event, shewed that he sung with a will, and in the highest strain of his muse. The royal pair were very poetically figured as the representatives of the national emblems.

THE THISTLE AND THE ROSE.

When March was with variand windis past,
  And Aperil* had, with her silver showers,
Tane leave at Nature with ane orient blast,
  And lusty May, that mothir is of flowers,
  Had made the birds to begin their hours †
Amang the tender odours red and white,
Whose harmony to hear it was delight,

In bed, at morrow, sleeping as I lay,
  Methought Aurora, with her crystal ene,
In at the window lukit by the day,
  And halsit ‡ me, with visage pale and green ;
  On whose hand a lark sang fro the spleen §—
Awauk, lovers, out of your slumbering !
See how the lusty morrow does upspring.

Methought fresh May before my bed upstood,
  In weed depaint of mony diverse hue,
Sober, benign, and full of mansuetude,
  In bricht attire of flow'rs forgit new,
  Heavenly of colour, white, red, brown, and blue,
Balmit in dew, and gilt with Phœbus' beams ;
While all the house illuminit of her lemes.||

Sluggard, she said, awauk anon for shame,
  And in mine honour something thou go write ;
The lark has done the merry day proclaim,

---

* So pronounced in Scotch.

† Morning orisons. From *Horæ*, in the Missal of the Romish
Church.

‡ Hailed.   § The heart. || Gleams.

To raise up lovers with comfort and delight ;
Yet nocht increases thy courage to indite,
Whose heart some time has glad and blissful been,
Sangis to mak under the leavis green.

Whereto, quoth I, sall I uprise at morrow,
   For in this May few birdis herd I sing ;
They have more cause to weep and plane* their
     sorrow ;
   Thy air it is not wholesome nor bening ;
   Lord Eolus does in thy season ring :
So busteous† are the blastis of his horn,
Amang thy boughs to walk I have forborne ?

With that this Lady soberly did smile,
   And said, Uprise, and do thy observance ;
Thou did promyt,‡ in Mayis lusty while,
   For to descrive the ROSE, of most pleasance.
   Go, see the birdis how they sing and dance,
Illuminit oure with orient skies bricht,
Enamelit richly with new azure licht.

When this was said, departit she, this Queen,
   And enterit in a lusty garden gent ;§
'And then methought, full hastily bescne,||
   In serk and mantle efter her I went
   Into this garth, most dulce¶ and redolent,
Of herb and flow'r, and tender plantis sweet,
And green leavis doing of dew down fleet.**

---

* Complain of.   † Violent, boisterous.   ‡ Promise.
§ Fine. || Attired, or provided.   ¶ Sweet.
** Quickly dropping dew.

The purpour sun, with tender beams reid,
    In orient bricht as angel did appear,
Through golden skies putting up his heid,
    Whose gilt tressis shone so wonder clear,
    That all the world took comfort, far and near,
To look upon his fresh and blissful face,
Doing all sable fro the heavens chase.

And, as the blissful soun' of cherarchy,*
    The fowlis sung through comfort of the licht ;
The birdis did with open voices cry,
    Oh, lovers' foe ! away, thou dully nicht,
    And welcome day, that comforts every wicht ;
Hail May, hail Flora, hail Aurora sheen !
Hail Princess Nature, hail Venus, love's queen !

Dame Nature gave ane inhibition there,
    To fierce Neptunus, and Eolus the bauld,
Not to perturb the water nor the air,
    And that no shouris snell nor blastis cauld
    Effreng † suld flouris nor foulis on the fold : ‡

---

* Both Lord Hailes and Mr Laing interpret this line as the "blissful *sone* [sun] of cherarchy," thanksgiving of angels. In the original it is the "blissful *soune* of cherarchy," and should read thus—

    "And, as the blissful *sound* of cherarchy,
      The fowlis sung through comfort of the licht."

The difference in the meaning, we think, is very obvious.

† Assail. Flowers could not well be *terrified*, as in Laing's edition, by snell showers.

‡ This word, in place of *earth*, as Laing has it, must mean in the *bud* or *blossom*. We are not aware that flowers and fowls are to be found anywhere else than *on the earth*.

She bad eik Juno, goddess of the sky,
That she the heaven suld keep amene* and dry.

She ordered eik that every bird and beast,
   Before her Hieness suld anon compeir,
And every flow'r of virtue, most and least,
   And every herb by field far and near,
   As they had wont in May, fro year to year,
To her, their maker, to mak obedience,
Full low inclining with all due reverence.

With that anon she send the swift Roe
   To bring in beasts of all conditioun ;
The restless Swallow commandit she also,
   To fetch all fowl of small and great renoun ;
   And to gar flow'rs compeir of all fassoun,†
Full craftily conjurit she the Yarrow,‡
Whilk did furth swirk§ as·swift as ony arrow.

All present were, in twinkling of an e'e,
   Baith beast and bird, and flow'r, before the Queen;
And first the Lion, greatest of degree,
   Was callit there, and he, most fair to seen,
   With a full hardy countenance and keen,
Before Dame Nature came, and did incline,
With visage bauld, and courage leonine.

This awful beast full terrible was of cheer,
   Piercing of look, and stout of countenance,
Richt strong of corps, of fashion fair, but feir,‖
   Lusty of shape, licht of deliverance,
   Red of his colour, as is the ruby glance ;

---

* In amenity.　　　† Fashion.　　　‡ The herb sneeswort.
§ Spring.　　　‖ Without companion.

On field of gold he stood full michtily,
With flour-de-lisis circulit lustily.

This Lady liftit up his cluvis* clear,
    And let him listly† lean upon her knee,
And crownit him with diadem full dear,
    Of radious stones, most royal for to see ;
    Saying, The King of Beastis mak I thee,
And the chief protector in woods and shaws ;
Unto thy lieges go furth, and keep the laws.

Exercie‡ justice with mercy and conscience,
    And let no small beast suffer skaith nor scorne,
Of great beastis that bene§ of more piscence ;
    Do law alike to apes and unicorns,
    And let no bowgle,|| with his lusteous ¶ horns,
The meek pleuch ox oppress, for all his pride,
But in the yoke go peaceable him beside.

When this was said, with noise and soun' of joy,
    All kind of beastis into their degree,
At once cryit, Laud !—Vive le Roy !
    And till his feet fell with humilitie ;
    And all they made him homage and fewtie,**
And he did them receive with princely laitis,††
Whose noble ire is *proteir prostratis.* ‡‡

---

* Hoofs.   † Lightly.   ‡ Exercise.   § Are.
|| Wild ox.   ¶ Rough.   ** Fealty.   †† Manners.
‡‡ Lord Hailes calls this an obscure expression ; and, from a hint which he supplies, Laing adopts the word *parcere* as having at least an intelligible meaning. But this does not mend the matter—*parcere prostratis* is next to nonsense. The word is more likely to be from *protero*, and *proteir prostratis* would mean that the lion's ire was trampled under, or subdued.

Syne crownit she the Eagle King of Fowls,
   And as steel dertis sharpit she his pens,
And bade him be as just to apes and owls,
   As unto peacocks, papingoes, or crens,
   And mak a law for wicht fowls and for wrens ;
And let no fowl of ravyne * do efferay,†
Nor devour birdis but his awin prey.

Than callit she all flouris that grew on field,
   Discerning all their seasons and effeirs': ‡
Upon the awful THISTLE she beheld,§
   And saw him keepit with a bush of spears ;
   Consid'ring him so able for the weirs,
A radius croun of rubies she him gave,
And said, In field, go furth and fend the lave.

And sen thou art a king, thou be discreet ;
   Herb without virtue thou hald not of sic price
As herb of virtue, and of odour sweet ;
   And let no nettle vile, and full of vice,
   Her fallow‖ to the guidly flour-de-lis ;
Nor let no wild weed, full of churlishness,
Compare her to the lilie's nobleness :

---

* No ravenous fowl. † Assail—same word as affray.
‡ What belonged to them.
§ Pinkerton remarks, in his History of Scotland, that this is the first authentic appearance of the Thistle as a Scottish badge. Quoting " Cleland's Collection," in reference to the marriage of James IV. and the Princess of England, it is said : " Under was a licorne and a greyhound, that held a difference of one charden florysched, and a red rose interlassed."
‖ Make herself equal to.

Nor hald no other flow'r in sic deuty
    As the fresh ROSE, of colour red and white:
For gif thou does, hurt is thine honesty ;
    Considering that no flow'r is so perfite,
    So full of virtue, pleasance, and delight,
So full of blissful, angelic beauty,
Imperial birth, honour and dignity.*

Than to the ROSE she turnit her visage,
    And said, O lusty dochter, most bening,
Above the lily, illustare † of lineage,
    Fro the stock royal rising fresh and ying,
    Bot ‡ ony spot, or macull doing spring :§
Come, bloom of joy, with jemis to be crown'd,
For oure the lave thy beauty is renown'd.

A costly croun, with clarified stones bricht,
    This comely Queen did on her head inclose,
While all the land illuminit of the licht ;
    Wherefore, methought, the flow'rs did rejoice,
    Crying, at once, Hail, be thou richest ROSE !
Hail herbs' Empress, hail freshest Queen of Flow'rs,
To thee be glory and honour at all hours.

Then all the birds sang with voice on hicht,
    Whose mirthful soun' was marvellous to hear ;
The mavis sang, Hail, ROSE, most rich and richt,
    That does up flourish under Phœbus' sphere ;

---

* As Lord Hailes remarks, "This is an ingenious exhortation to conjugal fidelity, drawn from the high birth, beauty, and virtues of the Princess Margaret."

† More illustrious.   ‡ Without.
§ Spot or blemish, upspringing.

Hail, plant of youth, hail, Princess, dochter dear;
Hail, blosom breaking out of the bluid royal,
Whose precious virtue is imperial.

The merle she sang, Hail, ROSE of most delight,
   Hail, of all flow'rs queen and sovereign:
The lark she sang, Hail, ROSE both red and white,
   Most pleasant flow'r, of michty colours twane:*
   The nichtingale sang, Hail, Nature's suffragane,
In beauty, nurture, and every nobleness,
In rich array, renown, and gentleness.

The common voice up raise of birds small,
   Upon this wise, Oh, blessit be the hour
That thou was chosen to be our principal;
   Welcome to be our Princess of honour,
   Our pearl, our pleasance, and our paramour,
Our peace, our play, our plain felicitie;
Christ thee comfort from all adversitie.

Than all the birds sung with sic a shout,
   That I anon awoke where that I lay,
And with a braid † I turnit me about
   To see this court; but all were went away;
   Then up I leanit, haflingis in affray,
And thus I writ as ye have heard to-forrow,‡
Of lusty May upon the nynt morrow.

---

* In allusion, probably, to the houses of York and Lancaster,
which were united in the persons of Henry VII. and his queen.
At the same time the poet frequently uses the same expression—
"red and white"—where no such application could be intended.
   † Start.   ‡ Before.

As the author tells us in the concluding line, this truly beautiful poem was written on the ninth of May, while the marriage between James IV. and the Princess Margaret of England did not take place till the 8th of August 1503. It was no vulgar conception to represent the royal parties in this union by the national emblems of the *Thistle* and the *Rose.* By so doing he judiciously avoided that direct and personal flattery which a poet of less imagination would have adopted, at the same time that it afforded him an opportunity of inculcating sound advice, both political and moral. The queen must have appreciated highly the compliments paid to her under the designation of the ROSE, and she seems to have ever been, in after-life, though unstable in politics and even morals, the steady friend of the bard. The poem is altogether a remarkable piece of composition, both for the descriptive powers which it exhibits, and the ingenious manner in which the heraldic characters that constitute the arms of Scotland are made to act. Lord Hailes, Warton, Ellis, all are lavish in praise of the poem. " Every reader," says Hailes, " will remember Langhorne's encomium—

In nervous strains Dunbar's bold music flows,
And *Time still spares the ' Thistle and the Rose.'* "

TO THE MERCHANTS OF EDINBURGH.

Why will ye, merchants of renoun,
Let Edinburgh, your noble town,
For laik of reformatioun
The common profit tyne and fame ?
  Think ye not shame,
That ony other regioun
Sall with dishonour hurt your name ?

May nane pas through your principal gaits,*
For stink of haddocks and of skates ;
For cries of carlings † and debates ;
For fensum flytings of defame : ‡
  Think ye not shame,
Before strangers of all estates,
That sic dishonour hurt your name ?

Your stinking style § that stands dirk,
Halds the licht fra your Parish Kirk ;
Your forestairs ‖ maks your houses mirk,

---

* Streets.   † Old women.

‡ Offensive scolding in defamation of one another—a practice
apparently hereditary among the lower class of fish-women.

§ The " Stinkand Style " is described by Mr Laing as " a
narrow passage which extended from the north side of St Giles's
Church, between the Tolbooth and the houses which formed the
Krames, to the opposite side of the street, now called the
Luckenbooths. It long continued to be a place noted for filth,
robberies, and assaults."

‖ Stairs in front of the houses, some of which still exist.

Like na country but here at hame :
  Think ye not shame,
Sae little policy to wirk
In hurt and slander of your name ?

At your Hie Cross,* where gold and silk
Suld be, there is but cruds and milk ;
And at your Tron† but cockle and wilk,
Panshes, puddings of Jock and Jame :‡
  Think ye not shame,
Sen as the world says that ilk
In hurt and slander of your name ?

Your common minstrels§ have no tune,
But "Now the day dawis," and " Into June ;"
  Cunninger men maun serve St Clown,

---

  * The octagonal building called the High Cross of Edinburgh, so celebrated in the annals of the city, and immortalised in " Marmion," was rebuilt in 1617, and altogether removed in 1756. The site is indicated by the radiated pavement ; and here all public proclamations continue to be made.

  † The Tron Church now occupies the site where stood the Tron, or public weighing-beam. The *Weigh-house*, now also removed, was subsequently built at the foot of the Castle Hill.

  ‡ *Jock* and *Jame* were names, probably local, given to certain kinds of puddings, now unknown.

  § What were called the *common minstrels* were the town pipers, possessed by, at least, all the royal burghs in Scotland, whose duty it was to perambulate the civic boundaries at certain hours in the morning and evening, and to accompany, or rather precede, the authorities on particular official occasions. If the feudal chief had his piper, so had the magistrates of burghs, who, while in office, were the superiors of all within their boundaries. They were paid either from the common fund, or by the gratuity

And never to other crafts claim :
  Think ye not shame,
To hald sic mowars* on the moon,
In hurt and slander of your name ?

Tailyours, soutars, and crafts vile,
The fairest of your streets do fyle, †
And merchants at the Stinking Style
Are hampered in ane honey-kaim ;
  Think ye not shame,
That ye have neither wit nor will
To win yourself ane better name ?

Your burgh of beggars is ane nest ;
To shout thae sweyngcours ‡ will not rest ;
All honest folk they do molest,
Sae piteously they cry and rame :
  Think ye not shame,
That for the poor has nothing drest, §
In hurt and slander of your name ?

---

of the inhabitants.   In some instances they were hardly enough
dealt with ; for, if they failed in their duty, unless by the in-
temperateness of the weather, they were "to get na meet that
day."   It could scarcely be expected that such minstrels should
be of the first order ; but, according to Dunbar, the pipers of
Edinburgh could play only two tunes, "Now the day dawis,"
and "Into June."   The first of these, of ancient date, is now
better known as the air of "Bruce's Address."   We know not
if the latter exists under any title.   Better minstrels, Dunbar
asserts, were to be found in the service of "Sanct Clown," or the
"Merry-Andrew."   The complaint that they could only play
two tunes would infer that there were a great many others which
they ought to have been master of.

  * Jesters.   † Defile.   ‡ Idle fellows.
  § Provided.   There was no poor-law in Scotland at this

Your profit daily does incress,
Your godlie workis less and less ;
Through streets nane may mak progress,
For cry of cruikit, blind, and lame :
   Think ye not shame,
That ye sic substance do possess,
And will not win ane better name?

Sen for the Court and the Sessioun,*
The great repair of this regioun
Is in your burgh, therefore be boun
To mend all faults that are to blame,
   And eschew shame ;
Gif they pass to ane other toun
Ye will decay, and your great name !

Therefore strangers and lieges treat,
Tak not our meikle for their meat,
And gar your merchants be discreet,

---

period, though what were called hospitals were provided by
private behests, and by the communities, in various districts of
the country.   Hence the meaning of Dunbar's accusation—

> "Think ye not shame,
> That for the poor has nothing drest?"

So long as there was no legal provision for the poor, Scotland
was overrun with beggars of all kinds—*swcyngeours* as well as the
lame and proper objects of charity ; and acts of parliament were
passed in vain to put down the nuisance.

* Edinburgh became the seat of government, and the higher
courts, in the course of the fifteenth century, and, consequently,
the city rose rapidly in importance.

That na extortioners be proclaim,
  Offering ane shame :
Keep order, and poor neibours beit,*
That ye may get ane better name !

Singular† profit so does you blind,
The common profit goes behind :
I pray that Lord remeid to find
That deit in to Jerusalem ;
  And gar you shame,
That some reason may you bind,
For to reconquest you guid name !

We are greatly indebted to Mr Laing, who was the first to print this interesting poem from the Reidpeth MS. " It is the more curious," he remarks, " as we have no description of Edinburgh of so early a date ; for the brief notice which occurs in Froissart refers to a period when the city consisted of houses chiefly of wood, and presented an appearance which must have been totally unlike what it assumed during the fifteenth, and retained till the close of the last century. Even those who remember the High Street and Luckenbooths, previous to the first alterations which took place in the Parliament Square and the neighbourhood of St Giles's Cathedral, and before the removal of the Tolbooth, the Krames, and other adjacent buildings, will be fully sensible of the correctness of the poet's description. I have ventured to suggest that

---

* Help, or supply.   † Individual.

this poem might have been composed about the year 1500.   Sir David Lyndsay, in a poem written in 1530, thus alludes to the merchants of Edinburgh, in lines which may be contrasted with Dunbar's satire—

'Adew, Edinburgh, thou heich tryumphand toun,
    Within quhose boundis richt blythful have I bene;
Of trew merchandis, the rute of this regioun,
    Most reddy to ressave Court, King, and Quene,
    Thy policie and justice may be sene;
War, devotioun, wysedome, and honestie,
And credence tint, thay micht be found in thee.'

It is extremely probable that this poem was written about the time suggested by Mr Laing—perhaps a year or two later than 1500.   Dunbar may be supposed to have taken up his residence permanently in Edinburgh in that year, and it is written with all the spirit and vigour of a first impression.   Having travelled a good deal abroad, the contrast between the cities he had seen in foreign lands and the capital of his own country evidently stimulated him in the powerful remonstrance addressed to the merchant burgesses; and it must have had a very decided effect, since, in less than thirty years afterwards, another poet was enabled to address the same class in such terms of laudation as Sir David Lyndsay did.   Possibly both poets exaggerated a little; still, making every allowance, the picture sketched by Dunbar is perhaps not less graphic than true.   The cries and scoldings of the fishwives, the High Cross surrounded by dealers in curds and milk, the Tron by the disposers of cockles, wilks, tripe, and puddings, the streets defiled by the operations of all kinds of craftsmen, and the merchants confined, as in a honeycomb, round the Church of St Giles's, each in his own little hole, or *kaim*, numerous beggars piteously crying and *raming*, and the common minstrels mocking the moon in their evening perambulations through the city, depictures a scene which any artist might paint with an accuracy that would shew what groups the High Street daily presented at the beginning of the sixteenth century.

OF SOLICITORS AT COURT.

By divers ways and operations
Men maks in Court their solicitations :
Some by service and diligence ;
Some by continual residence ;
Some on his substance does abide,
While * fortune do for him provide ;
Some sings, some dances, some tell stories ;
Some late at even brings in the morris ; †
Some flirds, some fenyeis, ‡ and some flatters ;
Some play the fool, and all out clatters ;
Some man, musing with the wa',
Looks as he micht not do with a' ;

---

* Until.   † The morris-dancers.   ‡ Dissembles.

Some stands in to a neuk and rouns ; *
For covatyce † ane other near swoons ;
Some bears as he wald gae wud
For heit ‡ desire of warld's guid ;
Some at the mass leaves all devotion,
And busy labours for promotion ;
Some has their advocates in cham'er,§
And taks them self thereof no glamer.‖
  My simpleness, amang the laiff,¶
Wait of na way, so God me save !
But, with ane humble cheer and face,
Refers me to the king's grace :
Methinks his gracious countenance
In riches is my sufficience.

Dunbar was evidently at this time but a young, though not unobservant, courtier. As Pinkerton remarks, " the poem affords a curious picture of the court of James IV. ;" and the picture, as we have seen, is fully substantiated by the Treasurer's Accounts.

NEW-YEAR'S GIFT TO THE KING.

My Prince ! in God gif thee guid grace,
Joy, gladness, comfort, and solace,
Play, pleasance, mirth, merrie cheer,
  In hansel of this guid New Year.

----

* Whispers.   † Covetousness.   ‡ High or intense.
§ " Pretty wives," says Pinkerton.
‖ Glamour, as here used, must mean observance or sight.
¶ Remainder.

God gif to thee ane blessed chance,
And of all virtue abundance,
And grace aye to persevere,
   In hansel of this guid New Year.

God give thee guid prosperitie,
Fair fortune and felicitie,
Ever mair in earth while thou art here,
   In hansel of this guid New Year.

The heavenly Lord his help thee send,
Thy realm to rule and to defend,
In peace and justice it to steer,
   In hansel of this guid New Year.

God gif thee bliss quhere ever thou bouns,
And send thee many Fraunce crowns,
Hie, liberal heart, and hands not swear,
   In hansel of this guid New Year.

Such new-year addresses were, and still are, not uncommon. Buchanan is known to have offered similar congratulations to Queen Mary and the Regent Murray. Of course, largess was usually expected, which was generally made in French crowns, value 14s. each in Scottish money—hence the point of the poet's wish, " And send thee many Fraunce crowns." French money appears to have been comparatively plentiful in Scotland in the reign of James IV., brought in by traffic, or partly, perhaps, by subsidies.

OF THE LADIES SOLICITORS AT COURT.

Thir ladies fair,
That maks repair,
And in the Court are kend ;
Three days there,
They will do mair
Ane matter for to end,
Than their guidmen
Will do in ten,
For ony craft they can ;
So weel they ken,
What time and when,
Their manes * they sould mak than.

With little noy
They can convoy
Ane matter finally,
Richt mild and moy,
And keep it coy,
On evens quietly ;
They do not miss,
But gif they kiss,
And keepis collatioun,
What rek of this ?
Their matter is
Brocht to conclusioun.

Ye may wit weel,
They have great fiel'

---

* Complaints.

Ane matter to solist ;
 Trest * as the steal,
 Sync never a deal
When they come hame are mist.
 Thir lairdis are
 Me think richt far
Sic ladies behalden to,
 That sa weel daur
 Go to the bar
When there is ocht ado.

 Therefore I read,
 Gif ye have plead,
Or matter into pley,†
 To mak remeid,
 Send in your stead
Your ladies graithit up gay :
 They can defend
 Even to the end
Ane matter furth express ;
 Suppose they spend,
 It is unkend,
Their geir is not the less.

 In quiet place,
 Though they have space
Within less nor twa hours,
 They can, percase,
 Purchase some grace
At the compositours ;

---

* Trusty.   † Plea, debate.

Their composition,
Without suspicion,
There finally is endit
With expedition,
And full remission,
And their seals to are pendit.

Alhail almost,
They mak the cost
With sober recompence ;
Richt little lost,
They get indost,
Alhail their evidence ;
Sic ladies wise,
They are to prise,
To say the veritie,
Sae can devise,
And nocht surprise
Them, nor their honestie.

These satirical verses, bordering on indelicacy,
were no doubt fully borne out by the practices of
the day, as they have been at a much later period.
At the same time, we must not fancy that the poet,
while he abhorred such as "stooped to [interested]
folly," was insensible to the mighty claims which
the fair sisters of creation have on the manhood of
the world.   Hear him

IN PRAISE OF WOMEN.

Now of women this I say for me,
Of earthly things nane may better be :
They should have worship and great honouring
Of men, above all other earthly thing ;

Richt great dishonour upon himself he taks
In word or deed wha ever women laks,
Sen that of women comin all are we ;
Women are women, and sae will end and die :
Wo worth the fruit would put the tree to nocht !
And wo worth him richt so that sayis ocht
Of womanhood that may be ony lak,
Or sic great shame upon him for to tak !
They us conceive with pain ; and be them fed,
Within their breasts there we boun to bed :
Great pain, and wo, and mourning marvellous,
Into their birth they suffer sair for us ;
Than, meat and drink to feed us got we nane,
But that we souk out of their breast's bane :
They are the comfort that we all have here;
There may no man be till us half so dear :
They are our very nest of nourishing.
In lack of them, wha can say ony thing,
That foul his nest he fyles ! and for thy*
Exilit he suld be of all guid company ;
There suld nae wise man give audience
To sic ane without intelligence.
Christ to His father He had not ane man ;
See what worship women suld have than !
That Son is Lord, that Son is King of kings,
In heaven and earth His Majesty aye rings !
Sen she has borne Him in her haliness,
And He is well, and grund of all guidness,
All women of us suld have honouring,
Service and love above all other thing !

---

* That.

These lines, it must be admitted, are considerably below the standard of Dunbar's muse; still, as they are ascribed to him both by Bannatyne and Maitland, we have no right to say that they are not his. The sentiment all must applaud; and we heartily echo the line—

" Wo worth the fruit would put the tree to nocht !"

TIDINGS FRAE THE SESSION.

Ane muirland's man, of uplands mak
At hame thus to his nichtbour spak—
What tidings, gossip, peace or weir ?*
The tother rownit† in his ear,
   I tell you this under confession,
But lately lichtit aff my mere,‡
   I come of Edinburgh frae the Session.

What tidings heard you there, I pray you ?
The tother answerit, I sall say you :
Keep this all secret, gentle brother,
Is na man there that trusts ane other :
   Ane common doar of transgression,
Of innocent folks prevents a futher :§
   Sic tidings heard I at the Session.

Some with his fallow‖ rowns him to please,
That wald for envy bite off his neis ;¶

---

* War.   † Whispered.   ‡ Mare.
§ Prevents a fusion, or union.
‖ Whispers in an insinuating manner.   ¶ Nose.

His fae some by the oxter leads ;
Some patters with his mouth on beads,*
  That has his mind all on oppression ;
Some becks full law, and shaws bare heads,
  Wald look full heich were not the Session.

Some biding the law, lays land in wed ;†
Some super expendit, goes to his bed ;
Some speeds, for he in Court has means ;
Some of partiality complenes,
  How feud and favour flemis‡ discretion ;
Some speaks full fair, and falsely feins :
  Sic tidings heard I at the Session.

Some casts summons, and some excepts ;
Some stands beside, and skailed§ law keps ;
Some is continuit ; some wins ; some tynes ;
Some makes him merry at the wines ;
  Some is put out of his possession ;
Some herriet,‖ and on creddens ¶ dines :
  Sic tidings heard I at the Session.

Some swears, and some forsake God ;
Some in ane lambskin is ane tod ;
Some in his tongue his kindness turses ;**
Some cuts throats, and some picks purses ;
  Some goes to gallows with procession ;
Some sanes the sait,†† and some them curses :
  Sic tidings heard I at the Session.

---

* Mutters his prayers.   † Mortgages his estate.
‡ Inflames.   § Spilled.   ‖ Robbed.
¶ Credit.   ** Bundles up.
†† Blesses the judges.

Religious men of diverse places
Comes there too woo, and see fair faces ;
Baith Carmelites and Cordilleris*
Comes there to gen'er and get ma friers,
   And are unmindful of their profession ;
The younger at the elder leirs ;
   Sic tidings heard I at the Session.

There comes young monks of hie complexion,
Of devout mind, love, and affection ;
And in the Court their hate-flesh dantis,†
Full father-like, with pechs and pantis ;‡
   They are so humble of intercession,
All merciful women their errands grantis :
   Sic tidings heard I at the Session.

This is another sarcastic poem, expository of the manner in which justice was administered in the time of Dunbar. It is difficult, however, as Mr Laing remarks, to hazard even a guess as to which of the courts the poet alludes—whether to the old court, abolished March 1503-4, or to the court of daily council then established. We should incline to think that it aimed at the latter, and that, consequently, the verses were written subsequently to the date mentioned.

* These were the severer orders of regular clergy—hence the more pungent the sarcasm.

   † Subdues.   ‡ Short breathings.

THE TESTAMENT OF MR ANDRO KENNEDY.

I, Maister Andro Kennedy,
    Curro quando sum vocatus,
Gotten with sum incuby,
    Or with some freir infatuatus ;
In faith I can nocht tell readily,
    Unde aut ubi fui natus,
But, in truth, I trow truly,
    Quod sum diabolus incarnatus.

Cum nihil sit certius morte,
    We maun all die, when we have done,
Nescimus quando, vel qua sorte,
    Na, blind, alane, wait* of the mone.†
Ego patior in pectore,
    This night I might not sleep a wink;
Licet æger in corpore,
    Yet wald my mouth be wet with drink.

Nunc condo testamentum meum,
    I leave my saul for evermair,
Per omnipotentem Deum,
    In to my Lordis wine cellair ;

---

* To wait—to know, or have knowledge.
† Mr Laing prints this line as follows—

    "Na blind Allane wait of the mone"—

of which it seems impossible to make sense.   The way we print
it, it would read thus—

    "Nay, blind, alone, to know, or have knowledge of the moon."

This is intelligible, especially taken in connexion with the previous
lines—as to the certainty of our all dying.

Semper ibi ad remanendum
  While doomsday, without dissever,
Bonum vinum ad bibendum,
  With sweet Cuthbert that lovit me never.

Ipse est dulcis ad amandum,
  He wad oft ban me in his breath,
Det mihi modo ad potandum,
  And I forgive him laith and wraith :*
Quia in cellario cum servisia,
  I had lever† lie baith air and late,
Nudus solus in camisia,
  Na in my Lordis bed of state.

A barrel bung aye at my bosum,
  Of warldis guid I had na mair ;
Et corpus meum ebriosum,
  I leave into the toun of Air ;
In a draff midding for ever and aye,
  Ut ibi sepeliri queam,
Where drink and draff may, ilka day,
  Be cassyne ‡ super faciem meam.

I leave my heart, that never was sicker,
  Sed semper variabile,
That never mair wald flow nor flicker,§
  Consorti meo Jacobe ;

---

* Disgust and anger.   † Rather.   ‡ Cast.
§ It is generally understood that the circulation of the blood
was not discovered till Hervey did so in the reign of James I. of
England. Does this expression of Dunbar—that the heart of
Andro would "never more *flow* nor flicker"—not indicate a
knowledge of the movement of the heart in accordance with such

Though I wald bind it with a wicker,
  Verum Deum renui ;
But and I hecht* to toom a bicker,
  Hoc pactum semper tenui.

Syne leave I the best aucht† I bocht,
  Quod est Latinum propter caupe‡
To head of kin, but I wait nocht
  Quis est ille, then I schrew§ my scawpe : ‖
I call't my lord, my head, but hiddill,¶
  Sed nulli alii hoc dixerunt,
We were as sib as sieve and riddle,**
  In una silvæ quæ creverunt.

Omnia mea solatia
  They were but leisings all and ane,

---

circulation? The word *flow*, as applied to the heart, would be unintelligible otherwise. In scientific discoveries we take many things for granted that are not consistent with fact, and this, apparently, is one of the fallacies. It is not to be supposed that the action of the lungs and heart upon the blood should have remained a secret throughout all time, down to the reign of James VI. of Scotland.

* Promised.   † Property.

‡ Caupes, or calpes, were the gifts given to the head of a clan to support his dignity as chief.

§ Curse.   ‖ Head.

¶ Secret. Lord Hailes reads this line thus :—"I privately informed the Earl of Cassillis, chief of the name of Kennedy." But this does not seem to be the correct reading. The word *but* signifies *without* ; therefore the meaning is, "I called my Lord, my head, without secrecy," because he was as sib with him as "sieve and riddle."

** This old proverbial saying is not yet obsolete.

Cum omni fraude et fallacia,
  I leave the maister of Sanct Antane,*
Willelmo Gray, sine gratia,
  Mine awn dear cousin, as I ween,
Qui nunquam fabricat mendacia,
  But when the holly growis green. †

My feigning and my false winning,‡
  Relinquo falsis fratribus ;
For that is Godis awn bidding,
  Dispersit, dedit pauperibus.
For menis saulis they say and sing,
  Mentientes pro muneribus ;
Now God gif them ane evil ending,
  Pro suis pravis operibus.

To Jock Fule,§ my folly free,
  Lego post corpus sepultum ;
In faith I am mair fule than he,
  Licet ostendit bonum vultum:
Of corn and cattle, gold and fee,
  Ipse habet valde multum,
And yet he bleris‖ my lord's e'e
  Fingendo eum fore stultum.

---

* The preceptor of St Anthony's Hospital.

† A proverbial saying of persons addicted to falsehood—meaning that they tell lies at all times, for the holly is always green.

‡ He leaves his false *whining* to the knavish friars.

§ The fool of the court of James IV. appears, from the Treasurer's Accounts, to have been a person of the name of John Wallace. He is sometimes styled "Daft Jok the Fule." He died in 1508, when, June 19, 16s. were paid "for Jok Wallass tyrment."   ‖ Blears.

To Master John Clerk* syne,
  Do et lego intime,
God's hie malisone and mine:
  Ipse est causa mortis meæ.
Were I a dog and he a swine,
  Multi mirantur super me,
But I suld gar that lurdane quhryne,†
  Scribendo dentes sine de.

Residuum omnium bonorum,
  For to dispone my lord sall have,
Cum tutela puerorum
  Adce, Kyttee, and all the lave.
In faith I will na langer rave:
  Pro sepultura ordino
On the new gys,‡ sa God me save,
  Non sicut more solito.

In die meæ sepulturæ
  I will none have but our awn gyng,§
Et duos rusticos de rure
  Bearing a barrel on a styng ;§

---

* Lord Hailes's suggestion, that "Maister Johne Clerk was probably an ignorant practitioner in physic," seems perfectly certain from the lines which follow. Mr Laing did not think the explanation satisfactory; but it is only necessary to read the verse to be satisfied. Andro Kennedy attributes his death to "Maister Johne Clerk," and, in consequence, pours forth his malediction upon him. *Maister* was only applied to the learned professions, such as ecclesiastics, lawyers, and doctors; and it is evident that Clerk must have belonged to the latter class.

† That lazy fellow cry out.

‡ Fashion.   § Gang.   ‖ A pole.

Drinking and playing cup out even,
  Sicut egomet solebam ;
Singing and greeting with hie stevin*
  Potum meum cum fletu miscebam.

I will na priestis for me sing,
  Dies illa, Dies iræ ;
Na yet na bellis for me ring,
  Sicut semper solet fieri ;
But a bagpipe to play a spring,
  Et unum ailwisp ante me ;
Instead of banners for to bring
  Quatuor lagenas servisiæ :

Within the grave to set sic thing,
  In modum crucis juxta me.
To flee the fiends, then hardily † sing
  De terra plasmasti me.

If this is not macaronic poetry, and a very fine specimen of it too, the dictionaries of the English language do not rightly explain what macaronic means. Octavius Gilchrist, in mentioning Theophilus Folengo of Mantua, as the supposed inventor of that kind of verse, says, in his " Opus Macoronicum," first printed in 1517, " He was preceded by the laureat Skelton, whose works were printed in 1512, who was himself anticipated by the *great genius of Scotland, Dunbar,* in his ' Testament of Andro Kennedy,' and the last must be

---

* Voice or sound.   † With confidence.

considered as the reviver or introducer of macaronic or burlesque poetry." *

Mr Laing was of opinion that Gilchrist was " not quite correct, as the mixture either of Latin and English words, or in alternate lines, as used by Skelton and Dunbar, does not constitute what is called macaronic verse, the peculiarity of which consists in the use of Latin words and of vernacular words with Latin terminations, usually in hexameter verse." And he claims Drummond of Hawthornden's " Polemo-middinia " as " one of the earliest and most celebrated pieces of the kind which is known in this country." This is surely a very nice distinction. A macaronic poem, we should opine, is simply a mixed, burlesque production, not limited to Latin and English, or vernacular English, but may be composed of any mixture of language, Latin, English, Scotch, High Dutch or Low Dutch; and assuredly the " Testament of Andro Kennedy " is a mixture of Latin and English, and a burlesque poem of great purity and humour. Lord Hailes remarks of it :—" This is a singular performance ; it represents the character of a drunken, graceless scholar. The alternate lines are composed of shreds of the Breviary, mixed with what we call *Dog Latin*, and the French *Latin de Cuisine*."

That Andro Kennedy was no myth we may rest assured from the general character of Dunbar's

---

* The " Testament of Andro Kennedy " was printed in 1508— hence its precedency of the works of Skelton.

satirical pieces.   Mr Laing informs us that his name repeatedly occurs in the Treasurer's Accounts between 1502 and 1504, as, for instance: 21 Aug. 1502, "for ane hors bocht to Jok Bailye,* and syne was geffin to Andro Kennedy, be the kingis command, 50s."   But if this is the Andro of the poem, it is unaccountable how he should not have been styled *Maister* Andro, the invariable title of men of learning.   How he was employed at court is not understood, but that he belonged to Ayrshire, and was one of the Carrick Kennedies,† is obvious from the lines—

> " Et corpus meum ebriosum,
>   I leif into the *toune of Air.*"

The probability is, that Mr Andro was one of the Earl of Cassillis's retainers, and that the poem was composed while " my lord " and his *sib* adherent were at court.

AGAINST TREASON.

AN EPITAPH FOR DONALD OWRE.

In vice most vicious he excels
That with the vice of treason mells;
Though he remission
Have for prodission,
Shame and suspicion aye with him dwells.

------

* Bailie was one of the king's henchmen.

† There used to be a small clan of Kennedies in the Highlands.

And he ever odious as ane owl,
The fault sa filthy is and foul;
Horrible to Natour
Is ane tratour,
As fiend in fratour,* under a cowL

Wha is a traitor, or ane thief,
Upon himself turns the mischief;
His fraudful wiles
Himself beguiles,
As in the Isles is now a preif.

The fell strong traitor Donald Owre,
Mair falset † had nor other four;
Round Isles and seas
In his suppleis,
On gallow treis, yet does he glour.

Falset no feet has, nor defence,
Be power, practice, nor puisance,
Though it fra licht
Be smored with slicht,
God shaws the richt, with sore vengeance.

Of the false fox dissimulator,
Kind has every thief and traitor,
Efter respite
To work despite,
Mair appetite he has of nature.

---

* Fratour or fraterie, the hall of a monastery, where the monks
eat together. Hence the comparison—"As fiend in fratour,
under a cowl."
† Falsehood.

Were the fox ta'en a thousand fauld,
And grace him given aye when he wald;
Were he on plain,
All were in vain,
From hens again micht none him hauld.

The murderer aye murder mais,*
And ever, while he be slain he slays;
Wives thus maks mocks,
Spinnand on rocks,
Aye rins the fox while he foot has.†

"This Donald Owre," Mr Laing tells us, "was a natural son of Angus, the natural son of John, Lord of the Isles; and, having usurped that title, he was, with some of his abettors, forfeited in 1503, when the Western Islands became the property of the Crown. The name Donald Owre, in the Gaelic, signifies 'Donald, the dark-brown man.' He is incidentally mentioned by this name in the Treasurer's Account: 1496, April 28, 'Item, to Donald Owris man, at the kingis command, 18s.' 1497–8, March 1, 'Item, to Donald Owr, at the kingis command, in the toun of Air, £2, 16s. 8d.' 'Item, to ane man of Donald Awris, the king send away errandis, 14s.' The king had two hensmen, [henchmen] Donald and Ronald of the Isles; and Margaret of the Isles, a sister of theirs probably, was also at court during the greater part of his reign."

* Must.   † A proverbial saying.

DUNBAR'S DIRGE TO THE KING AT STIRLING.

We that are here in heaven's glory,
To you that are in purgatory,
Commends us on our heartily wise :
I mean we folk in paradise,
In Edinburgh with all merriness,
To you in Strivilling in distress,
Where nowther pleasance nor delight is,
For pity thus ane apostle writis :
    O ye heremits and hankersaddles,*
That taks your penance at your tables,
And eats not meat restorative,
Nor drinks no wine confortative,
But ale, and that is thin and small ;
With few courses in to your hall,
But † company of lords or knights,
Or ony other guidly wichts,
Solitor walking your alone,
Seeing nothing but stock or stone ;
Out of your painful purgatory,
To bring you to the bliss of glory,
Of Edinburgh, the merry toun,
We sall begin ane careful soun ;
Ane dirige, devoit and meik,
The Lord of bliss doing beseek ‡
You to deliver out of your noy,
And bring you soon to Edinburgh joy,
For to be merry amang us ;
And sa the dirige begins thus :

---

* Anchorites.   † Without.   ‡ Beseeching.

LECTIO PRIMA.

The Father, the Son, and Haly Ghaist,
The mirthful Mary, virgin chaste,
Of angels all the orders nine,
And all the heavenly court divine,
Soon bring you fra the pine and wo
Of Strivilling, every court man's foe,
Again to Edinburgh's joy and bliss,
Where worship, wealth, and weelfare is,
Play, plesance, and sik honesty:
Say ye Amen, for charitie.

RESPONSIO.

Tak consolation in your pain,
In tribulation tak consolation,
Out of vexation come hame again,
Tak consolation in your pain.
   Out of distress of Strivilling toun
   To Edinburgh's bliss, God mak you boun !

LECTIO SECUNDO.

Patriarchs, prophets, and apostles dear,
Confessors, virgins, and martyrs clear,
And all the Saitt Celestiall,*
Devoutly we upon them call,
That soon out of your pains fell,
You may in heaven here with us dwell;
To eat swan, cran, patrik, and plever,
And every fish that swims in river;

---

* Heavenly Court.

To drink with us the new fresh wine
That grew upon the river of Rhine ;
Fresh, fragrant clarets out of France,
Of Angiers, and of Orleans,
With mony ane course of grit daintie :
Say ye Amen, for charitie.

RESPONSIO.

God and Saint Gile * hear you convoy
Baith soon and weel, God and Saint Gile,
To sonce † and seill, ‡ solace and joy,
God and Saint Gile hear you convoy.
　Out of Strivilling pains fell,
　In Edinburgh's joy soon mot § ye dwell !

LECTIO TERTIO.

We pray to all the saints of heaven,
That are above the stars seven,
You to deliver out of your penance,
That you may soon play, sing, and dance,
Here in to Edinburgh, and mak guid cheer,
Where wealth and weelfare is but weir,‖
And I, that does your pains descrive,
Thinks for to vissy ¶ you belive ;
Not in desert with you to dwell,
But as the angel Saint Gabriel,
Does go between, fra heaven's glory,
To them that are in purgatory,

---

* Saint Giles, the patron saint of Edinburgh.
† Plenty.　　　　　　　‡ Felicity.　　　　　　§ May.
‖ Without war.　　　　¶ Visit.

And in their tribulation
To give them consolation,
And shaw them when their pains are past
They sall till heaven come at last ;
And how nane deserves to have sweatness
That never tasted bitterness :
And, therefore, how suld you consider
Of Edinburgh's bliss when ye come hidder,
But gif ye tasted had before
Of Strivilling toun, the pains sore ?
And, therefore, tak in patience
Your penance, and your abstinence,
And ye sall come, or Yule begin,
In to the bliss that we are in :
Whilk grant the glorious Trinitie !
Say ye Amen, for charitie.

RESPONSIO.

Come hame, and dwell no more in Strivilling,
From hideous hell come hame and dwell,
Where fish to sell is non but spriling,*
Come hame, and dwell no more in Strivilling.

Et ne nos in temptationem de Strivilling :
Sed libera nos a malo ejusdem.
Requiem Edinburgi dona eis, Domine,
Et lux ipsius luceat eis.
A porta tristitiæ de Strivilling,
Erue, Domine, animas et corpora eorum.
Credo gustare vinum Edinburgi,

---

* Sprats.

In villa vinentium.
Requiescant statim in Edinburgo.   Amen.
Domine, exaudi orationem meam :
Et clamor meus ad te veniat.

OREMUS.

Deus qui justos et corde humiles ex omni eorum tri-
bulatione liberare dignatus es, libera famulos tuos apud
villam de Strivilling versantes a pœnis et tristitiis ejusdem,
et ad Edinburgi gaudia eos perducas.   Amen.

This dirge, or mournful song, Lord Hailes deemed
so " lewd and profane " that no poet durst address
it to his sovereign, if that sovereign " retained any
the least appearance of devotion."   But Hailes
thought of James V., while the poem refers to
James IV., a strange blunder in one so finically
critical.   It is well known that profanity of this
kind was not regarded in the light we should suppose by a priesthood who not only tolerated such
extravagances as the " Abbot of Unreason," but en-
couraged the performance of dramas which could
be regarded in no other light than as sacred bur-
lesques.   The poem, apart from its profanity, in so
far as it is a parody of the litanies of the Romish
Church, is curious as illustrative of the court and
the private life of the king.

It is a historical statement that James IV. was
subject to frequent fits of morose repentance, which
the Treasurer's Accounts prove by his repeated visits
and gifts to the shrines of St Ninian, in Galloway,

and of St Duthac, in Ross-shire.   In moods of this kind he often withdrew from the court to Stirling, where he had established a convent of St Franciscans in 1494, and, in a letter to Pope Julius II., declared himself to be their special patron.   With these monks he used to live until the qualms of conscience were over, and then he would return to the world and his courtly amusements with new zest.   It was upon one of these occasions that Dunbar penned his dirge, which he no doubt intended should divert the king; and, notwithstanding the profanity of the thing, as Hailes is pleased to consider it, it must be admitted that the poet succeeded very humorously in his parody. It was no bad conception to represent the king as in purgatory at Stirling, where fish were but sprats, and ale " thin and small," and to set the machinery of the Church in motion, with a view to transport him from his place of penance to the paradise of Edinburgh, there

> " To eat swan, cran, patrik and plever,
> And every fish that swims in river;
> To drink with us the new fresh wine
> That grew upon the river of Rhine;
> Fresh, fragrant clarets out of France,
> Of Angiers, and of Orleans."

Here we have a picture of court fare at the commencement of the sixteenth century; and are informed that the clarets most in repute were from Angiers and Orleans.

LEARNING VAIN WITHOUT GUID LYFE.

WRITTEN AT OXINFURDE.

To speak of science, craft, or sapience,
 Of virtue, moral cunning, or doctrine;
Of jure,* of wisdom, or intelligence;
 Of every study, lear, or discipline;
 All is but tynt,† or ready for to tyne,
Not using it as it should usit be;
 The crafter exerceing,‡ considering not the fine:
Ane perilous seikness is vain prosperitie.

The curious probation logical;
 The eloquence of ornate rhethorie;
The natural science philosophical;
 The dark appearance of astronomie;
 The theologis sermon; the fables of poetrie;
Without guid life all in the self does die,
 As May's flours does in September dry:
A perilous life is vain prosperitie.

Wherefore, ye Clerks, greatest of constance,
 Fullest of science and of knawlegeing,§
To us be mirrors in your governance;
 And in our darkness be lamps in shining:
 Or then in frustar‖ is all your lang learning;
Gif to your sawis¶ your deeds contrar be,
 Your maist accusar sall be your awn cunning.
A perilous seikness is vain prosperitie.

---

* Law.   † Lost.   ‡ Exercising.
§ Of what belongs to knowledge.   ‖ In vain.
¶ Wise sayings.

There is an Oxenford in Scotland, which once gave the title of Viscount, but, as Pinkerton observes, "the Oxinford mentioned in the colophon must be the University of Oxford;" and Ellis supposes that the poem was written in Dunbar's youth, during his travels in England. Perhaps it might; yet it has the strain of greater maturity, and was probably composed on visiting Oxford at a later period of life. It is known that he was in England, prior to the affiancing of the Princess Margaret, at the close of 1502, and may have been there years afterwards, although the Treasurer's Books bear no evidence of the fact.

OF DEEMING.*

Musing alone this hinder nicht
Of merry day, when gone was licht;
  Within ane garth under a tree,
I heard ane voice, that said on hicht,
  May na man now undeemit be:

For though I be ane crownit King;
Yet sall I not eschew deeming;
  Some calls me guid, some says they lie,
Some craves of God to end my sing,
  So sall I not undeemit be.

---

* Judging.

Be I ane lord, and not lord like,
Than every pelour* and purse-pike †
  Says, Lands were better wairt on me ;
Though he dow nocht to lead a tyk,‡
  Yet can he not let deeming be.

Be I ane lady fresh and fair,
With gentle men making repair,
  Than will they say, baith she and he,
That I am jaipit § late and air :
  Thus sall I not undeemit be.

Be I ane courtman, or ane knicht,
Honestly clad after my micht,
  Ane prideful man than call they me ;
But God send them a widdy wicht‖
  That cannot let sic deeming be.

---

* Thief.   † Pickpocket.

‡ Lord Hailes explains this line thus :—" ' Although he has not the abilities nor the spirit necessary for the meanest of all employments—that of leading a dog in a string.' There is no single word in modern English which corresponds with *dow*: that which approaches the nearest to it is *list*, from which the adjective *listless*. The force of the word *dow* is well expressed in a modern Scottish ballad—

> ' And now he gangs *dandering* about the dykes,
> And all he *dow* do is to *hund the tykes*."

Mr James Chalmers adds :—" The line literally means, ' Though he deserves not to lead a dog ; ' or, ' Though he is not worthy of leading a dog.' " And it may be added, as the real meaning, " Though he is not able to lead a dog."

§ Derided.   ‖ Strong.

Be I but little of stature,
They call me cative creature ;
    And be I great of quantitie,
They call me monstrous of nature :
    Thus can they not let deeming be.

And be I ornate in my speech,
Than Towsy says I am so streech,*
    I speak not like their house menyie ;†
Suppose her mouth misters a leech, ‡
    Yet can she not let deeming be.

But wist§ thir folk that other deems,
How that their saws to other seems,
    Their vicious words and vanitie,
Their tratling‖ tongues that all furth teems,
    Some time wald lat their deeming be.

Were nocht the matter wald grow the mair,
To work vengeance on ane deemer,
    But doubt I wald cause mony die ;
And mony cative and in care,
    Or some time let their deeming be.

Guid James the Ferd,¶ our noble king,
When that he was of years ying,
    In sentence said full subtillie,
Do weel, and set nocht by deeming,
    For no man sall undeemit be.**

---

* Affected.   † Menyie—the house men.
‡ Requires a surgeon to abridge its proportions.
§ Observe.   ‖ Tattling.   ¶ Fourth.
** From these lines, Chalmers, in his " Poetical Remains of the

And so I sall, with God's grace,
Keep His command in to that cace,
   Beseeking aye the Trinitie,
In heaven that I may have ane place,
   For there sall no man deemit be.

Evil thinkers and censorious speakers were, it appears, as common in Dunbar's time as they are now; and the only way to render their shafts less ·harmless and annoying is to adopt Dunbar's resolution, and pay no attention to them—" for no man sall undeemit be."

ON HIS HEADACHE.

TO THE KING.

My head did yak* yesternicht,
This day to mak† that I na micht,
   So sair the magrim does me menyie,‡
   Piercing my brow as ony ganyie,§
That scant I luik may on the licht.

And now, sir, lately, after mess,
To dite,‖ though I begouth to dress,
   The sentence lay full evil till find,
   Unsleepit in my head behind,
Dullit in dulness and distress.

Scottish Kings," presumed that James IV. was himself an author which is very likely; but there is no writing extant that can be shewn to be his.

  * Ache.   † To write poetry.   ‡ Injure.
  § Dart.   ‖ Indite.

Full oft at morrow I uprise,
When that my courage sleeping lies,
　For mirth, for minstrelsy, and play,
　For din, nor dancing, nor deray,
It will not wauken me no wise.

These verses tell their own story, and clearly
shew that Dunbar was retained at court as a poetical entertainer of the king. He apologises, on account of his headache, for the non-production of
some poetical effusion which possibly had been
promised. They also shew that, like most persons
of poetical temperament, he was occasionally subject to such lowness of spirits, that mirth, minstrelsy, nor pastime could not elevate him.

OF A DANCE IN THE QUEEN'S CHALMER.

Sir John Sinclair begouth to dance,
For he was new come out of France ;
For ony thing that he do micht,
The ane foot gaed aye unricht,
　And to the tother wald not gree.
Quoth ane, Tak up the Queen's knicht :
　A merrier dance micht na man see.

Than cam in Maister Robert Shaw :
He luikit as he could learn them a' ;
But aye his ane foot did waver,
He staggered like ane strummel-aver,*

.* Stumbling horse.

That hap-shakellit* abone the knee :
To seek fra Strivilling to Stranaver,
    A merrier dance micht na man see.

Than cam in the Maister Almaser,
Ane homelty-jomelty juffeller,†
Like a stirk staggering in the rye ;
His hippis gave mony hideous cry.
    John Bute, the fule, said, Wa is me !
He is bedirtin—Fy ! fy !
    A merrier dance micht na man see.

Than cam in Dunbar the makar ;‡
On all the floor there was nane frakar,§
And there he dancit the dirrye dantoun ;
He hoppit like a fillie wantoun,
    For love of Musgraiffe, men tells me ;
He trippit, while he tint his pantoun :‖
    A merrier dance micht na man see.

Than cam in Mistress Musgraiffe ;
She micht hae learnit all the laiffe ;¶
When I saw her sa trimly dance,
Her guid convoy** and countenance,
    Than, for her sake, I wist to be
The greatest earl, or duke, in France :
    A merrier dance micht na man see.

---

* With the head and foot fastened to prevent the animal from straying.

† A clumsy, awkward shuffler.   ‡ The Poet.

§ More active.   ‖ His shoe.   ¶ The rest.

** Carriage.

Than cam in Dame Dontibour ;
God wait* gif that she luikit sour !
She made sic murgeons † with her hips,
For lauchter nane micht hald their lips ;
  When she was dancing busilie,
Ane blast of wind soon fra her slips :
  A merrier dance micht na man see.

When there was come in five or sax,
The Queen's Dog‡ begouth to rax ;
And of his band he made a bred,§
And to the dancing soon he him made ;
  How mastive like about gaed he !
He stinkit like a tyke, some said :
  A merrier dance micht na man see.

We must plead guilty here to the admission of
what, in one or two instances, may be objected to
as unsuited to "ears polite." But it must be re-
collected that in the works of Ramsay, Burns, and
others, unhesitatingly admitted into the best society,
many expressions more rude occur; and we could
not afford to dispense with so graphic a picture of
the free and easy, and, it may be, gross, pastimes
which amused even a queen at the beginning of the
sixteenth century. Of course, in times past, indelicacy must be judged by the standard of the day ;
and, upon this principle, there was perhaps no impropriety in Queen Margaret witnessing the uncon-

* Knows.   † Grumblings.
‡ James Doig, the queen's wardrobe-keeper.
§ Sprung away.

strained, if not comical, attempts of her attendants to " trip it on the light fantastic toe."

In noticing the principal persons who figure in the dance, Mr Laing says he chiefly avails himself of the researches of his friend Mr Chalmers. With his leave, we shall also glean from the same source, with as much brevity as possible, what may serve our purpose.

Sir John Sinclair of Dryden was one of the king's attendants or courtiers. His name occurs in the Treasurer's Accounts as early as 1490; and it frequently appears down to 1512–13. In 1503, he was furnished with clothes, preparatory to the king's marriage, and was one of his attendants. He probably afterwards became the " queen's knicht," as Dunbar styles him. The king and he frequently played at " rowbowlis " and " the cartis." November 3, 1506, he had a gratuity of £28, by the king's command. His wife received £10 as a new-year's gift, 1511–12, and a similar sum next January.

Maister Robert Schaw frequently appears in the Treasurer's Accounts from 1502 to 1508. He was an ecclesiastic, but, as most priests were, acquainted with medicine: May 28, 1504, " Item, to Maister Robert Schaw, be the kingis command, quhen he passit to Bothwile to the Lady liand seik, £7." Feb. 9, 1504–5, " Item to the said William [Foular, potingair] for ane blude stane, and three vnce other stuf for the Quene, for bleding of the ness

[nose], after a R. of Maister Robert Schaw, 22s."
On May 14, 1508, he performed his first mass before the king, when he was presented with ten French crowns, or £7, a very high offering, from which it may be inferred that he was much esteemed by his majesty. He probably obtained some preferment immediately afterwards, as his name does not again occur in the books.

The *Maister Almaser* was Doctor Babington, who came from England with the queen at the time of her marriage, August 1503, as her almoner, and remained, with a salary of £20 English, or £70 Scottish, yearly. This sum he continued to receive for three years, the last half-yearly payment being made on the 8th of February 1506. Soon after he was appointed to the Deanery of Aberdeen. In the Treasurer's Accounts, between August 6, 1506, and September 6, 1507, there is a payment of £39, "gret Flemish money, for expediting the Bullis of the Denery of Aberdene to Doctor Babingtoun."

John Bute was one of the king's fools. His name has not been met with earlier than November 1506. In December that year, for his dress he received a doctor's gown of chamlot, lined with black gray, and purfellit with skins, with a hoode, a doublet of fustian, hose, and a gray bonnet; and at the same time, "Spark, John Butis man," received a goun of russet, doublet of fustian, and hose of carsay. The names of "John of Bute" and

his man Spark occur repeatedly in the Treasurer's
Accounts during the rest of James's reign; and
that of " John Butis brother," September 20, 1512.

Dunbar the makar is, of course, the poet himself. In accordance with the boisterous spirit of
the dance, he describes himself as one of the most
active on the floor, tripping it with such glee that
he at length tripped, and lost one of his slippers.
And all this joyousness for the love of Mrs Musgrave, who next occupies the floor. The kind of
dance called the " dirrye dantoun " is not known.

Maestris Musgraeffe is supposed to have been
the wife of Sir John Musgrave, who came to Scotland with the queen in 1503. She seems to have
been the principal lady in attendance on her majesty, and, besides her salary, which was £46, 13s.
4d. Scots yearly, she often received clothes, presents, and new-year's gifts. She is usually styled
" the Lady Maestress," and, in one instance, " Sir
John Musgrave's wife," a knight's wife being then
usually styled Maistress and not Lady. For bringing tidings to the king of the prince's birth, February 21, 1506-7, she received 100 unicorns, equal
to £90 Scots, along with a great cup of silver,
which the Bishop of Murray had given to the king.
The names of Maistres Musgray and Agnes Mus-
graif often occur in the years 1511 to 1513.

Dame Dontibour, it would appear from Sir
David Lyndsay and John Knox, is a cant name for
a profligate woman. Singers before the king are

frequently entered in the Treasurer's Books under the cognomen of " wantonness," &c.

OF SIR THOMAS NORRAY.

Now lythis* of ane gentle Knicht,
Sir Thomas Norray, wise and wicht,
  And full of chivalrie ;
Whase father was ane grand Keine †
His mother was ane fairie queen,
  Gotten be sorcerie.

Ane fairer Knicht nor he was nane,
On ground may neither ride nor gane,
  Na bear buckler nor brand ;
Or come in this court but‡ dread ;
He did full mony valiant deed
  In Ross and Murray land.

Full many cathereins§ has he chaste,
And cummered‖ many a Hieland ghaist,
  Amang thae dully glens :
Of the Clan Chattan twenty score
He drave as oxen him before ;¶
  This deed though na man kens.

---

* Listen.   † Perhaps khan, a Persian lord.
‡ Without.   § Highland plunderers.   ‖ Vexed.
¶ This has been interpreted to mean cattle ; but such is not the sense of the passage. Of the Glen or rather Clan Chattan he drove twenty score as oxen (as if they had been oxen) him before.

At feasts and bridals up-aland,*
He wan the gree, and the garland ;
   Dancit none so on deis : †
He has at warslings been ane hunder,
Yet lay his body never at under :
   He knaws gif this be lies.

Was never weild ‡ Robin § under bewch,
Nor yet Roger of Clekkinsklewch,||
   So bauld a bairn as he ;
Guy of Gysburne, ¶ na Adam Bell, **
Na Simon's sons of Whinfell, ††
   At shot were never so-slie.

This anterous ‡‡ Knicht, wherever he went,
At jousting, or at tournament,
   Ever more he wan the gree ;
Was never of half so great renoun
Sir Bewis the Knicht of South Hamptoun : §§
   I shrieve him gif I lie.

---

* Among the hills.

† Upper place in a hall, where the floor is raised.

‡ Free living.   § Robin Hood.

|| The subject, no doubt, of some of the popular ballads in Dunbar's time, but now unknown.

¶ "Guy of Gysburne," or "Gisborne," is one of the Robin Hood ballads, first printed in "Percy's Reliques."

** Adam Bell, with Clym of the Cleughe and Wyllyam of Cloudeslie, is celebrated in an early tale, printed by Ritson in his "Pieces of Ancient Popular Poetry."

†† The memory of these worthies, save the notice of them here, is lost.

‡‡ Adventurous.

§§ This is another of the mediæval knights whose light has gone out.

Therefore Quhentyne* was but ane lurdane,
That callit him ane full plum jurdane†
  This wise and worthy Knicht ;
He callit him fouler than ane fule,
He said he was ane lecherous bull,
  That crooned baith day and nicht.

He wald have made him Currie's‡ knave
I pray God better his honour to save,
  Na to be lichtliet sua !
Yet this far furth I daur him prais,
  He filed never saddle in his days ;
  And Currie befiled twa.

Wherefore, ever at Pasch and Yule,
I cry him Lord of every fule,§
  That in this region dwells ;
And, verily, it war great richt,
For, of ane hie renowned knicht,
  He wants no thing but bells.

---

* Quintine, who probably had written some sarcastic verses against Norray.

† Jourdane, a chamber convenience.

‡ Currie's servant. Currie, another of the king's fools, is repeatedly mentioned in the Treasurer's Accounts, from 1496 to 1506, in which latter year he seems to have died. On the 2d June of that year was paid "for the tyrment and expenses maid on the furthbringing of Curry, deliverit to Sir Andro Makbrek, 46s. 8d." In the same accounts Curry's mother, Daft Anne, Curry's wife, Peter Curry, Curry's brother, and Law, Curry's man, frequently occur.

§ There were a great many fools or jesters in the king's service. Besides the illustrious Sir Thomas Norray, there were Curry, Law (Curry's man), John Bute, Spark (his man), John Wallas, Cuddy Rig, &c.

The subject of this very clever *jeu d'esprit*, which must have been composed before 1506, was Thomas Norry, one of the king's fools. He was a favourite attendant of the king, and, taking due licence of his calling, seems to have been quite a Baron Munchausen in his way. "He knaws gif this be lies" is a happy explanation of his character. He occurs in the Treasurer's Books, where he is sometimes actually called *Sir* Thomas Norry, from 1503 to 1511–12. March 24 of that year, there is paid "to Thomas Norry, fule,—in elimose, at his passage to Saint James, 56s.;" and Aug. 5, "to Schir Thomas Norry, one pair schone, price 16d." Norrie is still a name in Fife, and the north-east of Scotland.

COMPLAINT AGAINST MURE.

TO THE KING.

Sir, I complain of injuries :
A rising son of raking MURIS
Has mangelit my making,* through his malice,
And present it into your palace ;
   But, sen he pleases with me to plead,
I sall him knawin mak hyne † to Calais,
   But giff ‡ your Hieness it remeid.

That full dismembered has my metre,
And poisoned it with strong saltpetre, §

-----

* His poetry.   † Hence.   ‡ Unless.
§ In allusion to the curing of butcher meat with saltpetre.

With richt defamous speech of lords,
Whilk with my colours all discords :
    Whose cruel slanders servis* deid ;
And in my name all leis records,
    Your Grace beseek I of remeid.

He has endorsit mine inditing,
With verses of his ain handwriting ;
Wherein baith slander is and treason :
Of ane wud full far out of season,
    He wants nocht but a roundit heid,†
For he has tint baith wit and reason :
    Your Grace beseek I of remeid.

Punish him for his deed culpable ;
Or gar deliver him ane babble,
That Cuddy Rig, the Dumfries fule,
May him receive again this Yule,
    All roundit into yellow and reid ;‡
That lads may bait him like a bull :
    For that to me were some remeid.

It is not known who this " rising son of raking
Mure's " was ; but, from the name, it is probable
that he was from the west country—the Mures of
Ayrshire or Renfrewshire. It would appear that
he had altered some of Dunbar's verses, and in-
serted some of his own, probably by way of joke ;
for we cannot, with Mr Laing, regard the complaint of Dunbar as either very serious or " indig-

---

* Deserves.   † His ears clipped off.
‡ Yellow and red was the king's livery.

nant." The punishment prayed for, that he might be made to babble, and handed over to Cuddy Rig, the Dumfries fool, "all rounded into yellow and red," that the boys might bait him like a bull, does not look as if the poet was seriously annoyed. The name of "Cuddy Rig," the fool, repeatedly occurs in the Treasurer's Accounts from 1504 to 1512. 17th Sept. 1504, there was paid "to the crukit vicar of Dumfreiss that sang to the king in Lochmaben, 14s.;" and a similar sum, by the king's command, to "Cuddy Rig."

OF JAMES DOIG, KEEPER OF THE QUEEN'S WARDROBE.

TO THE QUEEN.

The wardrober of Venus' bow'r,
To gif a doublet * he is as doure
As it were of ane foot side frog :†
Madam, ye have a dangerous Dog !‡

---

* It would thus appear that Dunbar had been in the habit of receiving, or had been ordered on this special occasion, a doublet or dress, by order of the queen, from the royal wardrobe; but the keeper, James Doig, careful of the royal interest, took it upon him to refuse the demand, even although shewn the queen's mark.

† An overcoat.

‡ The name of Doig is as frequently written and pronounced *Dog* in Fife, and further north, as it is the proper way.

When that I shaw to him your marks,*
He turns to me again and barks
As he were worrying ane hog :
    Madam, ye have a dangerous Dog !

When that I shaw him your writing,
He girns that I am red † for biting ;
I wald he had ane heavy clog :
    Madam, ye have a dangerous Dog !

When that I speak till him friendlike,
He barkis like ane midden tyke
Were chasing cattle through a bog :
    Madam, ye have a dangerous Dog !

He is ane mastiff, meikle of micht,
To keep your wardrobe over nicht,
Fra the great Sowdan ‡ Gog-ma-gog :
    Madam, ye have a dangerous Dog !

He is oure meikle to be your messan,
Madam, I red you get a less ane ;
His gang gars all your chalmers shog :
    Madam, ye have a dangerous Dog !

---

* This, says Pinkerton, "seems to mean *seal*. The seal of
Margaret appears at many letters of hers in the Cotton Library.
It is a lady sitting, and either a lamb or a dog by her."
† Free, in order, provoked.   ‡ Sultan.

OF THE SAID JAMES,

WHEN HE HAD PLEASED HIM [THE POET.]

O gracious Princess, guid and fair !
Do weel to James your wardropair ;
Whase faithful brother maist friend I am :
  He is nae Dog ; he is a Lamb.

Though I in ballad did him bourd,*
In malice spak I never ane word,
But all, my Dame, to do you game :
  He is nae Dog ; he is a Lamb.

Your Hicness can not get ane meter †
To keep your wardrobe, nor discreeter,
To rule your robes, and dress the same :
  He is nae Dog ; he is a Lamb.

The wife that he had in this inns,‡
That with the tangs wad break his shins,
I wald she drownit were in a dam :
  He is nae Dog ; he is a Lamb.

The wife that wald him cuckold mak,
I wald she were, baith side and bak,
Weel batterit with ane barrow tram :
  He is nae Dog ; he is a Lamb.

He has sa weel done me obey
In till all thing, therefore I pray
That never dolour§ mak him dram :‖
  He is nae Dog ; he is a Lamb.

---

* Jest. † Fitter. ‡ Lodging.
§ Grief. ‖ Melancholy.

M

The subject of this biting satire was, as the poet tells us, keeper of the queen's wardrobe. Of his history, Mr Laing gives the following account, as the result of Mr Chalmers's indefatigable researches :—

" James Dog, or Doig, appears in the Treasurer's Accounts as one of the king's domestic servants in 1489, and from the numerous subsequent entries where his name occurs, he must have been regarded as a trusty, active, and confidential person; and he was enabled by his savings to purchase the lands of Duntober, in Perthshire, May 12, 1500. After the king's marriage, in 1503, he was transferred to the establishment of the queen's household, whom he long continued to serve with fidelity. In proof of this it may be noticed that, in 1523, August 4, a grant was made to the king's (James V.) 'lovit servitour, James Dog,' of the ward, non-entries, and relief of the lands of the late Dormond Johnston of Drongy, and the marriage of his heir. Though here called the king's servitour, he was, in fact, still the servant of the queen-dowager, and had been so for twenty years. In an autograph letter from the Earl of Surrey, at Newcastle, October 24, 1523, to Cardinal Wolsey, he says, ' Plesith your grace to be advertised, that this present houre is come to me, James Dog, the Quene of Scott's servante,' &c. His name also occurs in December 1526, but how long he may have survived is uncertain. His son, James Dog, younger,

was, on September 17, 1524, appointed ' yeman of
the king's wardrope, with leveray, clothing, busche
of court, and duties used and wont,' " &c.

Pinkerton, who was the first to publish the satire,
says, in reference to the *per contra*, " This is a
sharp satire in the piercing mode of pity, and was
written, as the colophon tells us, when Doig *had
pleisit him*.   If so, whether was it most dangerous
to displease, or to please Dunbar ? "

WELCOME TO THE LORD TREASURER.

I thocht lang while some Lord come hame,
Fra whom fain kindness wald I claim ;
His name of comfort I will declare,
 Welcome, my ain Lord Thesaurair !

Before all raik* of this regioun,
Under our Roy of most renoun,
Of all my micht, though it were mair,
 Welcome, my ain Lord Thesaurair.

Your noble payment I did assay,
And ye hecht† soon without delay,
Again in Edinburgh till repair ;
 Welcome, my ain Lord Thesaurair !

Ye keepit tryst so wonder weel,
I hald you true as ony steel ;
Needs nane your payment till despair ;
 Welcome, my ain Lord Thesaurair !

---

 * Ranks or estates.   † Promised.

Yet in a pairt I was aghast,
Or ye the nearest way had past
Fra town of Stirling to the air : *
   Welcome, my ain Lord Thesaurair !

Than had my dyt † been all in dule,
Had I my wage wanted till Yule ;
Where now I sing with heart on sair,‡
   Welcome, my ain Lord Thesaurair !

Welcome, my benefice, and my rent,
And all the lyflett § to me lent ;
Welcome, my pension most preclair ;‖
   Welcome, my ain Lord Thesaurair !

Welcome, as heartily as I can,
My ain dear maister to your man ;
And to your servant singulair,
   Welcome, my ain Lord Thesaurair !

We learn from this "welcome" the utter dependence of Dunbar's circumstances. The Lord Treasurer, or rather his pension, was to him his benefice, his rent, in short, "all the *lyflett* to [him] lent." Which of the Lord Treasurers was the object of his greeting is uncertain. It may have been Sir David Beatoun of Creich, who filled the office from 1502 to 1504, or James Beatoun, abbot of Dunfermline, who held it from 1504 to 1509. The next poem is in the same strain.

* Justice, or court of justice.   † Inditing.
‡ Unsair.   § Means of subsistence.   ‖ Supereminent.

TO THE LORDS OF THE KING'S EXCHEQUER.

My Lords of Chacker, please you to hear
My compt, I sall it mak you clear,
   But* ony circumstance or sunyie ;†
   For left is neither corce nor cunyie‡
Of all that I took in the year.

For reckoning of my rents and roumes,§
Ye need not for to tire your thoumes ;
   Nor for to gar your counters clink,
   Nor paper for to spend, nor ink,
In the receiving of my soumes.

I took fra my Lord Thesaurair,
Anc soume of money for to wair :
   I cannot tell you how it is spendit,
   But weel I wit that it is endit ;
And that me think ane compt oure sair !

I trowit, in time, when that I took it,
That lang in burgh I sould have bruikit,‖
   Now the remains are eith ¶ to turs ;**
   I have na proof here but my purse,
Whilk wald not lie and it were luikit.

There is no evidence that Dunbar ever drew
money from the Exchequer, so that this address
may be regarded solely as a jocular mode of making
known the low condition of his finances. We have

---

* Without.   † Excuse.   ‡ Cross nor coin.
§ Lands.   ‖ Lived, enjoyed.   ¶ Easy.
** Pack up.

no date for these and the preceding verses, but they point to a period probably soon after the king's marriage, when a benefice appeared still distant, and the smallness of his income rendered his position irksome, and his patience less obedient.

TO A LADY.

WHEN HE LIST TO FEIGN.

My heart's treasure, and sweet, assured fo,
  The final ender of my life for ever ;
The cruel breaker of my heart in two,
  To go to death, this I deservit never :
  O man slayer! while* saul and life dissever ;
Stint of your slauchter ; alace! your man am I,
A thousand times that does you mercy cry.

Have mercy, love ! have mercy, lady bricht !
  What have I wrocht agains your womanheid,
That ye suld murder me, a sakeless wicht,
  Trespassing never to you in word nor deed ?
  That ye consent thereto, O God forbid !
Leave cruelty, and save your man for shame,
Or through the warld quite losit is your name.

My death chases my life so busilie,
  That weary is my ghost to flee so fast ;
Sic deadly dwaums so mischievouslie
  Ane hundred times has my heart ourepast ;
  Me think my spirit rins away full ghast,

---

* *While*, thus used, must mean *until.*

Beseeking grace, on knees you before,
Or that your man be lost for ever more.

Behald my wod* intolerable pain,
  For ever more whilk sal be my damage !
Why, under trust, your man thus have ye slain ?
  Lo ! death is in my breast, with furious rage,
  Whilk may no balm, nor tryacle † assuage,
But your mercy, for lack of whilk I die ;
Alace : where is your womanlie pitie ?

Behald my deadly passion dolorous !
  Behald my hideous hue, and wo, alace !
Behald my mane, and mourning marvellous,
  With sorrowful tears falling from my face !
  Rewth, ‡ love, is nocht, help ye not in this case,
For how suld ony gentle heart endure
To see this sicht on ony creature ?

White Dow, where is your sober humilness ?
  Sweet, gentle Turtle, where is your pitie went ?
Where is your rewth ? the fruit of nobleness,
  Of womanheid the treasure, and the rent ;
  Virtue is never put out in meek intent,
Nor out of gentle heart is fundin § pitie ;
Sen merciless may no wicht noble be.

In to my mind I sall you mercy cry,
  While that my tongue sall fail me to speak ;
And while that nature me in sicht deny ;

---

* Mad.   † Treacle.
‡ Pity.   § Found.

And while my e'en for pain enclose and steik ;
And while the death my heart in sunder break ;
And while my mind may think, and tongue may steir ;
And syne, fareweel, my heartis lady dear !

The author scarcely required to mention that these verses were written "when he list to feign." They are too extravagant for sincerity, and must have been the production of advanced life, when "true love" had lost its pathos, and forgotten its tones of silver sweetness.   Indeed, it may have been written *for* some one who was in the hopeless condition described, and whose obdurate and not overly-refined captivator required a strong cosmetic to move her compassion.   Such appeals for mercy, however, were in much repute long after the time of Dunbar.

THE VISITATION OF ST FRANCIS.

This nicht, before the dawing clear,
Me thocht Sanct Francis did to me appear,
  With ane religious habit in his hand,
  And said, In this go claith thee, my servand,
Refuse the warld, for thou maun be a freir.

With him and with his habit baith I skarrit,[*]
Like to ane man that with a ghaist was marrit :[†]
  Me thocht on bed he laid it me abone ;
  But on the floor deliverly[‡] and soon
I lap there fra, and never wald come nar it.

----

[*] Was startled.   [†] Interrupted.   [‡] Nimbly.

Quoth he, Why skars thou with this holy weed?
Claith thee therein, for wear it thou must need;
  Thou that has lang done Venus lawis teach,
  Sall now be freir, and in this habit preach;
Delay it not, it maun be done but* dread.

Quoth I, Sanct Francis, loving be thee till,
And thankit mot† thou be of thy gude will
  To me, that of thy claithis are so kind;
  But them to wear it never come in my mind;
Sweet Confessor, thou tak it not in ill.

In haly legends have I heard allevin,‡
Mae sancts of bishops, nor freirs, be sic seven;
  Of full few freirs that has been sancts I read;
  Wherefore, gae bring to me ane bishop's weed,
Gif ever thou wald my saul gaed unto heaven.

My breither of thes made thee supplications,
Be epistles, sermons, and relations,
  To tak this habit; but thou did postpone;
  But further process, come on therefore anon,
All circumstance put by, and excusations.

Gif ever my fortune was to be a freir,
The date thereof is past full mony a year;
  For into every lusty toun and place
  Of all England, from Berwick to Calais,
I have into thy habit made gude cheer.

In freir's weed full fairly have I fleechit,
In it have I in pulpit gone and preechit

---

* Without.   † May.   ‡ Alleged.

In Derntoun kirk, and eik in Canterberry;
In it I past at Dover oure the ferry,
Throw Piccardy, and there the people teachit.

As lang as I did wear the freir's style,
In me, God wit, was mony a wink and wyle;
In me was falset* with every wicht to flatter,
Whilk micht be flemit † with nae haly water;
I was aye ready all men to beguile.

The freir that did Sanct Francis there appear,
Ane fiend he was in likeness of ane freir;
He vanished away with stink and fiery smoke;
With him me thocht all the house end he took,
And I awoke as wy‡ that was in weir.§

This poem is of peculiar interest, as throwing the almost only light we have on the early history of Dunbar. That he was a preaching friar he plainly tells us, and in that habit had travelled over England and France. He is also honest enough to admit that he was no better than he should be—

"In me, God wit, was mony a wink and wyle."

But we should rather think that this admission was aimed more against the malpractices of the preaching friars as a body than in exposition of his own particular failings. The whole poem, indeed, is satirical of the order of friars; and his making the

---

* Falsehood.
‡ A person, one.
† Basted.
§ War, trouble.

arch-fiend appear in the disguise of St Francis,
urging him to assume the friar's habit, would imply
that the devil had a particular interest in recruiting
for a service which he found so useful. It is certainly surprising that Dunbar should have spoken
out so freely; and still more so that he should have
escaped the censures of the Church. We do not
coincide with Mr Laing in thinking that these
verses were not written till towards the close of the
reign of James IV. They were probably written
about 1504 or 1505, when the poet was beginning
to get impatient of the expected benefice, yet had
not the boldness, as in after-years, to address the king
in a direct manner on the subject. If his employ-
ment in the king's service began, as we have reason
to believe, in 1491, he was quite entitled to say—

> " Gif ever my fortune was to be a freir,
>   The date thereof is past full mony a year ;"

without waiting till the close of the king's reign.
The sarcastic humour of the poet is admirable—

> " Of full few freirs that has been sancts I read ;
>   Wherefore gae bring to me ane bishop's weed."

THE BIRTH OF ANTICHRIST.

Lucina shining in silence of the nicht,
The heaven all being full of sterns bricht,
     To bed I went ; but there I took no rest,
     With heavy thocht so sore I was opprest,
That sair I langit after the day's licht.

Of fortune I compleinit heavily,
That she to me stood so contrariously:
   And at the last, when I turnit oft
   For weariness, on me ane slumber soft
Come, with ane dreaming and a phantasy.

Me thocht dame Fortune, with ane fremmit* cheer,
Stood me before, and said on this maneir:
   Thou suffer me to work gif thou do weel,
   And press thee not to strive agains my wheel,
Whilk every warldly thing does turn and steer.

Full mony ane man 1 turn unto the hicht,
And maks as mony full low down to licht;
   Up on my staigs † or that thou ascend,
   Trust weel thy trouble is near at ane end;
Seeing thir tokens, wherefore thou mark them richt.

Thy troublit ghaist sall ne'er more be degest,‡
Nor thou into no benefice possest,
   While that ane abbot him claith in iron's pens,
   And flee up in the air amang the crens,
And as ane falcon fair fro east to west.

He sall ascend as ane horrible griphon,
Him meet sall in the air ane she dragon;
   Thir terrible monsters sall together thrist,
   And in the cluds get the Antichrist,
While all the air infect of their pusion.

Under Saturnus' fiery region
Symon Magus sall meet them, and Mahoun;§

---

* Foreign or strange.   † Young horses.   ‡ Composed.
§ The devil. Lord Hailes makes it pretty clear that *Mahoun*

And Merlin, at the moon, sall him be bydand ;
And Janet, the widow, on ane besom rydand,
Of witches with ane wonder garesoun.*

And syne they sall descend with reek and fire,
And preach in earth the Antichrist's empire ;
  Be than it sall be near this warld's end.
  With that this lady soon fra me did wend :
Sleeping and waking was frustrate my desire.

When I awoke, my dream it was so nice,
Fra every wicht I hid it as a vice ;
  While I heard tell, be mony southfast wy,
  Flee wald ane abbot up in to the sky,
And all his fethreme † made was at device.

Within my heart comfort I took full soon, .
Adieu, quoth I, my dreary days are done :
  Full weel I wist to me wald never come thrift,
  While that twa moons were seen up in the lift,
Or while an abbot flew above the moon.

This poem has reference to a very curious circumstance—the attempt of the abbot of Tungland
to fly from the ramparts of Stirling Castle. Although put in the form of a dream, and foreshadow-
ing an event to come, which the poet ingeniously
makes subservient to his own expected rise in the
world, there can be no doubt that the satire was

---

is derived from *Mahomet*, and has been in use probably since the
days of the crusades.
  * Following, body of troops.   † Dress of feathers.

written after the event, which happened in 1507. The abbot, as we have elsewhere remarked, was no other than " Maister John, the French medicinar," whom the king found such an amusing fellow, that they often played at cards together; and he professed such a knowledge of alchemy that he induced his majesty to expend considerable sums in what he called *multiplyinge,* or refining the baser metals. He had the abbacy of Tungland conferred upon him early in 1504, a circumstánce which must have weighed heavily on the mind of Dunbar. That a foreigner, with perhaps no solid claims to merit or sound sense, as his attempt to fly indicated, should have such preference, while he, who had served the king in his earlier years, and knew and felt his own mental superiority, as well as educational fitness for a benefice, must have been galling indeed.   Hence the origin of those numerous poetical appeals to the king's sense of justice and generosity, which we find addressed to him about this time, or perhaps subsequently.

OF THE FENYEIT* FREIR OF TUNGLAND.

As young Aurora, with her crystal hale,
In orient shew her visage pale,

----

* This is interpreted to mean feigned, or pretended ; but there is another meaning, which we think it bears, and which the author intended to convey, nearly expressed in the word *wowf;* so that we would read it—" The *Mad* Freir of Tungland."

A swevying swyth* did me assail,
　　Of sons of Satan's seed ;
Me thocht a Turk of Tartary
Come out of the land of Barbary,
And lay forloppin† in Lombardy,
　　Full lang in waith-man‡ weed :

Fra baptizing for till eschew,§
There a religious man he slew,
And clad him in his habit new,
　　For he could write and read.‖
When kend was his dissemulans,
And all his cursit governans,
For fear he fled, and come in France,
　　With little of Lombard leid.¶

To be a leech he feigned him there,
Whilk mony a man micht rue evermair ;
For he left neither sick nor sair
　　Unslain, or he hyne** gaed.

---

* A vision suddenly.　　　　† Fugitive.　　　　‡ Wanderer.
§ If discovered he would have been compelled to turn a
Christian, or become a slave.
‖ Because of these accomplishments he could pass as a friar.
¶ Lord Hailes interprets this passage thus :—" Either with
small knowledge of the Italian language, or with a little, or a
smattering of Italian literature, or with some knowledge of the
Lombard business of broker."　We must not forget, however,
that the abbot was in reality a *native* of Lombardy, and must
have known the Italian language, if not its literature, well ; and,
therefore, the probability is that Dunbar simply meant that he
had but little of the reputed wealth of Lombardy.
** Thence.

Vein organs he full cleanly carvit ;*
When of his stroke so many starvit,†
Dread he had gotten that he deservit,
   He fled away gude speed.

In Scotland than, the nearest way,
He came, his cunning till essay,
To some men there it was no play
   The proving of his science.

In potingary he wrocht great pyne,‡
He murderit in to medicine ;
The jow§ was of a great ingyne,
   And generit was of gyans.‖

In leechcraft he was homicide,
He wald have, for a nicht to bide,
Ane hackney and the hurt man's hide,¶
   So meikle he was of myans. **

---

* The veins he fully, cleanly carved.

† Lord Hailes explains this obscure passage satisfactorily :—
"When so many died by his stroke. The word *straik*, or *stroke*,
seems to confirm the notion that cupping-glasses are here meant.
Starvit is a word still preserved in English, implying a violent
death by hunger. *To starve of cold*, is still a Scottish expression,
from the word *storven*, to die."

‡ As an apothecary he wrought great mischief.

§ The *jow*, or juggler.

‖ Neither Hailes nor any one else has thrown light on this
obscure term. *Gy*, amongst other meanings, signifies a hob-
goblin-looking fellow. This *jow*, or juggler, was generated of
hobgoblins; or, in another sense of the word *gy*, of those who
wore masks, and acted the part of *gys* or *gysars*.

¶ Lord Hailes reads this passage thus :—"His fees were so
exhorbitant, that one night's attendance cost a horse—the most
sumptuous of presents in those days—and the skin of the patient."

** *Moiens*, or *moyens;* so great was he in expedients for making
money.

His irons were rude as ony rauchter,
Where he let bluid it was no lauchter;
Full many instruments for slauchter*
    Was in his gardyvians.†

He could give cure of laxative,
To gar a wicht horse want his life;
Wha ever essay wald, man or wife,
    Their hips gaed hiddy-giddy. ‡
His practicks never were put to preif,
But§ sudden death, or great mischief;
He had purgation to mak a thief
    To die without a widdy.

Unto no mess preissit‖ the prelat,
For sound of sacrying bell nor skellat;¶
As blacksmith bruikit** was his pellat††
    For battering at the study.
Though he come hame a new made chanon,
He had dispensit with matins canon,
On him come nouther stole nor fanon,
    For smoking of the smiddy. ‡‡

---

* The reading of these lines is, that his surgical instruments were of the rudest description. *Rauchter* means a beam, or the couple in the roof of a house.

† Gardevyance, a cabinet. It contained many instruments for slaughter—poisons, perhaps, as well as ill-made chirurgical weapons.

‡ Hither and thither.   § Without.   ‖ Pressed.

¶ A small bell or rattle, still called a *skellat*.

** Blackened.   †† Skin.

‡‡ The newly-made abbot was so busy with his chemical pursuits, and so begrimed with the smoke and dirt of his laboratory, that he was afraid of defiling his ecclesiastical vestments, so set

Me thocht fair fashions he assailit,
To mak the quintessence and failit ;
And when he saw that nocht availit,
    A federem * on he took :
And shape in Turkey for to flee ;†
And when that he did mount on hie,
All fowls ferlit what he suld be,
    That ever did on him look.

Some held he had been Dedalus,‡
Some the Minotaur marvellous,§
Some Mertis‖ blacksmith Vulcanus,
    And some Saturnus' cook.
And ever the cushets ¶ at him tuggit,
The rooks him rent, the ravens him druggit,
The hudit craws his hair furth ruggit,
    The heaven he micht not bruik.

---

aside the ecclesiastical law, which required him to say matins. But the real meaning of the poet is, that he was so indifferent as to his religious duties, that he outraged the laws of the Church and the decency of his order, by continually absenting himself from the duties of his position. Mr J. Chalmers says :—"James IV., who was a firm-built, athletic man, was fond of shewing his powers by *striking at the study*, or anvil. There are in the Treasurer's Accounts gratuities paid to blacksmiths, where the king *strak at the study*. Sir Anthony Darcie, the French knight, struck at the study with the king ; and the Abbot of Tungland probably did the same, which has occasioned Dunbar's ridicule."

  * Feathering.

  † Prepared to fly to Turkey, of which country Dunbar makes him a native.

  ‡ Dedalion, brother of Ceyx.   § Half man, half horse.

  ‖ Mertis—this term we do not know, unless it mean *Martius*, the month of March.   ¶ Wild pigeons.

The mittane* and Sanct Martin's fowl,†
Wend‡ he had been the hornit owl, §
They set upon him with a yowl,
    And gave him dint for dint.
The gowk,‖ the gormaw, ¶ and the gled,**
Beft†† him with buffets till he bled ;
The spar‡‡ hawk to the spring him sped§§
    As fierce as fire of flint.

The tarsal‖‖ gave him tug for tug,
The stanchel‖‖ hung in ilka lug,
The piet furth his pens did rug,
    The stork struck aye but¶¶ stint ;
The bissart,‖‖ busy but rebuke,
She was so clever of her cluik,
His . . . . he micht not langer bruik,
    She held them at ane hint.***

Thick was the clud of kays and craws,
Of merlins, mittanes, and of maws,†††
That bickerit at his beard with blaws,
    In battle him about :

---

* A kind of hawk.

† St Martin's fowl means the martlet. It is believed to quit the country about St Martin's day, in the beginning of winter.

‡ Thought.   § Great horned owl.   ‖ Cuckoo.

¶ Cormorant.   ** Kite.   †† Struck.

‡‡ Sparrow.   §§ To the flight.

‖‖ Kinds of hawks.   ¶¶ Without.

*** "Literally," says Lord Hailes, "held them by a hold"—*i.e.*, held them fast.

††† Mews.

They nibblit him with noyis* and cry,
The rerd † of them raise to the sky,
And ever he cried on Fortune, Fy!
　　His life was in to doubt.

The jay him skrippit with a skryke,‡
And scornit him as it was like ;
The eagle strong at him did strike,
　　And rawcht§ him mony a rout :
For fear uncunningly he cawkit,‖
While all his pens were drown'd and drawkit,
He made a hundred nolt all hawkit,¶
　　Beneath him with a spout.

He schewre his federem that was sheen,**
And slippit out of it full clean,
And in a myre, up to the e'en,
　　Amang the glaur did glide.
The fowls all at the federem dang,
As at a monster them amang,
While all the pens of it outsprang
　　In till the air full wide.

And he lay at the plunge evermair,
Sae lang as any raven did rair ;
The craws him socht, with cries of care,††
　　In every shaw beside.

---

* Annoyance.　　　† Uproar.　　　‡ Mocked with a screech.
§ Reached.　　　　　　　　　　‖ Betrayed himself.
¶ Cattle with streaks on their skin. *Hawkie* is a name for a
cow with such a skin.
** He put off his dress of feathers that was whole.
†† Chaucer uses a similar expression—
　　　"The ravyn, and the crow with her voice of care."

Had he revealed been to the rooks,
They had him riven all with their cluiks :
Three days in dub amang the duiks
   He did with dirt him hide.

The air was dirkit* with the fowls
That come with yammers, and with yowls,
With skryking, skrymming, and with scowls,
   To tak him in the tide.
I wauken'd with the noise and shout,
So hideous beir† was me about.
Sen syne I curse that canker'd rout,
   Wherever I go or ride.

In none of his poems does the poet's conception of the ridiculous appear to greater advantage than in this. The subject in itself was no doubt absurd enough; but the position in which he places the unhappy abbot—so assailed and held fast by the astonished and angry fowls of the air that he never got upon the wing at all—is truly laughable. How the satire must have annoyed the adventurous "multiplier!" Of course, it was not to be expected that Dunbar would quite adhere to the facts of the case; yet he has not made any unpardonable divergence from them. The story, according to Bishop Leslie, is this:—In September 1507, an embassy was sent by the king to France, on which occasion the abbot of Tungland "tuik in hand to flie with wingis, and to be in Fraunce befoir the

* Darkened.   † Uproar.

saidis ambassadouris. And to that effect he causet mak ane pair of wingis with fedderis, quhilkis beand fessinit apoun him, he flew of the Castell wall of Strivelling, bot shortlie he fell to the ground, and brak his thee bane; bot the wyt thairof he ascryvit to that thair was sum hen fedderis in the wingis quhilk yarnit and covet the mydding and not the skyis. In this doinge he preissit [essayed] to conterfute ane king of Yngland callit Bladud, quha, as thair histories mentiones, deckcd himself in fedderis, and presumed to flie in the aire as he did, bot, falling on the tempell of Apollo, brak his neck." Dunbar, to add to the pungency of his wit, assumes that the abbot, had he succeeded in his flight, never intended to return to a country where his quackery and covetousness had been so conspicuous.

The name of this adventurer—for he cannot be considered anything else—was JOHN DAMIAN. The research of Mr James Chalmers has enabled Mr Laing to supply several interesting facts regarding him. He appears in Scotland about 1501. In the Treasurer's Accounts he is variously styled: sometimes "the French Leich," "French Maister John," &c. In 1501-2 he received "leveray" along with other parties at court; from which it would appear that he then held the position of physician in the king's household. Bishop Leslie says he was an Italian, and from Lombardy, according to Dunbar's poem. From thence he had gone to France, where he practised surgery, and probably acquired some knowledge of the properties of metals, for chemistry could not then be said to have been understood as a science. He must have been a person of considerable address, for he gained much upon the king's feelings, and they were often engaged in pastimes together. It is supposed that it was from him that his majesty acquired so strong a taste for alchymy. But it is somewhat rash to draw such a conclusion. The dream of discovering the philosopher's stone, or the power of converting the baser metals into gold, was not confined to any one man or class of men, but pervaded all Europe, and all classes, crowned and coroneted, as well as humbler heads. He seems, if there is a shadow of truth in Dunbar's satire, to have been an ignorant and unscrupulous bungler in his own profession, and not at all above a belief in the expected results of " multiplyinge." He may, therefore, have been sincerely convinced of the power of the science which he called " Quintessence." At the same time, there can be little doubt that he was unscrupulous enough to take advantage of the king's munificence in straining after an impossibility. In whatever way the prosecution of the " Quint-essence " science was instituted, it appears that he was not long at the Scottish court until the king and he were heartily engaged—the one day in " multiplyinge," and the other at the card-table : 1501-2, " Item, the third day of Merch, send to

Strivelin iiij hary nobles in . . . . *to the Leich to multiply,* summa £9." The 4th of the same month, "Item, to the King and the French Leich to play at the cartis, £9, 5s." May 29, 1502, the treasurer paid to Robert Bertoun, one of the king's mariners, "for certaine droggis brocht home be him to the French Leich, £31, 4s." And next day he gave "to the French Liech, quhen he passit his way, 300 French crowns," or £210 Scottish money. The leech at this time had gone upon a temporary visit to the continent, for the purpose of acquiring some additional knowledge of the mysteries of "Quintessence." " In the Treasurer's Accounts," says Mr Chalmers, "there are numerous payments for the ' *Quinta Essentia,*' including wages to the persons employed; utensils of various kinds; coal and wood for the furnaces; and for a variety of other materials, such as quicksilver, aquavite, litharge auri, fine tin, brint silver, alum, salt, eggs, salpeter, salaramoniack, &c. Considerable payments were also made to several 'Potingairs, for stuff of various kinds to the Quinta Essentia.' On the 13th October 1507, the king's treasurer paid £6 for a *puncheon of wine to the abbot of Tungland, to mak Quinta Essentia.* The king sometimes got *gold coins* from the treasurer to *put into the Quinta Essentia.*" The wine and the gold coins, it is to be presumed, amalgamated somewhere else than in the *Quinta Essentia.* From these gleanings by Mr Chalmers, it seems clear

enough that the poet's character of the " Fenyeit Freir of Tungland" can hardly be over-
drawn.

The rapid strides to promotion by this adventurer must have been annoying to Dunbar. That
a person wholly unconnected with ecclesiastical
matters should have had an abbacy conferred upon
him, in the course of two or three years' attendance at court, while he who had conducted the national business as secretary in numerous embassies,
and celebrated the union of " The Thistle and the
Rose" in such inimitable strains, had difficulty
in cking out life upon £10 a-year, was, in the
highest degree, humiliating. And yet such was the
fact. On the 11th March 1503–4, the treasurer
paid " to Gareoch Pursevant, 14s. to pass to Tungland for the abbacy to French Maister John." On
the 12th of the same month, " by the king's command," he paid " to Bardus Altovite, Lumbard,
£25, for Maister John, the French Medieiner, *new
maid abbot of Tungland*, quhilk he aucht [was in-
debted] to the said Bardus." This item, perhaps,
speaks more than all the rest as to the character of
John Damian. It evidently was a debt which he
had left unsettled in Lombardy, when he went to
France. In addition to this, some few days later,
there was given " to Maister John, the new maid
abbot of Tungland, £7." There is another item,
characteristic of the man. July 27, 1507, " Item,
lent be the kingis command to the abbot of Tung-

land, *and can nocht be gottin fra him,* £33, 6s. 8d."

The probability is that Damian was a spendthrift, imposing upon the liberality of the king without greatly enriching himself. The failure of his egregious attempt to fly from the ramparts of Stirling Castle brought him into universal contempt. Still the king seems to have treated him with unfailing kindness. Between October 1507, the time of his unhappy flight, and August 1508, the Treasurer's Accounts shew that the king had frequently played at cards and dice with him; but he seems to have been at last fain to withdraw, probably from the ridicule Dunbar had helped to produce. On the 8th of September 1508, "Damiane, abbot of Tungland," had a licence granted to him to pass out of the kingdom for five years, to study or engage in any other lawful occupation, without incurring any hurt, prejudice, or skaith anent the abbey and place of Tungland. He again reappears on the 29th March 1513, when he is paid £20 " to pas to the myne at Crawfurd-moor."

TO THE KING, WHEN MONY BENEFICES VAKIT.*

Sir, at this feast of benefice,
Think that small parts maks great service,

---

* Became vacant.

And equal distribution,
Maks them content that has reason ;
And wha has nane are pleasit nae wise.

Sir, whether is it alms mair,
To give him drink that thirsts sair ;
    Or fill ane fou man while he brist ;
    And let his fallow * die for thrist
Whilk wine to drink as worthy were ?

It is no glad collation
Where ane maks merrie, ane other looks down ;
    Ane thrists, ane other plays cap out :
    Let ance the cap go round about,
And win the covanis † bennison.

No date can be given to these verses ; but they were probably amongst the first of Dunbar's direct appeals to the king on the subject of a benefice.

TO THE KING.

Sanct Salvator sent silver sorrow ;
It grieves me both even and morrow,
    Chasing frae me all charitie ;
It makes me all blitheness to borrow ;
    My painful purse so prickles me.

---

* Equal, or neighbour.

† Mr Laing guesses this to mean company ; and very likely he is right. *Covin-tree*, in the south country, means a large tree in front of the mansion, where the Laird met his visitors.

When I wald blithely ballats brieve,*
Languor thereto gives me no leave ;
　　Were not guid houp my heart uphie,†
My very corpse for care wald cleave ;
　　My painful purse so prickles me.

When I set me to sing or dance,
Or go to pleasant pastance,
　　Then pausing‡ of penuritie,
Reaves that frae my rememberance ;
　　My painful purse so prickles me.

When men that has purses in tone,
Passes to drink or to disjone,§
　　Then maun I keep ane gravity,
And say that I will fast while none ;‖
　　My painful purse so prickles me.

My purse is made of sic ane skin,
There will no corses¶ bide it within ;
　　Straight as frae the fiend they flee,
Wha ever tine, wha ever win ;
　　My painful purse so prickles me.

Had I ane man of ony nation,
Could mak on it ane conjuration,
　　To gar silver aye in it be,
The devil suld have no domination,
　　With pine to gar it prickle me.

---

* Write.　　　† My heart to uplift.　　　‡ Thinking.
§ Breakfast, or other early repast.　　　‖ Until noon.
¶ Scots money usually had the form of the cross.

I have inquired in mony a place,
For help and comfort in this case,
  And all men says, my Lord, that ye
Can best remeid for this mal-ease,
  That with sic pains prickles me.

Sibbald supposes "this to be one of the earliest of Dunbar's addresses to James IV., as it contains no request for a benefice;" and while he "was yet in the practice of setting himself to sing and dance." Possibly it was one of the poet's earliest addresses to the king, but the reasons adduced are no guide to such a conclusion. He does not mean, by "setting himself to sing and dance," that he was in the habit of doing so for the amusement of the king, but rather for his own. He could neither indite ballads, nor sing or dance, or pass to the tavern, because of the "silver sorrow," or empty purse, which so troubled him. Dunbar frequently had money given him, in addition to his pension, by order of the king. 1507–8, March 15, "Item, to Maister William Dunbar, be the king's command, vłi. And again, "Item, the xxij day of Junij, to Maister William Dunbar, be the king's command, iijłi. xs." It is possible, therefore, that the address was written about this time."

THE DANCE OF THE SEVEN DEADLY SINS.

Of Februar the fifteen nicht,
Full lang before the dayis licht,
   I lay in till a trance ;
And then I saw baith Heaven and Hell :
Me thoucht, amangis the fiends fell,
   Mahoun gart cry ane Dance
Of shrews that were never shriven,*
Agains the feast of Fastern's even,†
   To mak their observance.
He bad gallants gae graith a gyes,‡
And cast up gamountis§ in the skies,
   As varlets do in France.

    *   *   *   *   *

---

* Such as never had made confession.

† Fastern's even is the evening preceding Lent, and was a festival of much jollity at the Scottish court as the Treasurer's Accounts shew. Tournaments were frequently held in honour of the occasion. In 1504-5, Feb. 3, Peter More, the taubroner, prepared a dance, by order of the King :—" Item for xij cotis and xij pair hois, half Scottis blak, and half quhit, to xij dansaris, £13, 2s. 10d." Fastern's even was much celebrated throughout the country. At Kilmarnock, foot-races, and other amusements, were held on that day, down till about twenty years ago. These sports, patronised by the Magistrates and Council, had continued from time immemorial; but when the Reformed Town Councillors came into office, in 1833, they considered themselves too wise for such puerilities, and withheld their countenance. The inhabitants, however, carried them on for a few years voluntarily; but at last they were allowed to drop.

‡ Prepare a mask.   § Gambols.

Helie harlots on hawtane wise,*
Come in with mony sundry guise,
  But yet leuch never Mahoun,
While priests come in with bare shaven necks ;
Then all the fiends leuch, and made gecks,
  Black-Belly and Bawsy-Broun.†

      *   *   *   *   *

Let see, quoth he, now wha begins,
With that the foul Seven Deadly Sins
  Begoud to leap at anis.
And first of all in Dance was Pride,
With hair wyld‡ back, and bonnet on side,
  Like to make vaistie wanis ;§
And round about him, as a wheel,
Hang all in rumples to the heel

---

* "This is a bold line," says Hailes, "if it means, as I think it does, 'Holie whores in haughtie guise.'" And Laing adds :— "*Heillie harlottis* means proud, or haughty harlots : the epithet *harlot* was applied indiscriminately by early writers to persons of either sex." We think Hailes in the right ; because the other explanation would make the line tautology, in which Dunbar never indulges. By holy harlots the poet, no doubt, meant such as had assumed the garb of holiness while in life.

† These were the names of certain spirits—such as Robin Goodfellow in England, and *Brownie* in Scotland. Some lines of this verse are supposed to be awanting in the MSS.

‡ Trained.

§ This is an obscure expression, which none of the annotators have attempted to explain, unless that *vaistie* means *void, wasteful;* and *wanis,* a habitation. But wanis means also the *jaws;* and the reading may be, that Pride so combed back his hair, and so wore his bonnet, that he was like to leave his cheeks altogether *bare,* or void of covering.

His kethat* for the nanis :†
Mony proud trumpour‡ with him trippit ;
Through scalding fire, aye as they skippit
　They girned with hideous granis. §

Then Ire came in with sturt and strife ;
His hand was aye upon his knife,
　He brandished like a beir :‖
Boasters, braggars, and bargainers, ¶
After him passit in to pairs,
　All bodin in feir of weir ; **
In jacks, and scryppis,†† and bonnets of steel,
Their legs were chainit to the heel, ‡‡
　Frawart was their affeir : §§
Some upon other with brands beft,‖‖
Some jaggit others to the heft,
　With knives that sharp could shear.

Next in the Dance followit Envy,
Filled full of feud and felony,
　Hid malice and despite :
For privy hatred that traitor tremlit ;
Him followit mony freik dissemlit,
　With fenyeit ¶¶ wordis quite :

---

* Cassock.　　　　　　　† For the nonce, for the occasion.
‡ From the French, *trompeur*—a cheat, a deceiver.
§ Groans.　　　　　‖ Bear.　　　　　¶ Wranglers.
** A Scottish law phrase, meaning arrayed after the manner of
war.
†† Short coat of mail.　　‡‡ Covered with chain armour.
§§ Wild was their appearance.　　　　　‖‖ Gave blows.
¶¶ Feigned.

And flatterers in to mèn's faces ;
And backbiters in secret places,
   To lie that had delight ;
And rownaris of false lesings,*
Alace ! that courts of noble kings
   Of them can never be quit.

Next him in Dance came Covetyce,
Root of all evil, and ground of vice,
   That never could be content :
Catives, wretches, and ockeraris,†
Hudpikes,‡ hoarders, gatheraris,
   All with that warlock went :
Out of their throats they shot on other
Het, molten gold, me thocht, a futher §
   As fire-flaucht maist fervent ;
Aye as they toomit them of shot,
Fiends filled them new up to the throat
   With gold of all kind prent.||

Syne Swearness, at the second bidding,
Came like a sow out of a midding,
   Full sleepy was his grunyie : ¶
Mony swear bumbard belly huddroun,**
Mony slut, daw, and sleepy duddroun,
   Him servit aye with sonnyie ;††

---

* Whisperers of false and injurious reports.
† Usurers.   ‡ Misers.
§ A quantity. || Impression or device.
¶ Grunsie, a vulgar phrase for *face*.
** Many a lazy, tun-bellied sloven.   †† With care.

He drew them furth in till a chain,
And Belial with a bridle rein
  Ever lashed them on the lunyie :
In Dance they were so slaw of feet,
They gave them in the fire a heat,
  And made them quicker of cunyie.*

Then Lechery, that laithly corpse,
Came berand † like ane baggit horse, ‡
  And Idleness did him lead ;
There was with him ane ugly sort,
And mony stinking foul tramort, §
  That had in sin been dead :
When they were enterit in the Dance,
They were full strange of countenance,
  Like torches burning red ;
Ilk ane led other by the tarsis ; ||
Suppose they fylit with their ——
  It micht be no remeid.

Then the foul monster, Gluttony,
Of wame insatiable and greedy,
  To Dance he did him dress :
Him followit mony foul drunkart,
With can and collop, cup and quart,
  In surfit and excess ;
Full mony a waistless wally-drag, ¶
With wames unwieldable, did furth wag,

---

* Of apprehension.   † Neighing or snorting.
‡ An entire horse.   § Dead body.
|| Tails.   ¶ A silly, useless person.

In creesh that did incress :
Drink ! aye they cried, with mony a gaip,
The fiends gave them het lead to laip,*
   Their leveray† was na less.

  *   *   *   *   *

Nae minstrels played to them but doubt,
For gleemen there were halden out,
   Be day, and eik by nicht ;
Except a minstrel that slew a man,
So to his heritage he wan,
   And enterit by brieve of richt.‡

Then cried Mahoun for a Hielan' Padyane :§
Syne ran a fiend to fetch Makfadyane,
   Far northwast in a neuch ;
Be he the coronach had done shout,
Ersche men so gatherit him about,
   In hell great room they took :
Thae tarmigants, with tag and tatter,
Full loud in Ersche begoud to clatter,
   And roup‖ like raven and rook.
The Devil sae deaved was with their yell,
That in the deepest pot of hell
   He smorit them with smook !

This is certainly the production of a master hand.
Lord Hailes remarks :—" The drawing of this pic-

---

* Lap.

† *Loveray*, or *Leveray*, is explained to mean reward ; but this
cannot be the meaning here. Lord Hailes reads it thus :—
" Their desire was not diminished ; their thirst was insatiable."

‡ The *breve de recto.*   § Padyhean, a pageant.

‖ Croak.

ture is bold, the figures well grouped. I do not
recollect ever to have seen the 'Seven Deadly
Sins' painted by a more masterly pencil than that
of Dunbar. His designs·certainly excel the explanatory peacocks and serpents of Callot." Warton
is equally warm in his encomium ; and Campbell,
in his "Specimens of the British Poets," says—
"His [Dunbar's] 'Dance of the Seven Deadly Sins
through Hell,' though it would be absurd to compare it with the beauty and refinement of the
celebrated 'Ode on the Passions,' has yet an animated picturesqueness not unlike that of Collins.
The effect of both pieces shews how much more
potent allegorical figures become, by being made to
fleet suddenly before the imagination, than by being detained in its view by prolonged description.
Dunbar conjures up the personified Sins as Collins
does the Passions, to rise, to strike, to disappear.
They ' come like shadows, so depart ! ' "

It has been calculated by Mr J. Chalmers, from
a hint by Lord Hailes, that the only years, in the
reign of James IV., when Fastern's-even fell upon
the 16th of February, were 1496, 1507, and 1518.
" It therefore appears," he says, " most probable
that this poem was written either in 1496 or 1507.
I should prefer the last ; " and in this opinion we
agree.

That the Seven Deadly Sins formed one of the
religious pageants in early times is extremely probable ; but that any of these pageants took the

form of a dance through the infernal regions, as Dunbar has so powerfully portrayed, has never been alleged by any one. Hawkins, in his " Origin of the English Drama," states that the people of Italy are still fond of seeing the Seven Deadly Sins dance a saraband with the Evil Spirit; and Spenser, in his " Faerie Queene," has a " procession of the Deadly Sins" from the palace of Pride; but Dunbar's *Dance* seems to stand by itself in unquestioned originality. In some of our old ecclesiastical buildings, such as the Cathedral of Glasgow, the Seven Deadly Sins are sculptured in relief; but whether after the manner of a dance our memory is not so fresh on the subject as to be positive.

Dunbar, as Lord Hailes observes, properly leads off the dance with *Pride*, because " *by that sin fell the angels;* " and he winds up the wild entertainment by representing *Mahoun* as calling for a Highland *Padyane,* and describes the Celtic uproar which followed as so very terrible that even the Devil was deaved with the yell. His satire is the more pointed, that he selects Macfadyan to shout the coronach—Macfadyan being a name detested even by the Highlanders themselves. In Dunbar's time, the feeling of dislike was mutual between the Highlands and Lowlands, the offspring probably of the great battle of the Harlaw, and the numerous attempts of the Highlanders, under the Lords of the Isles, to shake off their allegiance to the Scottish kings.

THE JOUST BETWIXT THE TAILOR AND SOUTAR.

Next at a Tournament was tryit,
That lang before in hell was cryit,
    In presence of Mahoun ;
Betuix a Tailor and a Soutar,
A pricklouse and a hobbil cloutar,*
    Their barras† was made boun.‡
The Tailor, baith with spear and shield,
Convoyit was unto the field,
    With mony a limmer loun ;§
Of seam biters, and beast gnapparis,||
Of stomach stealers,¶ and claith knapparis,**
    A graceless garrison.††

His banner borne was him before,
Wherein were clouts a hundred score,
    Ilk ane of diverse hue ;
And all stolen out of sundry webs,
For, while the sea flood fills and ebbs,
    Tailors will never be true.
The boothman‡‡ on the barras blent ;§§
Alace ! he tint all hardiment,
    For fear he changit hue :
Mahoun him comfort and made him knicht,
No ferlie than his heart was licht,
    That to sic honour grew.

---

* A cobbler.   † Barrier.   ‡ Prepared.
§ Scoundrel. || Catchers.
¶ The meaning of this phrase is not at all obvious.
** Stealers.   †† Company.
‡‡ The keeper of a small stall or booth.   §§ Looked.

He hecht* hiely before Mahoun,
That he suld ding the Soutar doun,
  Though he were wicht as mast ;†
But when he on the barras blenkit,
The Tailor's courage a little shrenkit,
  His heart did all ourecast ;
And when he saw the Soutar come,
Of all sic wordis he was dumb,
  Full sair he was aghast ;
For he in heart took sic a scunner,
A rack of wind, like ony thunner,
  Went frae him blast for blast.

The Soutar to the field him drest,
He was convoyit out of the west,
  As a defender stout :
Suppose he had no lusty varlot,
He had full mony lousy harlot,
  Fast rinning him about.
His banner was a barkit hide,
Wherein Sanct Girniga‡ did glide
  Before that ribbald rout :
Full soutar-like he was of laits,§
For aye between the harness plaits,
  The oily burstit out.

Upon the Tailor when he did look,
His heart a little dwalming took,
  Unease he micht upsit ;

---

* Promised.　　　　　† Strong as a mast.
‡ Saint Crispin.　　　§ Manners.

In till his stomach was sic a steer,
Of all his dinner, that cost him dear,
    His breast held never a bit.
To comfort him, or he raid forder,
The Devil of knichthood gave him order ;
    For stink then he did spit ;
And he about the Devil's neck,
Did spew again a quart of bleck,
    So knichtlie he him quit.

Then forty times the Fiend cried, Fy !
The Soutar furth affraitlie,
    Unto the field he socht :
When they were servit with their spears,
Folk had a feile* by their efferis,†
    Their hearts were baith on flocht.‡
They spurrit upon either side,
The horse attour the green did glide,
    And them together brocht :
The Tailor was no thing weel sittin,
He left the saddle all be——,
    And to the ground he socht.

His birnes§ brak and made a brattle,
The Soutar's horse scarred with the rattle,
    And round about did reel ;
This beast that was afraid full evil,
Ran with the Soutar to the Devil,
    And there rewart him weel.

---

  * Knowledge. † Condition.
  ‡ Fluttering. § Cuirass.

Something frae him the Fiend eschewit,
He trowed again to be bespewit,
  So strainit he was in steel :
He thocht he wald again debate him,
He turned his back and all be—— him,
  Quite oure frae neck to heel.

He lowsit it with sic a rerd,
Baith horse and man flew to the erd,
  He —— with sic a feir :
Now, have I quit thee ! quoth Mahoun ;
The new made knicht lay into swoon,
  And did all arms forswear.
The Devil gart them to dungeon drive,
And them of knichthood to deprive,
  Discharging them all weir ;
And made them harlots again for ever,
Whilk style to keep they had far lever,*
  Nor any armis bear.

I had mair of their warks written,
Had not the Soutar been be——,
  With Belial's —— unblest ;
But that sae guid a bourd,† me thocht,
Sic solace to my heart it wrocht,
  For lauchter near I brist.
Where through I waukenit of my trance ;
To put in to rememberance,
  Micht no man me resist,
To dite how all this thing befell

---

* They liked better.   † Joke.

> Before Mahoun, the heir of Hell :
> Schirris,* trow it gif ye list.

The Joust of the Tailor and the Soutar is a continuation of what the poet saw in the trance into which, as he tells us, he fell on the 15th of February —the night before the eve of Lent. The whole is a cunningly-contrived satire on the festival of Fastern's-e'en, as celebrated at the Scottish court, and throughout Scotland generally. His Satanic majesty—not behind other royal personages—is represented as holding a sort of carnival on the occasion, and, as dances were fashionable in courtly circles, nothing could be more appropriate in " the dark dominion " than the " Dance of the Seven Deadly Sins." We have seen how that dance began and ended, not in the poet's wakening up from his vision, but only to enjoy a change in the performance. Nothing seems, in his day, to have been more in consonance than a dance and a tournament; so the Devil, in imitation of his earthly contemporaries, calls a tilt, which had long before been proclaimed throughout his sovereignty. The poet selects the champions from two of the most burlesqued of all the crafts in his day—the tailors and the shoemakers. The weavers, who came in for a pretty considerable share of ridicule in later times, do not seem to have been so obnoxious in the sixteenth century—at least they are

* Sheriffs—pronounced, *Shirras.*

never mentioned in Dunbar's poems; but that they existed, and from a much earlier period, must be admitted. Be this as it may, a tournament seems to have formed a natural incident in the Devil's amusement at the celebration of Lent. The humour of the poem is certainly of an unrefined character, nay, altogether coarse, though not, perhaps, indelicate. Yet such, it must be admitted, were the jokes most relished by our unsophisticated ancestors. Pinkerton says, " The flames alone can cleanse the filth of this poem. But such were the standing jokes of the time. Sir Thomas More has his epigrams, *De ventris crepitu*." Much, however, can be tolerated where the tendency is not immoral; and the omission of the joust would have been an unwarrantable interference with those illustrations of his times for which the poet will ever be celebrated. " It is not improbable," as Laing observes, " that Dunbar may have had some personal allusions in this mock poem, as among the numerous entries in the Treasurer's Accounts regarding tournaments, and jousting in the barres, or barriers, is the following: — 1502, October 24, ' Item, to the heraldis for their compositioun of the eschet of the barres, *quhen Christofer Tailyour faucht*, £6, 13s. 4d.'" But perhaps the greatest satire of the whole is what follows.

AMENDS TO THE TAILORS AND THE SOUTARS.

Betuix twal hours and eleven,
I dreamed ane angel cam fra heaven,
  With pleasant stevin,* saying on hie,
  Tailors and Soutars, blest be ye !

In heaven hie, ordained is your place,
Above all sancts in great solace,
  Next God, greatest in dignitie :
  Tailyeours and Soutars, blest be ye !

The cause to you is not unkend,
What God mismaks ye do amend,
  Be craft and great agilitie :
  Tailors and Soutars, blest be ye !

Soutars, with shoon weel made and meet,
Ye mend the fauts of ill-made feet ;
  Wherefore to heaven your sauls will flee :
  Tailors and Soutars, blest be ye !

Is not in all this fair a flyrok,†
That has upon his feet a wyrok,‡
  Knowll tais,§ nor mools in no degree,
  But ye can hide them, blest be ye !

And Taileors, with weel-made claes,
Can mend the warst-made man that gaes,
  And mak him seemly for to see :
  Tailors and Soutars, blest be ye !

---

* Sound.   † Is not in all this crowd an ill-made person.
‡ An excrescence.   § Swelled at the joints.

Though God mak ane misfashioned man,
Ye can him all shape new again,
  And fashion him better be sic three :
  Tailors and Soutars, blest be ye !

Though a man have a broken back,
Have ye a gude crafty tailor, what rack,—
  That can it cover with crafts slee !
  Tailors and Soutars, blest be ye !

Of God great kindness may ye claim,
That helps his people frae crook and lame,
  Supporting faults with your supplie :
  Tailors and Soutars, blest be ye !

In erd ye kyth* sic miracles here,
In heaven ye sall be sancts full clear,
  Though ye be knaves in this countrie :
  Tailors and Soutars, blest be ye !

Such is the *per contra*, or amends to the tailors and soutars. In the Maitland MS. the following note is appended :—" Quod Dunbar quhane he drank to the Dekkynnis for amendis to the bodeis [members] of their craft." That the craft were offended with the poet there can be little doubt; but if they were satisfied with the amends made, they must have been truly simple-minded.

* Produce.

HOW SALL I GOVERN ME?

How sould I rule me, or what wise,
I wald some wise man wald devise ;
  I cannot live in no degree,
But some will my manners despise :
  Lord God, how sall I govern me ?

Gif I be gallant, lusty, and blyth,
Than will they say on me full swyth,
  That out of mind yon man is he,
Or some has done him comfort kyth :
  Lord God, how sall I govern me ?

Gif I be sorrowful and sad,
Than will they say that I am mad,
  I do not droop as I wald die ;
Thus will they say, baith man and lad :
  Lord God, how sall I govern me ?

Be I liberal, gentle, and kind,
Though I it tak of noble strynd,*
  Yet will they say, baith he and she,
Yon man is like out of his mind :
  Lord God, how sall I govern me ?

Gif I be lusty in array,
Than love I paramours they say,
  Or in my heart is proud and hie,
Or else I have it some wrang way :
  Lord God, how sall I govern me ?

---

* Kindred.

Gif I be nocht weel as beseen,
Than twa and twa says them between,
   That evil he guides* yon man, truelie ;
Lo ! be his claiths it may be seen :
   Lord God, how sall I govern me ?

Gif I be seen in court oure lang,
Than will they murmur them amang,
   My friends they are not worth a flee,
That I sae lang but guerdon† gang :
   Lord God, how sall I govern me ?

In court reward than purchase I,‡
Than have they malice and envy,
   And secretly they on me lee,
And does me slander privilic :
   Lord God, how sall I govern me ?

I wald my guiding were devisit ;
Gif I spend little I am despisit,
   Gif I be noble, gentle, and free,
A prodigal man I am so prisit :
   Lord God, how sall I govern me ?

Now judge they me baith guid and ill,
And I may no man's tongue hald still,
   To do the best my mind sall be,
Let every man say what he will,
   The gracious God mot§ govern me !

---

* Evil guides him.   † Without reward.
‡ Purchase by money is not meant.   § May.

We have no guide as to the date of this poem;
but, from the allusions to Dunbar's own particular
position, we may presume that it was not written
till he had been some time at court.   It is ingeniously contrived, while complaining of the difficulty
of conducting one's self without censure, to stimu-
late his friends in procuring for him the preferment
wished.

> " Gif I be seen in court oure lang,
>   Than will they murmur them amang,
>   *My friends they are not worth a flee,*
>   That I sae lang but guerdon gang."

DUNBAR'S COMPLAINT TO THE KING.

Complain I wald, wist I whom till,
Or unto whom direct my bill;
Whether to God, that all thing steers,
All thing sees, and all thing hears,
And all things wrocht in days seven;
Or till His mother, Queen of Heaven;
Or unto worldly Prince here doun,
That does for justice wear a crown;
Of wrangis, and of great injures
That nobles in their days indures,
And men of virtue, and cunning,
Of wit, and wisdom in guiding,
That nocht can in this Court conqueis,
For lawtie,* love, or lang service.

---

* Loyalty.

But foul, jow-jowrdane-yhedit jevels,*
Cowkin-kenseis,† and culroun‡ kevels ;§
Stuffets,‖ strekours,¶ and stafische strummels ;**
Wild haschbalds,†† haggerbalds,‡‡ and hummelis ;§§
Drunkards, dysours,‖‖ divours,¶¶ drivels,*
Misguidit members of the devils ;
Mismade mandrags,† of mastiff strynd,‡
Crawdons,§ cowarts, and thieves of kind ;
Blait mowit blaidyeanes,‖ with bledder cheeks,
Club-faced cluccanes,¶ with cloutit breeks,
Chaff-midden churls, coming of cart-fillars,
Great glaschew-headit gorge** millers,
Evil, horrible monsters, false and foul ;
Some causeless cleiks to him ane cowl,
Ane great convent fra sin to 'tice ;
And he himself example of vice :
Entering for geir and no devotion,
The devil is glad of his promotion ;
Some ramyis ane rokkat†† fra the Roy,
And does ane dastard destroy ;
And some that gets ane parsonage,
Thinks it ane present for a page ;

---

* A foul epithet for nasty fellows.
† Idle beggars.　　　　　‡ Scoundrel.
§ Sorry fellows.　　　　‖ Lackeys.　　　　¶ Flatterers.
** Stubborn stumblers.　†† Gluttons.
‡‡ Coarse feeders.　　　§§ Drones.　　　　‖‖ Gamblers.
¶¶ Bankrupts.　　　　　* Drivellers.
† Mandrake.　　　　　‡ Race.
§ Base fellows.　　　　‖ Soft persons.
¶ Persons who seize, or *cleik*, with violence.
** Voracious, gorged.
†† By continual solicitation obtaining a surplice.

P

And on na wise content is he,
My Lord while that he callit be.
   But how is he contentit, or nocht,
Deem ye about into your thocht!
The learit* son of Earl or Lord,
Upon this ruffian to remord, †
That with all castings has him cled,
His errands for to rin and red?
And he is master native born,
And all his elders him beforn ; ‡
And meikle mair cunning be sic three,
Has to possess ane dignitie,
Saying his odious ignorance,
Panting ane prelate's countenance,
Sae far abone him set at table,
That wont was to muck the stable :
Ane pyk-thank§ in ane prelate's clais,
With his wauld‖ feet, and wirrok¶ tais,
With hopper hips,** and henches narrow ;
And bausie hands to bear ane barrow ;
With lout shoulders, and loutered back, ††
Whilk nature made to bear ane pack ;
With greedy mind, and glaschand‡‡ gain,
Mell-headit like ane mortar stane,
Feigning the feiris§§ of ane lord,
And he ane strummell, I stand ford ; ‖‖

---

* Learned.   † To produce remorse.
‡ Before.   § Parasite.   ‖ Plain-soled.
¶ Corns, or excrescences.   ** Uneven, unequal.
†† Bent shoulders and bent back.
‡‡ Unsatiated.   §§ Companionship.   ‖‖ For it.

And ever more as he does rise,
And nobles of bluid as he does despise,
And helps for to hald them doun,
That they rise never to his renoun.
   Therefore, O Prince, maist honorable !
Be in this matter merciable,
And to thy old servants have an e'e,
That lang has lippenit unto thee ;*
Gif I be ane of thae mysell,
Through all regions has tein hard tell,†
Of whilk my writing witness bears ;
And yet thy danger aye me dears :‡
But after danger comis grace,
As has been heard in mony place.

Pinkerton accuses Dunbar of having written this poem in a passion, and that it was consequently so indistinct that he could not explain many of the phrases. Still we seldom find Dunbar making use of expressions that were not intelligible and full of

---

* Trusted thee.

† *Tein hard tell.* The meaning of this is somewhat obscure. *Tein* signifies *anger*, or it may be *sorrow;* but "anger," or "sorrow, heard tell" does not read ; nor yet would *tein*, as signifying *taken.* The poet evidently means, however, that throughout all regions he had experienced trouble or difficulty in the king's service. At the same time, there is still another way of explaining it. In this poem, as well as elsewhere, the poet makes a distinction between the words *hard* and *herd*, both bearing the common English explanations of *hard* and *heard* He may therefore mean, that in all regions he has had hard *tell*, or hard discussions, in his ambassadorial capacity.

‡ Attaches him more to the sovereign.

meaning.   At the same time, it is quite possible
that it had been written when excited by the conduct of some of those ignoramuses who, by importunity or otherwise, had been unduly elevated.
It was certainly a bold complaint to lay before the
king, and the last four lines would almost infer
that his majesty had but recently escaped some
danger to which his good-nature, in the patronage
of low and designing individuals, had exposed
him.

DUNBAR'S REMONSTRANCE TO THE KING.

Sir, ye have mony servitours,
And officiars of diverse cures ;
Kirkmen, courtmen, and craftsmen fine ;
Doctors in jure and medicine ;
Diviners, rhethors, and philosophers,
Astrologers, artistes, and orators,
Men of arms, and valiant knichts,
Musicians, minstrels, and merry singers ;
Chevaliers, callandaris,* and French flingers ;
Cunyers, carvours, and carpenters ;
Builders of barks and ballingers ;†

---

* We only know of two meanings which can be given to this
word—keepers of yearly registers, or pressers of linen. It is
possible that it has reference to the Kalends rather than to
manufactures : and it is no bar to this idea that the word occurs
between chevaliers and French flingers. The poet was fond of
such transitions.

† A particular kind of ship.

Masons, lying upon the land,*
And ship-wrichts hewing upon the strand ;
Glazing wrichts, goldsmiths, and lapidaries,
Printers, painters, and polingaris ;
And all of their craft cunning,
And all at anis labouring,
Whilk pleasant is and honourable ;
And to your Hieness profitable ;
And richt convenient for to be,
With your hie regal majestie ;
Deserving of your Grace most ding,†
Baith thank, reward, and cherishing.

And though that I, amang the lave,
Unworthy be ane place to have,
Or in their number to be tald,
As lang in mind my wark sall hald !
As hale in every circumstance,
In form, in matter, and substance,
But‡ wearing, or consumption,
Rust, canker, or corruption,
As ony of their warkis all,
Suppose that my reward be small !

But ye sae gracious are and meek,
That on your Hieness follows eik
Ane other sort, more miserable,
Though they be not so profitable :

---

* Are we to infer from this expression—"lying upon the land "—that masons had a different mode of preparing stones in the reign of James IV. from what is practised now?

† Condign, worthy.   ‡ Without.

Fenyeors, fleechers, and flatterers ;
Criers, craikers, and clatterers ;
Soukars,* groukars,† gledars,‡ gunners ;§
Monsieurs of France, gude claret cunners ;||
Inopportune askers of Ireland kind ;¶
'And meet rievers,** like out of mind ;
Scaffers,†† and scamlers ‡‡ in the neuk,
And hall hunters of drake and deuk ;

---

* Idlers.   † Sharpers.

‡ Gleds, or hawks, of persons.

§ James IV. introduced artillery, or the use of great guns, in the Scots army. In "The Golden Targe" Dunbar speaks of his allegorical personages, when they had "up-sail" and departed, as having "fyrit gunnis with powder violent." The king frequently amused himself with shooting. In the Treasurer's Accounts, February 1, 1508, L.14, by the king's command, was paid for a gun, to James Bertoun, who, no doubt, had brought it from abroad. On the 4th of the same month there is, "Item, to the king, quhilk he tynt on schuting with the culveryn in the hall of Halyrud house, with Hannis, [or Hanse, the gunner] 28s." Next day, "Item, to the king, quhilk he tynt on schuting with the culveryn, in Sir George Newton's yard, 7 French crownis, summa L.4, 18s." Holyrood House had thus been finished—at least the hall—before February 1508.

|| Tasters.

¶ We are not, perhaps, to suppose that the court of James IV. was troubled with what is now known at head-quarters as "the brass band." Highlandmen were probably the "Ireland kind" meant by Dunbar.

** We should hardly interpret this, as Mr Laing has done, "meat-pilferers;" but rather *suitable* rievers, suitable to the askers. *Like out of mind,* equally mad or impudent.

†† Dishonourable gatherers of provisions.

‡‡ An impertinent intruder at table.

Thimlers * and thristers,† as they were wud,
Kokens and kens,‡ nae man of gude ;
Shoulderers, and shovers, that have no shame,
And to no cunning that can claim ;
And can none other craft nor cures
But to mak thrang, Sir, in your doors,
And rush in where they counsel hear,
And will at nae man nurture § lear :
In quintessence, eik, inginors ‖ jolly,
That far can multiply in follie ; ¶
Fantastic fules, baith false and greedy,
Of tongue untrue, and hand evil-dredie : **
Few daur of all this last addition,
Come in tolbuith, without remission.

    And though this noble, cunning sort,
Whom of before I did report,
Rewardit be, it were but reason,
Thereat suld no man mak enchesson : ††
But when the other fules nice,
That feastit at Cokelbeis gryce,‡‡
Are all rewardit, and not I,
Than on this false world I cry, Fy !
My heart near bursts for teyne,§§
Whilk may not suffer nor sustene

---

* Such as press violently into a crowd.
† Thrusters.   ‡ Idle, froward fellows.
§ Good breeding.   ‖ The ingenious.
¶ This is a rub at the abbot of Tungland.
** Given to evil deeds.   †† Exception.
‡‡ A coarse but humorous production called "Colkelbye sow."
Gryce means a pig, hence feasted at or on Cokelbeis pig.
§§ Vexation.

So great abusion for to see
Daily in court before my e'e !
  And yet mair patience wald I have,
Had I reward amang the lave ;
It wald me something satisfie,
And have less of melancholie,
And gar me mony falt oursee,
That now is braid before mine e'e :
My mind so far is set to flite,
That of nocht else I can indite ;
For outher maun my heart to break ;
Or with my pen I maun me wreak ;
And sen the tane must needs be,
Into melancholy to die,
Or let the venom ische* all out ;
Beware, anon, for it will spout,
Gif that the treacle† come not tyt‡
To 'suage the swalme§ of my despite.

This " Remonstrance " was, in some respects, a politic corollary of the " Petition."   Here we have the king's patronage of industry, and the arts and sciences, described in happy relief to the excessive abuse of the royal privilege complained of in the " Petition."   And yet Dunbar does not commit himself by sycophantish whining.   He claims reward as his due, and fails not to tell the king that

---

* Issue.

† Treacle seems, in Dunbar's time, to have been used for its soothing qualities.

‡ To it.   § Tumour.

he does not consult justice in the way he confers his favours. It is certainly curious that he should have so· long passed over the poet's known desire for a benefice, however small; unless, as Mr Laing supposes, it was that he might have the poet as a member of the royal household.

DUNBAR'S DREAM.

This hinder nicht half-sleeping as I lay,
Methocht my chalmer in ane new array
   Was all depaint* with many diverse hue,
   Of all the noble stories auld and new,
Sen our first father formed was of clay.

Methocht the lift all bricht with lampis licht,
And therein enterit mony lustie wicht,
   Some young, some old, in sindry wise arrayit,
   Some sang, some dancit, on instruments some playit,
Some made disports with heartis glad and licht.

Than thocht I thus, this is ane feloun fary,†
Or else my wit richt wondrouslie does vary;
   This seems to me ane guidlie companie,
   And gif it be ane friendlie fantasie,
Defend me Jesu, and His mother Marie!

---

* Before the introduction of tapestry the walls of the higher class of houses were painted in various colours and devices—a fact which shews that the limner's art was not unknown in Scotland at a very early period.

† Strange tumult.

Their pleasant sang, nor yet their pleasant toun,*
Nor yet their joy did to my heart redoun ;
  Methocht the drearie damiesal Distress,
  And eik her sorry sister Heaviness,
Sad as the lead, in bed lay me abone.

And Languor sat up at my bed's head,
With instrument full lamentable and dead ;
  She playit sangis so duleful to hear,
  Methocht ane hourie seemit aye ane year ;
Her hew was wan and wallowit as the lead.

Than came the ladies, dancing in ane trace,
And Nobleness before them came ane space,
  Saying, with cheer benign and womanly,
  I see ane heir in bed oppressit ly,
My sisters go and help to get him grace.

With that anon did start out of a dance,
Twa sisters, callit Comfort and Pleasance,
  And with twa harpis did begin to sing,
  But I thereof micht tak nae rejoicing,
My Heaviness opprest me with sic mischance.

They saw that I nocht gladder wax't of cheer,
And thereof had they wonder all but weir,†
  And said ane lady that Perceiving hecht,‡
  Of Heaviness he feelis sic a wecht,
Your melody he pleases not till hear.

She and Distress her sister does him grieve :
Quod Nobleness, How sall he them eschew ?

---

* Tune.   † Without doubt.   ‡ Named.

Than spak Discretion, ane lady richt benign,
Work after me, and I sall gar him sing,
And lang or nicht gar Languor tak her leave.

And then said Wit, Gif they work not be thee,
But ony doubt they sall not work be me.
Discretion said, I knaw his malady,
The stroke he feelis of melancholie,
And Nobleness, his leeching lies in thee.

Or ever this wicht at heart be hale and feir,*
Both thou and I must in the court appear;
For he has lang made service there in vain:
With some reward we maun him quit again,
Now in the honour of this guid New-year.

Weel worth thee, said Considerance,
And I sall help for to maintene the dance.
Than spak ane wicht callit Blind Affection,
I sall before you be, with mine election,
Of all the court I have the governance.

Than spak ane constant wicht callit Reason,
And said, I grant you have been lord a session,
In distribution, but now the time is gone,
Now I may all distribute mine alone;
Thy wrangous deeds did ever man enscheson.†

For time were now that this man had some thing,
That lang has been ane servant to the King,

And all his time never flatter could nor feign,
But humbly into ballat wise complain,
And patiently endure his tormenting.

I counsel him be merry and jocund ;
Be Nobleness his help maun first be found.
    Weel spoken, Reason, my brother, quoth Discretion,
    To set on dais with lordis at the session,
Into this realm you were worth mony ane pound.

Then spak anon Anopportunitie,
Ye sall not all gar him speed without me,
    For I stand aye before the Kingis face ;
    I sall him deave, or else myself mak chase,
But gif that I before him servit be.

Ane busy asker sooner sall he speed,
Nor sall twa busy servants out of dread,
    And he that asks not tynes' but his word,
    But for to tyne lang service is no bourd,*
Yet thocht I never to do sic folly did.

Then came anon ane callit Sir John Kirkpaker,
Of many cures, ane michtie undertaker,
    Quoth he, I am possest in kirkis seven,
    And yet I think they grow sall till eleven,
Or he be servit in ane, yon ballat-maker.

And then Sir Bet-the-Kirk, sae mot I thrive,
I have of busy servants four or five,
    And all directit unto sundrie steids,†
    Aye still awaiting upon kirkmen's deids,‡
Frae whom my tithings§ will I hear believe.

---

* Jest.   † Places.   ‡ Deaths.   § Tidings.

Quoth Reason than, the balance goes uneven,
That thou, alas, to serve has kirks seven,
    And seven as worth kirk, not having ane,
    With greediness I see this world ouregane,
And sufficience dwells not but in heaven.

I have not wit thereof quoth Temperance,
For though I hald him evenly the balance ;
    And, but ane cure, full even micht till him weigh,
    Yet will he tak ane other and gar it swey ;
Wha best can rule wald maist have governance.

Patience to me, my friend, said Mak-guid-cheer,
And on the Prince depend with heavenly fear,
    For I full weel does knaw his noble intent :
    He wald not, for ane bishopric's rent,
That you were unrewardit half ane year.

Than as ane fairy they to door did frak,*
And shot ane gun that did so rudely rak,
    While all the erd did rerd,† the rainbow under,
    On Leith sands me thocht she brak in sunder,
And I anon did wauken with the crak.

From what the author states, it would appear
that this " Dream " was composed as a New-year
Address to the king. It is curious to notice how
ingenious the writer is in his contrivances to enforce
his claim for past services; and he is evidently in
earnest. On ten pounds a year, (Scots money,)
with even occasional gratuities, it is impossible that

* Move quickly.   † Did resound.

he could be otherwise than in needy circumstances. And he even condescends to style himself, by way of ridicule, "yon ballat-makar." It is not at all impossible, that, in his character of poet, he was looked down upon by some of the ignorant nobility and the *Sir John Kirkpakars* of the day, as one who wasted his time in idle fancies, and felt careless, or wanted the influence necessary to secure a greater share in the gifts of the court. It is little wonder that his importunity increased as years began to steal upon him, and when he saw himself so strangely neglected.

OF DISCRETION IN ASKING.

Of every asking follows nocht
Reward, but gif some cause were wrocht;
　　And where cause is, men weel may see,
And where nane is, it will be thocht
　　In Asking sould Discretion be.

Ane fule, though he have cause or nane,
Cries aye, Gif me, into a 'drane;*
　　And he that drones aye as ane bee
Sould have ane hearer dull as stane:
　　In Asking sould Discretion be.

Some asks mair than he deserves,
Some asks far less than he 'serves;

---

* A rame, constant repetition.

Some shames to ask, and braids* of me,
And all without reward he sterves :
  In Asking sould Discretion be.

To ask but† service hurts guid fame,
To ask for service is not to blame ;
  To serve and live in beggartie,
To man and maister is baith shame :
  In Asking sould Discretion be.

He that does all his best service,
May spoil it all by cracks and cries,
  Be foul inopportunitie ;
Few words may suffice the wise :
  In Asking sould Discretion be.

Not needful is men sould be dumb,
Naething is gotten but words some,
  Nocht speed but diligence we see ;
For naething it alane will come :
  In Asking sould Discretion be.

Asking wald have convenient place,
Convenient time, leisure, and space ;
  But haste or press of great menyie,‡
But heart abasit, but tongue reckless :
  In Asking sould Discretion be.

Some micht have Yea, with little cure,§
That has oft Nay, with great labour ;
  All for that time not bide can he,
He tynes baith errand and honour :
  In Asking sould Discretion be.

---

* Shies.   † Without.   ‡ Company.   § To do.

Suppose the servant be lang unquit,
The Lord some time reward will it !
  Gif he does not, what remedy ?
To fecht with Fortune is no wit :
  In Asking sould Discretion be.

OF DISCRETION IN GIVING.

To speak of gifts or amous deeds :
Some gives for merit, and some for meeds ;*
  Some wardly honour to uphie ;
Some gives to them that nothing needs :
  In Giving sould Discretion be.

Some gives for pride and glory vain ;
Some gives with grudging and with pain ;
  Some gives on prattik† for supplie ;
Some gives for twice as guid again :
  In Giving sould Discretion be.

Some gives for thank, and some for threat ;
Some gives money, and some gives meat ;
  Some gives words fair and slie ;
And gifts fra some may nae man treat :
  In Giving sould Discretion be.

Some is for gift sae lang required,
While that the craver be so tired,
  That or the gift deliver't be,
The thank is frustrat‡ and expired :
  In Giving sould Discretion be.

------

* Praise.   † Design.   ‡ Interrupted.

Some gives so little full wretchedly,*
That all his gifts are nocht set by,
  And for a hud-pyke † halden is he,
That all the warld cries on him, Fy !
  In Giving sould Discretion be.

Some in his giving is so large,
That all oure-laden is his barge ;
  Than vice and prodigalitie,
Thereof his honour does discharge :
  In Giving sould Discretion be.

Some to the rich gives his geir,
That micht his gifts weel forbear ;
  And though the poor for falt ‡ sould die,
His cry nocht enters in his ear :
  In Giving sould Discretion be.

Some gives to strangers with face new,
That yesterday frae Flanders flew ;§
  And to auld servants list‖ not see,
Were they never of sae great virtue :
  In Giving sould Discretion be.

Some gives to them can ask and plenyie ;¶
Some gives to them can flatter and fenyie ;**

---

* Niggardly.   † Miser.   ‡ Want.

§ In allusion, probably, to some foreign " abbot of Tungland," who had recently experienced the kindness of the court. It was chiefly through the Netherlands that the intercourse with the Continent was carried on—England being then an enemy's country.   ‖ Chose not to regard.

¶ Complain.   ** Feign.

Some gives to men of honestie,
And halds all janglars * at disdenyie :
In Giving sould Discretion be.

Some gets gifts and rich arrayis,
To swear all that his master sayis,
    Though all contrar weel knaws he ;
Are mony sic now in thir days :
    In Giving sould Discretion be.

Some gives to guid men for their thews ;†
Some gives to trumpours‡ and to shrews ;
    Some gives to know his authoritie :
But in their office guid funden few is :
    In Giving sould Discretion be.

Some gives parochins§ full wide,
Kirks of St Bernard and St Bride,‖
    The people to teach and to ouresee,
Though he has nae wit them to guide :
    In Giving sould Discretion be.

OF DISCRETION IN TAKING.

Efter Giving I speak of Taking,
But little of ony gude forsaking ;¶

----

* Disputatious or talkative persons.
† For their good qualities.   ‡ Deceivers.   § Parishes.
‖ Probably some personal allusion was here meant.
¶ "The meaning seems to be," says Lord Hailes, "I may
speak of taking, but I need not say much of people's quitting any-
thing of value ; *that* is not common."

Some taks oure little authoritie,
And some oure meikle, and that is glaiking :*
  In Taking sould Discretion be.

The clerks taks benefices with brawls,†
Some of St Peter and some of St Paul's ;
  Tak he the rents, no care has he,
Suppose the Devil tak all their sauls :
  In Taking sould Discretion be.

Barons taks fra the tenants poor,
All fruit that growis on the feure,‡
  In mails§ and gersoms‖ rais't oure hie,
And gars them beg frae door to door :
  In Taking sould Discretion be.

Some merchants taks unleissum win,¶
Whilk maks their packs ofttimes full thin ;
  Be their succession as ye may see,
That ill win geir 'riches not the kin :
  In Taking sould Discretion be.

Some takis other mennis tacks,
And in the poor oppression maks,
  And never remembers that he maun die,
While that the gallows gar him rax :
  In Taking sould Discretion be.

---

* Absurd.
† Numerous examples of this occur in Scottish history.
‡ Furrow.   § Rents.
‖ Grassum, a sum of money paid by a tenant for the renewal
of his lease.   ¶ Unlawful gain.

Some taks be sea and some be land,
And never frae taking can hald their hand,
　　While he be tyit up to ane tree;
And syne they gar him understand,
　　In Taking sould Discretion be.

Some wald tak all his neibour's geir,
Had he of man as little fear
　　As he has dread that God him see;
To tak than sould he never forbear:
　　In Taking sould Discretion be.

Some wald tak all this warld on breid;*
And yet not satisfied of their need,
　　Through heart insatiable and greedie;
Some wald tak little, and cannot speed:
　　In Taking sould Discretion be.

Great men for taking and oppression,
Are set full famous at the session,
　　And poor takers are hangit hie,
Shamit for ever, and their succession:
　　In Taking sould Discretion be.

These three pieces, on Discretion in Asking, Giving, and Taking, were all, no doubt, intended as moral lessons, and as exposures of the malpractices of the times—inculcating at the same time a sound advice to the king, to discourage flatterers, sycophants, impostors, and oppressors. The poet even does not spare the then Court of Session—repre-

* At once.

senting its members as the greatest oppressors and appropriators of what was not their own, and the merciless punishers of less guilty offenders.

MEDITATION IN WINTER.

Into thir dark and drublie* days,
When sable all the heaven arrays,
   With mystic vapours, cluds, and skies,
   Nature all courage me denies
Of sangs, ballats, and of plays.

When that the nicht does lengthen hours,
With wind, with hail, and heavie shours,
   My dule spirit does lurk forschoir;†
   My heart for languor does forloir,‡
For laik of summer with his flours.

I wauk, I turn, sleep can I nocht,
I vexit am with heavy thocht;
   This warld all oure I cast about,
   And ever the mair I am in doubt,
The mair that I remeid have socht.

I am essayit on every side,
Despair says aye, In time provide,
   And get some thing whereon to leif;
   Or with great trouble and mischief,
Thou sall into this court abide.

---

* Probably drumly, dark, gloomy.
† Forshorn, desolate.   ‡ Becomes forlorn.

Than Patience says, Be nocht aghast;
Hald Hope and Truth within thee fast:
   And let Fortune work forth her rage,
   When that no reason may assuage,
While that her glass be run and past.

And Prudence in my ear says aye,
Why wald thou hald that will away?
   Or crave that thou may have no space,
   Thou tending to another place,
A journey going every day?

And than says Age, My friend, come near,
And be not strange, I thee requeir:
   Come, brother, by the hand me tak,
   Remember thou has compt to mak,
Of all the time thou spendit hear.

Syne Death casts up his yets wide,
Saying, Thir open sall ye bide;
   Albeit that thou were never so stout,
   Under this lintel sall thou lout;
There is nane other way beside.

For fear of this all day I droop;
No gold in kist, nor wine in cup,
   No ladie's beauty, nor love's bliss,
   May let* me to remember this:
How glad that ever I dine or soup.

Yet, when the nicht begins to short,
It does my sp'rit some part comfort,

---

* Hinder.

> Of thocht oppressit with the shours.
> Come, lustie simmer ! with thy flours,
> That I may live in some disport.

This is altogether a very superior poem. Pinkerton says, " The addresses of the several personifications to him [the poet] are fine; that of Age, pathetic; and that of Death, even sublime. Death's throwing up his gates wide, and telling the poet he must enter, are most grand and striking circumstances." And Ellis adds, " It is pleasant to observe in this fine poem the elastic spirit of Dunbar struggling against the pressure of melancholy : indeed, it appears that his morality was of the most cheerful kind." Dunbar was an ardent admirer of nature, and " the dark and drumlie' days" of winter were well calculated to depress a mind so sensitive as his. That he was distressed by his peculiar and unprovided-for condition, is apparent in almost all his verses at this time. The cause of his despondency forms the keynote of his meditations—

> " I am essayit on every side,
>   Despair says aye, In time provide,
>   And get some thing whereon to leif;
>   Or with great trouble and mischief,
>   Thou sall into this court abide."

The want of some provision for advancing age, and the precariousness of living at court, were the canker-worms that preyed at his heart. His complaint was put forth sometimes in banter, humour, or in downright melancholy, as in the present case. Yet how truly and beautifully he draws comfort, even in the depth of his despair from the coming of " lustie simmer, with his flours." The beauties of the external world are gratifying to all, especially to the more intelligent and sensitive. Amongst the last enjoyments of weary age, is to draw himself out into the sun, and bask for a time in his rays. Mr Laing thinks rightly that this poem was " written about the year 1507, or when Dunbar composed the 'Lament for the Makars.'"

LAMENT FOR THE MAKARS.

WHEN HE WAS SEIK.

I that in heil* was and glaidness,
Am troublit now with great seikness,
And feeblit with infirmitie :
   Timor mortis conturbat me.

Our pleasance here is all vain glory,
This false warld is but transitory,
The flesh is bruckle, the Fiend is slee ;
   Timor mortis conturbat me.

The state of man does change and vary,
Now sound, now seik, now blyth, now sary,†
Now dancing merry, now like to die ;
   Timor mortis conturbat me.

---

* Health.   † Grieved.

No state in erd* here stands sicker ;
As with the wind waves the wicker,
So waves this warld's vanitie ;
   Timor mortis conturbat me.

Unto the Death goes all estates,
Princes, Prelates, and Potestates,†
Baith rich and puir of all degree :
   Timor mortis conturbat me.

He taks the knichts into the field,
Anarmit‡ under helm and shield ;
Victor he is at all melee :
   Timor mortis conturbat me.

That strang unmerciful tyrand
Taks, on the mother's breast soukand,
The babe, full of benignitie :
   Timor mortis conturbat me.

He taks the champion in the stour,§
The captain closit in the tour,‖
The lady in bour full of beautie :
   Timor mortis conturbat me.

He spares no lord for his piscence,¶
Nor clerk for his intelligence ;
His awful straik may no man flee ;
   Timor mortis conturbat me.

---

* Earth.   † Potenates.   ‡ Armed.
§ Of battle.   ‖ The captain of a fortress.
¶ Puisance.

Art-magicians, and astrologys,
Rethors, logicians, theologys,
Them helps no conclusions slee :
    Timor mortis conturbat me.

In medicine the most practicians,
Leeches, surgeons, and physicians,
Them self from death may not supplie :
    Timor mortis conturbat me.

I see that makars,* amang the lave,
Plays here their padyanes,† syne goes to grave,
Sparit is not their facultie :
    Timor mortis conturbat me.

He has done piteously devour,
The noble Chaucer, of makars flow'r,
The Monk of Berry, and Gower, all three :‡
    Timor mortis conturbat me.

The gude Sir Hew of Eglintoun,
And eik Heryot, and Wyntoun,
He has ta'en out of this countrie :
    Timor mortis conturbat me.

That scorpion fell has done infek§
Maister John Clerk, and James Afflek,
Frae ballat-making and tragedie :‖
    Timor mortis conturbat me.

---

* Poets.   † Pageants.

‡ These three English poets, Chaucer, Lydgate, and Gower, were greatly admired in Scotland.

§ Taken away.

‖ In Dunbar's time *tragedy* was not limited to the dramas, as in our day, but meant any moral or descriptive poem.

Holland and Barbour he has berevit ;
Alace ! that he nocht with us leavit
Sir Mungo Lockhart of the Lee :
   Timor mortis conturbat me.

Clerk of Tranent eik he has ta'en,
That made the awnteris* of Gawane ;
Sir Gilbert Hay endit has he :
   Timor mortis conturbat me.

He has Blind Harry, and Sandy Traill
Slain with his shot of mortal hail,
Whilk Patrik Johnstoun micht not flee :
   Timor mortis conturbat me.

He has left Merseir his indite,
That did in love so lively write,
So short, so quick, of sentence hie :
   Timor mortis conturbat me.

He has ta'en Roull of Aberdeen,
And gentle Roull of Corstorphine ;
Two better fallows did no man see :
   Timor mortis conturbat me.

In Dunfermline he has ta'en Broun,
With Maister Robert Henrisoun ;
Sir John the Ross embraced has he :
   Timor mortis conturbat me.

And he has now ta'en last of aw,
Gude, gentle Stobo, and Quintine Schaw,

---

* Adventures.

Of whom all wichtis has pitie :
    Timor mortis conturbat me.

Gude Maister Walter Kennedy,
In point of deid lies verily,
Great ruth it were that so suld be :
    Timor mortis conturbat me.

Sen he has all my brether ta'en,
He will not let me live alane,
On forse* I maun his next prey be :
    Timor mortis conturbat me.

Sen for the Death remeid is none,
Best is that we for death dispone,†
After our death that live may we :
    Timor mortis conturbat me.

This is an affecting poem, heightened by the ever-recurring and solemn burden, " Timor mortis conturbat me," supposed by Ritson to have been suggested by one of Lydgate's poems, beginning " So as I lay the other night." But this we consider hypercritical. The same idea might have occurred to hundreds—and does occur to hundreds unacquainted either with Lydgate or Dunbar. The poem was composed, as the author tells us, " when he was sick," and his thoughts naturally turned to the contemplation of death. His moralising as to the world's vanity, and the instability of all things, is clothed in quaint but beautiful language—

* Compulsion.   † Dispose ourselves.

> " He taks the champion in the stour,
>   The captain closit in the tour,
>   The lady in bour, full of beautie :
>   Timor mortis conturbat me."

And from generalising in this way, he is led, by a fine species of ratiocination, to reflect that his own class, the poets, are not exempt from the stroke of the tyrant—

> " I see that makars, amang the lave,
>   Plays here their padyanes, syne goes to grave."

And then he enumerates how many have been laid low, until he comes to " Gude Maister Walter Kennedy," then at the point of death, and himself, ill in health and depressed in mind—

> " Sen he has all my brether ta'en,
>   He will not let me live alane."

The poem, printed at the press of Chepman and Myllar, in 1508, is rendered of extreme interest because of this " Lament for the Makars," many of whose names would otherwise have been wholly lost to fame. The first mentioned are

Chaucer, Lydgate, and *Gower,* well-known early English poets.

Sir Hew of Eglintoun is believed to have been that Sir Hugh de Eglintoun of Eglintoun, in Ayrshire, who married Egidia, daughter of Walter, Lord High Steward of Scotland, and who died about 1381, without male issue. His only daughter and heiress, Elizabeth, married John Montgomerie of Eaglesham, from which union sprung the noble house of Eglintoun. "Hucheon of the Awle Ryale," (Hall Royal,) mentioned hy Wyntown as the author of several poems, is supposed to have been Sir Hew of Eglintoun, but upon very insufficient grounds.

Heryot and *Wyntown.* Of the first of these poets nothing whatever is known. The second is *Andrew of Wyntown,* author of "The Chronicle Originale," in Scottish metre, first published by Macpherson, in 1795. He was Prior of Lochleven.

Maister *John Clerk* and *James Afflek.* Of the former, nothing is known beyond the fact that there were several Scottish poets of the same name. Afflek is supposed to have been "servitour to the Earl of Rosse" in 1494, and afterwards had the Chantory of Caithness, which, becoming vacant on the death of "Maister James Auchinleck," in 1497, was bestowed on Maister James Beton. Mr Laing says "there is a poem entitled ' The Qair of Jelousy,' preserved in the Selden MS., which has at the end, 'Explicit quod Auchin . . . .' " The poem consists of 607 lines.

Holland and *Barbour.* Holland was a priest, and flourished in the reign of James II. He was the author of a curious allegorical poem, called "The Buke of the Howlat," written about 1453. It is preserved in the MSS. of Asloane and Bannatyne. Hailes says, " It is a verbose work, but must have merit with antiquaries, from the stanzas describing ' the kyndis of instrumentis, the sportaris [jugglers], the Irish bard, and the fulis.' " *John Barbour* was Archdeacon of Aberdeen, in the reign of David II., and author of the " Acts of Robert the Bruce."

Sir Mungo Lokert of the Lee. Hailes supposed that this person must have been an ecclesiastic, one of the Pope's knights, as he could find no trace of him in the family pedigree. In the Acts of Council, however, 27th February 1489, occurs, " Agnes Lindesay, spouse of *umquhile Sir Mongo Lokart, Knyct,*" and " Robert Lokert of the Leie, *his son and are.*" He died before 1493, in which year Robert is mentioned as his successor. None of his writings are known.

Clerk of Tranent, " that made the awnteris of Gawane," Dunbar tells us. As " Hucheon of the Awle Ryale " is said to have been the author of the " Adventures of Gawane," the suggestion seems probable that *Hew* or *Hucheon* was Clerk's first name. This is countenanced by the fact that Dunbar does not speak of Hucheon. No doubt he omits several well-known names, such as Thomas the Rhymer, James I., and Gawin Douglas; still as he positively states that Clerk made the " Adventures of Gawane," it seems extremely likely that Hucheon and he were one and the same person.

Sir Gilbert Hay, chamberlain to Charles VI. of France. He was the author of several translations from the French. A MS. version of his, of the

French metrical romance of "Alexander the Great," consisting of 20,000 lines, is in the library of the Earl of Ormelie. This translation was probably completed about 1460.

Blind Harry and *Sandy Traill.* The former was the author of "The Life and Acts of Sir William Wallace." He was coexistent with Dunbar. The Treasurer's Accounts shew that small gratuities were occasionally given to the minstrel during the reign of James IV., between the years 1489 and 1493. Of the latter, *Sandy Traill*, no traces have been found.

Patrik Johnstoun, according to the Bannatyne MS., was the author of a poem called "The Three Deid Powis," but which, in the Maitland MS., is attributed to Robert Henryson. It is impossible, therefore, to decide who has the best claim to the poem. It is perhaps more in the style of Henryson than any other poet of the period; but that Johnston was a "makar" of some repute is evident. His name occurs repeatedly in the Treasurer's Accounts between 1488 and 1492. He "and his fallowis" "playt a play to the king in Lythgu," in 1489.

Merseir or *Merser.* This poet is celebrated by Lyndsay, as well as Dunbar, and yet so little is known of him that even his Christian name has not been ascertained. Peter, James, William, and Andro Merser, all occur in the Treasurer's Accounts.

Roull of Aberdeen, and "gentle *Roull of Corstorphine."* Neither of these parties has been identified. Sir John Rowl was the author of a poem called "Rowlis Cursing." Perhaps he was "Roull of Aberdeen," for such a production could hardly be the work of "*gentle* Roull of Corstorphine."

Broun. Bannatyne's MS. contains two copies of a poem, entitled "Judgment to Come," by, in the one case, *Walter* Broun, and in the other, *Sir William Brown.* But, as Laing shews, the original edition of the "Lament for the Makars," printed in 1508, does not contain any such name. The lines read thus—

> "In Dunfermline he has doun roune
> Gud Maister Robert Henrysoun;"

which expression—"*doun roune*"—Sibbald interprets to mean, "has rounded, or whispered in the ear." It would have been a more direct and simple explanation if he had merely modernised the spelling, and said, "*he has down run,*" that is, death had run down gud Maister Henrysoun. As the poem was printed under Dunbar's own eye, the conclusion is obvious, that Brown was not in the original version.

Maister Robert Henrisoun was preceptor in the Benedictine Convent of Dunfermline, hence his appellation of "Scolmaister of Dunfermling." He was the author of "Robene and Makyne," one of the earliest pastorals in the Scottish language, which has been much admired for its poetical merits. He is also the author of a number of fables. Many of his pieces have been printed separately; but a collected edition, by Mr David Laing, is now, we understand, nearly completed.

Sir John the Ross, probably another of the Pope's Knights. He was the party to whom Dunbar addressed the first portion of the " Flyting" with Kennedy. In the Treasurer's Accounts there is a payment, 8th May 1490, " Item, to John the Ross, be a precept of the kingis, xx unicornis," (£18 Scots.) This may have been the party, but it is impossible to identify him.

" Gentle *Stobo,* and *Quintyne Schaw.*" Of Stobo's writings nothing is known. He was an ecclesiastic, but acted as a notary-public both in the reigns of James III. and IV. His name was *Reid,* although perhaps better known as *Stobo.* He had a pension granted to him by James III., of £20, in 1477–8, the words of which are—" dilecto nostro familiari servitori et scribe Johanni Red *nuncupato* Stobo." It had originally been only £5. In the Treasurer's Accounts his name occurs in 1505. May 6, " Item, be the kingis command, to Stobo *liand seik,* £5." Again, on the 27th of the same month, " Item, to Stobo, liand seik, be the kingis command, 5 French crownis, £3, 10s." This, no doubt, was immediately before his death, for the " Lament" must have been written prior to

1508. The only known poem of *Quintyne Schaw* is the "Advyce to a Courtier," first printed by Pinkerton. He was a native of Ayrshire. *Quintin Schaw*, son of *John Schaw of Haily*, had a charter under the great seal, dated June 20, 1489, confirming a charter of 1475, by the Lord of Dernley, to John Schaw of Haily, and the heirs male of his body. There are numerous entries in the Treasurer's Accounts shewing that he had a pension, and had been long at court. "Item, the samyn day [July 8, 1504] to Quintin Schaw, in his pensioun, be the kingis command, quhilk he hes ilk yeir, £10." As his name does not occur again, the probability is that he did not long survive this date.

Maister Walter Kennedy, as already stated in the introduction to this volume, was the sixth son of Lord Kennedy of Cassillis and Duñure, in Ayrshire. He was educated for the Church, and Mr Laing thinks it probable that he was appointed Provost of Maybole, on the death of Sir David Robertson, about 1494, the patronage of which collegiate church continued in the Kennedy family, who originally founded it. But this was not the case: for although at one time an expectant of Church preferment, he seems to have abandoned his views in this respect. When he and Dunbar wrote the "Flyting" he was Depute-Clerk of Carrick, which he held under his brother David, Earl of Cassillis; and he acquired the property of Glentig, from John Wallace, in 1504. He married Christian Hynd, but of what family, is unknown, and had two sons, *Walter* and *Alexander*. In 1510, Walter is mentioned in a deed as parson of Douglas. He was incorporated a member of the College of Glasgow in 1511, and appointed rector of Douglas in 1517. He was chosen rector of the University of Glasgow in 1525, at which time he was provost of Maybole, and canon of Glasgow. *Alexander* was designed of Glentig. He married Janet Wallace, and had issue, *William Kennedy of Glentig*, called in the entail of the Earl of Cassillis, in 1540. William of Glentig had a daughter, *Janet*, who is stated in a contract, dated 3d April 1562, between Gilbert, fourth Earl of Cassillis, and her, to be the heir of Alexander Kennedy of Glentig, Walter Kennedy, parson of Douglas, her grandfather, and James Kennedy, in Kirkdomini. She married William Kennedy of Gillespie. Glentig seems to have passed from the family before the end of the sixteenth century. Besides the " Flyting " with Dunbar, Walter Kennedy is known as the author of " The Praise of Aige," " Ane Aigit Man's Invective," " Ane Ballet of our Lady," " The Passion of Christ," " Pious Counsale," &c. But it is presumed that much of his writing has disappeared. He seems to have been a poet of very considerable talent. His share of the " Flyting " is by no means unworthy of his opponent. Indeed, it is difficult to say which of the combatants has the advantage. He is even placed, by Dou-

glas, before Dunbar, and is called, in his " Court
of the Muses," " Great Kennedy." Could it be
that a spirit of enmity existed between Dunbar and
Douglas? They were contemporaries, and yet
Douglas is not mentioned in Dunbar's " Lament."
Of course, Douglas was alive at the time,* and
could not be *lamented;* still it was not proper for
Dunbar to say—

> " Sen he has *all my brether tane*
> He will not let *me live alane,*"

if he recognised Douglas as a brother poet. The
oversight must have annoyed the worthy Bishop of
Dunkeld.

OF THE WARLD'S INSTABILITY.

TO THE KING.

This wavering warld's wretchedness,
The failing and fruitless business,
The misspent time, the service vain,
    For to consider is ane pain.

The sliding joy, the gladness short,
The feignit love, the false comfort,
The sweet abayd,† the slichtful trane,‡
    For to consider is ane pain.

The sugarit mouths, with minds therefra,
The figurit speech, with faces twa,
The pleasant tongues, with hearts unplain,
    For to consider is ane pain.

---

* He lived till 1522. † Delay. ‡ Snare.

The leal labour lost, and leal service,
The lang avail on humble wise,
And the little reward again,
  For to consider is ane pain.

Not I say all be this countrie,*
France, England, Ireland, Almanie,
But all be Italy and Spain ;
  Whilk to consider is ane pain.

The change of warld frae weel to wo,
The honourable use is all ago,
In hall, in bour, in burgh and plain ;
  Whilk to consider is ane pain.

Belief does hope, trust does not tarry,
Office does flit, and courts do vary,
Purpose does change, as wind or rain ;
  Whilk to consider is anc pain.

Gude rule is banished oure the border,
And rangat† rings but‡ any order,
With rerd§ of ribalds, and of swane ;‖
  Whilk to consider is ane pain.

The people so wickit are of fears,
The fruitless erd all witness bears,
The air infectit and profane ;
  Whilk to consider is ane pain.

---

* He did not confine himself to this country.
† Tumult.   ‡ Without.   § Roar.
‖ Probably sweyngeours, sturdy vagabonds.

The temporal state to grip and gather,
The son disheris * wald the father,
And as ane divour wald him demean ;
   Whilk to consider is ane pain.

Kirkmen so halie are and gude,
That on their conscience, rowne and rude,†
May turn aucht oxen and ane wane ;
   Whilk to consider is ane pain.

I knaw not how the Kirk is guidit,
But benefices are not weel dividit ;
Some men has seven, and I not ane ;
   Whilk to consider is ane pain.

And some, unworthy to bruik ane stall,
Wald climb to be ane cardinal,
Ane bishopric may not him gane ;‡
   Whilk to consider is ane pain.

Unworthy I, amang the lave,
Ane kirk does crave, and nane can have;
Some with ane thraif§ plays passage plain ;
   Whilk to consider is ane pain.

It comes be king, it comes be queen,
But aye sic space is us between,

---

* Disinherit.

† Mr Laing queries this expression without attempting any explanation. It seems to mean, simply, that the consciences of kirkmen were so *round and rude*, so wide, coarse, and ignorant, that eight oxen and a waggon might turn upon them.

‡ Suffice.

§ Twenty-four sheaves of corn—a heap of anything.

That nane can shoot it with ane flane ;*
Whilk to consider is ane pain.

It micht have comin in shorter while
Frae Calyecot and the new-found Isle,†
The parts of Transmeridiane ;
   Whilk to consider is ane pain.

It micht be this, had it been kynd,‡
Comin out of the deserts of Inde,
Oure all the great sea oceane ;
   Whilk to consider is ane pain.

It micht have comin out of all airts,
Frae Persia and the Orient parts,
And frae the Isles of Africane ;§
   Whilk to consider is ane pain.

It is so lang in comin me till,
I dreid that it be quite gane will,
   Or backward is turnit again ;
   Whilk to consider is ane pain.

---

* An arrow.

† *Calicut*, a town in Hindostan, the first part visited by Europeans. It was with the view of finding a shorter passage to India that led to the discovery of America, which was at first considered an island, and called the New Isle. Sebastian Cabot, a native of Bristol, though of foreign parentage, discovered America in 1497, whereas Columbus did not get within sight of the continent till the following year. In the Privy Purse Accounts of Henry VII. there is the following entry : Aug. 10, 1497, "To him that found the New Isle, L.10."

‡ Natural.   § Isles of Africa.

Upon the heid of it is hecht,*
Baith unicorns, and crowns of wecht,†
When it does come all men does frane ;‡
   Whilk to consider is ane pain.

I wit it is for me providit,
But sae done tiresome it is to bide it,
It breaks my heart, and brists my brain ;
   Whilk to consider is ane pain.

Great abbeys' graith I nill§ to gather,
But ane kirk scant coverit with heather ;
For I of little wald be fain :
   Whilk to consider is ane pain.

And for my cures‖ in sundrie place,
With help, Sir, of your noble Grace,
My sillie saul sall never be slain ;
   Nor for sic sin to suffer pain.

Experience does me so inspire,
Of this false, failing warld I tire,
That evermore flits like ane phane ;¶
   Whilk to consider is ane pain.

The foremost hope yet that I have
In all this warld, sae God me save,
Is in your Grace, baith crop and grain,
   Whilk is ane lessoun** of my pain.

---

* Promised.   † Coins of different values.
‡ Insist, get impatient.   § I care not.
‖ Benefice, business.   ¶ Phantom.   ** Lessening.

The moral reflections, and the poet's earnest cry for a benefice, are very curiously and ingeniously blended. · The transition, from the disparity of things in general, to his own particular case is, as Pinkerton remarks, arch—

> " I knaw not how the Kirk is guidit,
>   But benefices are not leal dividit ;
>   Some men has seven, and I not ane."

Nor is his humour, as to the postponement of the gift, less pungent. He had no doubt that his cure was provided, but then it might have come from Calicut or the New-found Isle; and he was afraid, from the time that had elapsed, that it was on the way backward. Dunbar probably speaks truly, when he tells us, that on the faith of getting a benefice, he had made promises of payments, both in *unicorns* and *crowns,* and that his creditors were getting impatient.

WELCOME TO BERNARD STEWART,

LORD OF AUBIGNY.

Renownit, royal, right reverend, and serene
     Lord, hie triumphing in worship and valour,
Fro Kings down, most Christian Knight, and keen,
     Most wise, most valiant, most laureat* hie victour,

----

* Laurelled.

Unto the stars uphcit is thine honour ;
In Scotland welcome be thine excellence
  To king, queen, lord, clerk, knight, and servitour,
With glory and honour, laud and reverence.

Welcome, in stour* most strong, incomparable knight,
  The fame of armies, and flow'r of vassalage ;
Welcome, in weir most worthy, wise, and wight ;
  Welcome, the son of Mars of most courage ;
  Welcome, most lusty branch of our lineage,
In every realm our shield and our defence ;
  Welcome, our tender blood of hie parage,†
With glory and honour, laud and reverence.

Welcome, in weir the second Julius,
  The prince of knighthood and flow'r of chivalry ;
Welcome, most valiant and victorious ;
  Welcome, invincible victor most worthy ;
  Welcome, our Scottish chieftain most doughty ;
With sound of clarion, organ, song, and sence,‡
  To thee at once, Lord, welcome all we cry ;
With glory and honour, laud and reverence.

Welcome, our indeficient § adjutory,‖
  That ever our nation helpit in their need ;
That never saw Scot yet indigent nor sorry,
  But thou did him support, with thy guid deed ;
  Welcome, therefore, above all living leyd,¶
With us to live, and to make residence,

---

* Battle.   † Parentage.   ‡ Incense.
§ Not deficient.   ‖ Help.   ¶ Man.

Whilk never sall sunyhie* for thy sake to bleed :
To whom be honour, laud, and reverence.

Is none of Scotland born, faithful and kind,
   But he of natural inclination
Does favour thee, with all his heart and mind,
   With fervent, tender, true intention ;
   And wald, of inward, hie affection,
But† dread of danger, die in thy defence,
   Or death, or shame, were done to thy person ;
To whom be honour, laud, and reverence.

Welcome, thou knight, most fortunable in field ;
   Welcome, in arms most aunterus‡ and able,
Under the sun that bears helm or shield ;
   Welcome, thou champion, in fecht unourcumable ;
   Welcome, most doughty, digne,§ and honourable,
And most of laud, and hie magnificence,
   Next under kings to stand incomparable ;
To whom be honour, laud, and reverence.

Through Scotland, England, France, and Lombardy,
   Flies on wing thy fame, and thy renown ;
And oure all countries underneath the sky,
   And oure all strands, fro the stars down ;
   In every province, land, and region,
Proclaimit is thy name of excellence,
   In every city, village, and in toun,
With glory and honour, laud and reverence.

---

   * Refuse.   † Without.
   ‡ Adventurous.   § Dignified.

O fierce 'Achil, in furious, hie courage!
  O strong, invincible Hector, under shield!
O valiant Arthur, in knightly vassalage!
  Agamemnon, in governance of field!
  Bold Hannibal, in battle to do beild.*
Julius, in jupert,† in wisdom and experience!
  Most fortunate chieftain, both in youth and eild,
To thee be honour, laud, and reverence!

At parliament thou suld be hie renownit,
  That did so mony victories obtene;
Thy crystal helm with laurel suld be crownit,
  And in thy hand a branch of olive green;
  The sword of conquest, and of knighthood keen,
Be born suld hie before thee in presence,
  To represent sic man as thou has been;
With glory and honour, laud and reverence.

Hie, furious Mars, the god armipotent,
  Rong‡ in the heaven at thine nativitie;
Saturnus doun, with fiery e'en did blent,§
  Through bloody visor, men menacing to gar die;
  On thee fresh Venus cast her amorous e'e;
On thee Mercurius furthiet‖ his eloquence;
  Fortuna major did turn her face on thee,
With glory and honour, laud and reverence.

Prince of freedom, and flow'r of gentleness,
  Sword of knighthood, and choice of chivalry,
This time I leave, for great prolixitness,¶
  To tell what fields thou wan in Piccardy,

---

* Shelter.   † Jeopardy.   ‡ Reigned.
§ Glance.   ‖ Put forth.   ¶ Prolixity.

In France, in Bretagne, in Naples, and Lombardy;
As I think after, with all my diligence,
Or thou depart at length for to descry ;*
With glory and honour, laud and reverence.

B, in thy name, betokens batalrus ;
   A, able in field ; R, right renown most hie ;
N, nobleness ; and A, for aunterus ;
   R, royal blood ; for doughtiness is D ;
   V, valiantness ; S, for strenewitie ;
Whose knightly name, so shining in clemencie,
   For worthiness in gold suld written be ;
With glory and honour, laud and reverence.

.   .   .   .   .   .

This poem is not preserved in any of the MS. collections, but printed from the black letter of Chepman and Myllar, published in 1508. The last verse has been defaced. It probably contained an illustration of the surname, similar to that of *Bernardus*. The subject of the poem was a descendant of the house of Darnley, and inherited the title and estates of Aubigny, in France. He was one of the most celebrated men of his time, and called, by the French, " Le Chevalier sans Reproche." He came to Scotland in 1484, as ambassador from Charles VIII. of France, to renew the ancient league between the two countries; and next year he distinguished himself as commander of the French auxiliaries of the Duke of Richmond

* Describe.

at the battle of Bosworth Field. He subsequently
performed valiant deeds, in the interest of France,
in the various places mentioned by the poet.. The
welcome was occasioned by Lord Aubigny's second
and last embassy to Scotland, on the 9th May
1508, when he came through England with a following of eighty troopers. He was then advanced
in years, and ill in health, so that Dunbar's pane-
gyric was speedily changed to an elegy, in consequence of the death of the distinguished visitor.

ELEGY ON THE DEATH OF BERNARD STEWART,

LORD OF AUBIGNY.

Illuster Lodovick, of France most Christian King,
    Thou may complain with sighs lamentable,
The death of Bernard Stewart, noble and ding,*
    In deed of arms most anterous† and able ;
    Most michty, wise, worthy, and comfortable,
Thy men of weir to govern and to gy :‡
    Fortune, alace ! now may thou wear the sable,
Sen he is gone, the Flow'r of Chivalrie.

Complain sould every noble, valiant knicht
    The death of him that douchtie was in deed ;
That many ane fo in field has put to flicht,
    In weirs wicht, be wisdom and manheid ;
    To the Turk sea all land did his name dreid,
Whose force all France in fame did magnific ;

---

* Worthy.   † Adventurous.   ‡ Guide.

Of so hie price sall nane his place posseid,＊
For he is gone, the Flow'r of Chivalrie.

O duleful Death ! O dragon dolorous ;
　Why has thou done so dulefullie devour
The prince of knichtheid, noble and chivalrous,
　The wit of weirs, of-arms and honour,
　The cropt † of courage, the strength of arms in stour,
The fame of France, the fame of Lombardy,
　The choice of chieftains, most awful in armour,
The charbuckell ‡ chief of every chivalrie ?

Pray now for him, all that him lovit here !
　And for his saul mak intercession
Unto the Lord, that has him bocht so dear,
　To give him mercy and remission :
　And, namelie, we of Scottish nation,
Intill his life whom most he did affy,§
　Forget we never into our orison
To pray for him, the Flow'r of Chivalrie.

Lord Aubigny died at the seat of Forrester of
Corstorphine, in the beginning of July, about a
month after his arrival in Scotland. His last
will and testament, the inventory of his effects,
taken after his decease, is dated 8th June 1508.
On the 15th of that month, the treasurer gave 14s.
" as the kingis offerand at my Lord Aubigne's
saule mess." His body is said to have been in--
terred in the south aisle of Corstorphine church,

＊ Possess.　　　　　　　　　　　　　　† Top.
‡ The most brilliant amongst gems.　　　§ Esteem.

where his tomb, with a recumbent figure in armour, is still pointed out; but this is extremely doubtful, because, in his will, he expressly desired to be buried in the church of the Black Friars of Edinburgh, which was burned down in 1528. The arms on the monument at Corstorphine are those of Forrester.

The reader will remark that both the " Welcome " and the " Elegy " are strained, as if the poet had tasked himself beyond the requirements of the subject. It is very probable, as Mr Laing remarks, that Dunbar had experienced the liberality of Lord Aubigny when he was abroad, and gratitude, as well as admiration, prompted him to exceed even himself in the earnestness of his welcome.

OF ANE BLACKAMOOR.*

Lang have I made † of ladies white,
Now of ane black I will indite,
    That landit furth of the last ships ;
Who fain wald I descrive perfite,
    My Ladie with the meikle lips.

How she is tute mowit ‡ like an ape,
And like a gangarel § unto graip ;‖

---

* Negro.   † Written.
‡ The under jaw jutting out.   § Stroller.
‖ " And like a gangarel unto graip," is very obscure. To *graip* in the Scottish language is to *grope*. In no manner can

> And how her short cat nose up-skips ;
> And how she shines like ony saip ;
> My Ladie with the meikle lips.
>
> When she is clad in rich apparel,
> She blinks as bricht as ane tar barrel ;
> When she was born the sun tholit 'clips,
> The nicht he fain faucht in her quarrel :
> My Ladie with the meikle lips.
>
> Wha for her sake, with spear and shield,
> Proves maist michtilie in the field,
> Sall kiss, and with her go in grips ;
> And fra thence furth her love sall wield :
> My Ladie with the meikle lips.
>
> And wha in field receivis shame,
> And tynes there his knichtlie name,
> Sall come behind and kiss her hips ;
> And never to other comfort claim :
> My Ladie with the meikle lips.

This is a graphic delineation from nature. As
the poet tells us, it is the first time he ever indited
anything about black ladies. She had just "landit
furth of the last ships." The Bertrams—well
known as adventurous seamen in the reign of James
IV.—had letters of marque from the king against
the Portuguese, whose vessels they often captured
on the return of the latter from their settlements in

this be twisted to make sense, unless in a far-off way, that she
was like a wanderer going to darkness.

Africa and India. Blackamoors were consequently not unknown in Scotland before Dunbar celebrated this dark beauty. Mr Laing observes that, in 1501, one of the king's minstrels was " Peter the Moryen," or Moor; but *moryen* simply means swarthy, so that Peter was perhaps not an African. In 1504, two blackamoor girls arrived, and were educated at court, where they waited on the queen. They were baptized Elen and Margaret. In June 1507, a tournament was held in honour of the queen's black lady, Elen More, which was conducted with great splendour. But neither of these girls could have stood for the picture by Dunbar. His subject must have been a fully-matured and genuine specimen of African produce. A number of return ships were captured from the Portuguese in 1509, and brought into the Scottish ports. It is probable that some of these were the last ships meant by the poet. Although he joked of a tournament in her honour, it is not necessary that such an affair should actually have taken place.

TO THE KING.

Of benefice, sir, at every feast,
Wha moniest has maks maist request :
  Get they not all, they think ye wrang them ;
Aye is the oure-word of the guest,
  Gif them the pelf to part amang them.

Some swaillis* swan, some swaillis deuk,
And I stand fasting in a neuk,
  While the effect of all they fang them :
But, Lord ! how piteously I look,
  When all the pelf they part amang them.

Of sic hie feasts of sancts in glory,
Baith of common and proper story,
  Where lords were patrons, oft I sang them
Caritas pro Dei amore ;†
  And yet I gat naething amang them.

This blind warld ever so pays his debt,
Rich before poor spreads aye their net,
  To fish all waters does belang them :
Wha naething has can naething get,
  But aye as cipher set amang them.

Sa some the kirk had in their cure,
They fors‡ but little how it fure,§
  Nor of the buiks, nor bells wha rang them :
They panse‖ not of the parochin puir,
  Had they the pelf to part amang them.

So variant is this warld's rent,
That men of it are never content ;
  Of death while¶ that the dragon stang them,
Wha maist has than sall maist repent,
  And has maist compt to part amang them.

---

* Devours.	† Part of the Litany.	‡ Care.
§ Fared.	‖ Think.	¶ Until.

Pinkerton was of opinion that this poem was written about the same time that Dunbar addressed the king when many benefices became vacant. It is impossible, however, to fix the date of either the one or the other; and it could hardly be that all his verses " To the King " immediately followed one another. This would not have been politic, but rather a violation of his own ideas of " discretion in asking."

TO THE KING.

Sir, yet remember, as of before,
How that my youth is done forlore,*
   In your service, with pain and grief,
Gude conscience cries, Reward therefore !
   Excess of thocht does me mischief.

Your clerks are servit all about,
And I do like ane red hawk shout,
   To come to lure that has no leif,†
While my plumes begin to break out :‡
   Excess of thocht does me mischief.

Forgot is aye the falcon's kind ;
But ever the mittane is hard in mind,
   Of whom the gled does prectikis§ preif;

---

* Utterly wasted.
† Who is not permitted to come to *lure*, a term in falconry.
‡ His plumage begins to get into disorder.
§ Stratagems or tricks.

The gentle goshawk goes unkind :
Excess of thocht does me mischief.

The pyet, with her pretty coat,
Feigns to sing the nichtingale's note ;
But she can never the crochet cleif,
For harshness of her carlich* throat :
Excess of thocht does me mischief.

Aye fairest feathers has fairest fowls ;
Suppose they have no sang but yowls,
In silver cages they sit at chief ;
Kind native nest does cleck but owls :
Excess of thocht does me mischief.†

O gentle Eagle,‡ how may this be,
That of all fowls does hiest flee !
Your lieges why will ye not relief,
And cherish after their degree ?
Excess of thocht does me mischief.

When servit is all other man,
Gentle and semple of every clan,
Kin of *Rauf Colyear*, and *John the Reif*,§
Naething I get, nor conqueis can :
Excess of thocht does me mischief.

---

* Coarse, vulgar.

† This is a hit at the King's preference of foreigners.

‡ The King.

§ Two ballads, popular in Dunbar's day. An edition of
" Rauf Colyear, with the thrawin brow," was printed by Robert
Lekprewik, at St Andrews, in 1572. We are not aware that
any copy of "Johne the Reif" has been discovered. The poet
meant that, when people of the class of these two worthies had
all been served, he could obtain nothing.

Though I in court be made refuse,
And have few virtues for to roose ;
  Yet am I comin of Adam and Eif ;
And fain wald live as others does :
  Excess of thocht does me mischief,

Or I suld live in sic mischance,
Gif it to God were no grievance,
  To be a pyk-thank* I wald preif,
For they in warld want no pleasance :
  Excess of thocht does me mischief.

In some part on myself I plenyie ;†
When other folks does flatter and fenyie,
  Alace ! I can but ballads brief ;‡
Sic bairnhood bids my bridle renye :§
  Excess of thocht does me mischief.

I grant my service is but licht ;
Therefore of mercy, and not of richt,
  I ask you, sir, no man to grief,
Some medicine give that ye micht :
  Excess of thocht does me mischief.

May nane remeid my malady
Sae weel as ye, sir, verily ;
  For with a benefice ye may preif,
And gif I mend not hastily :
  Excess of thocht does me mischief.

I was in youth, on nurse's knee,
Dandely ! Bishop, dandely !

---

* A spy, or informer.   † Complain.
‡ Ballads write.   § Curb.

And when that age now does me grief,
Ane simple vicar I cannot be :
  Excess of thocht does me mischief.

Jock that was wont to keep the stirks,
Can now draw him ane cleik of kirks,
  With ane false card into his sleif,*
Worth all my ballads under the birks :
  Excess of thocht does me mischief.

Twa cures or three has Upolands † Michell,
With dispensations bund in a knitchell ; ‡
  Though he fra nolt had new ta'en leif,
He plays with totum, and I with nichell !§
  Excess of thocht does me mischief.

How suld I live that is not landit, ||
Nor yet with benefice am I blandit,
  I say not, sir, you to repreif ;
But doubtless I gae richt near hand it :
  Excess of thocht does me mischief.

As saul is here in purgatory,
Living in pain and houp of glory ;
  So is myself, ye may belief,
In houp, sir, of your adjutory : ¶
  Excess of thocht does me mischief.

---

* Perhaps, as Lord Hailes suggests, the poet does not mean
false play at cards, but secret calumny and false suggestion.   But
it is by no means improbable that benefices were staked and won
at the card table.

† Hills or muirlands.   ‡ A bundle.

§ He plays with *Te-totum*, and I with nothing.

|| Had no landed property.   ¶ Intercessor.

We have here another evidence, in the poet's own statement, that he was wholly without patrimony, and entirely dependent on the king. How could he live, he asks, not being possessed of land? Land or a benefice was then the great stoop of a comfortable existence.

TO THE KING,

THAT HE WERE JOHN THOMSON'S MAN.

Sir, for your grace, baith nicht and day,
Richt heartily on my knees I pray,
With all devotion that I can,
   God gif ye were John Thomson's man!

For, were it so, than weel were me,
But* benefice I wald not be;
My hard fortune were endit than:
   God gif ye were John Thomson's man!

For it micht hurt in no degree,
That one, so fair and gude as she,
Through her virtue sic worship wan,
   As you to mak John Thomson's man!

I wald give all that ever I have,
To that condition, so God me save,
That ye had vowit to the swan,†
   Ane year to be John Thomson's man!

---

* Without.

† This was a vow well understood in chivalry. The knights used to make vows to God over a roasted swan or other fowl.

The mercy of that sweet, meek *Rose*,
Suld soft you, *Thistle*, I suppose,
Whose pikes through me so ruthless ran ;
   God gif ye were John Thomson's man !

My advocate, baith fair and sweet,
The hale rejoicing of my sp'rit,
Wald speed into my errands than ;
   And ye were anis John Thomson's man !

Ever when I think you hard or dour,
Or merciless in my succour,
Than pray I God, and sweet Sanct Ann,
   Gif that ye were John Thomson's man !

This is a happy play of humour in furtherance of the poet's hint for a benefice. He was a favourite with the queen, and his prayer is, that the king should become " John Thomson's man," were it only for a twelvemonth. The phrase is proverbial for a person who is ruled by his wife; and probably the name originally was *Joan* in place of *John*. Were the king a henpecked husband, even for a year, Dunbar was confident that his benefice would be immediately realised.

TO THE KING.

THE PETITION OF THE GRAY HORSE, AULD DUNBAR.

Now lovers come with largess loud,
Why sould not palfreys than be proud,

When gillets will be schourd and schroud,*
That ridden are baith with lord and lad?
   Sir, let it never in toun be tald,
   That I sould be ane Yule's yald!†

When I was young and into ply,
And wald cast gambols to the sky,
I had been bocht in realms by,
Had I consentit to be sauld.
   Sir, let it never in toun be tald,
   That I sould be ane Yule's yald!

With gentle horse when I wald knyp,‡
Than is there laid on me ane whip,
To colleveris§ than maun I skip,
That scabbit are, has cruik and cauld.
   Sir, let it never in toun be tauld,
   That I sould be ane Yule's yald!

Though in the stall I be not clappit,
As coursers that in silk been trappit,

---

* The meaning of this line is, that at this season, why should not palfreys be proud when *gillets* (young horses) will be *schourd*, clipped, and *schroud*, covered or decorated.

† Yule's yald or *yaud*. Yald or yaud means a worn-out horse. It was a superstition amongst the peasantry, not yet wholly extinct, that whatever work was in hand should be finished before Yule, or, in later times, when Christmas ceased to be observed in Scotland, the New-year, otherwise nothing would go well with them throughout the incoming twelvemonth. The meaning of the poet, therefore, is, that the king should not let it be said that he was a *Yule's yaud*, an old horse that had not finished his task and been provided for, otherwise reward was not likely to come in the year following.

‡ Nip, or nibble grass.

§ Coal-avers, coal-horses; Laing explains it *coal-heavers.*

With ane new house I wald be happit,
Agains this Christmas for the cald.
   Sir, let it never in toun be tald,
   That I sould be ane Yule's yald!

Suppose I were an auld yaid aver,[*]
Shot furth oure cleuchs to pull the claver,[†]
And had the strength of all Stranaver,[‡]
I wald at Yule be housit and stall'd.
   Sir, let it never in toun be tald,
   That I sould be ane Yule's yald!

I am ane auld horse, as ye knaw,
That ever in dule does dring[§] and draw;
Great court horse puts me frae the staw,
To fang[||] the fog be frith and fald.
   Sir, let it never in toun be tald,
   That I sould be ane Yule's yald!

I have run lang furth in the field,
On pastures that are plain and peild;
I micht be now ta'en in for eild,
My beiks[¶] are spruning[**] hie and bauld.
   Sir, let it never in toun be tald,
   That I sould be ane Yule's yald!

My mane is turnit into white,
And thereof ye have all the wyte,[††]

---

[*] A worn-out *cart*-horse.   Sibbald explains it to mean simply a worn-out horse.

[†] Clover.   [‡] A district in Sutherlandshire.
[§] Drag.   [||] Endure.
[¶] Beiks, or boks—corner teeth.   [**] Rising.   [††] Blame.

When other horse had bran to bite
I gat but grass, nip if I wald.
   Sir, let it never in toun be tald,
   That I sould be ane Yule's yald!

I was never dautit into stable,
My life has been so miserable,
My hide to offer I am able
For evil shorn strae* that I reive wald.
   Sir, let it never in toun be tald,
   That I sould be ane Yule's yald!

And yet, suppose my thrift be thine,
Gif that I die your aucht within,
Let never the soutars have my skin,
With ugly gums to be knawin.
   Sir, let it never in toun be tald,
   That I sould be ane Yule's yald!

The court has done my courage cuil,
And made me ane foridden† mule ;
Yet, to wear trappours‡ at this Yule,
I wald be spurrit at every speld.§
   Sir, let it never in toun be tald,
   That I sould be ane Yule's yald!

RESPONSIO REGIS.

After our writings, Thesaurar,
Tak in this gray horse, auld Dunbar,

---

* Ill shorn straw.   † Over-ridden.
‡ Trappings.   § In every limb.

> Whilk in my aucht, with service true,
> In lyart changit is his hue ;
> Gar house him now agains this Yule,
> And busk him like ane bishop's mule :
> For, with my hand, I have indost
> To pay what ever his trappours cost.

This, it must be admitted, was a very dexterous and happy turn the poet gave to his often-repeated remonstrances and prayers on the subject of a benefice. The time, the approach of Yule, with its festivities, the dead of winter, and his unprovided-for condition, are all most humorously and pithily blended for the furtherance of his one great object. Nor are we to suppose that it altogether failed of its purpose. In the " Responsio Regis," or response of the king, we have the royal mandate that the petition should be complied with. That these lines were the genuine production of James IV. has been assumed by Chalmers, who gives them as such in his " Poetical Remains of the Scottish Kings," printed in 1824; and Mr Laing is so undecided in his opinion that he leaves the question to the reader. It appears to us, however, not to admit of a doubt, that they were written by Dunbar himself, as a jocular mode of exciting the king's attention.

Whether resulting from this, the sort of crowning supplication of the poet, no judgment can be hazarded ; but it is true that Dunbar had his pension augmented from £10 to £20, in 1507—the

" new eik " having been paid on the 12th November of that year; and on the 26th August 1510, a letter passed the " Privy Seal Register," enlarging his pension to £80 yearly. It is as follows :—

" A Lettre maid to Maister William Dunbar, of the gift of ane yeirly pensioun of iiij^{xxli.} to be pait to him at Mertymes and Witsonday, of the kingis cofferis, be the Thesaurar that now is, and beis for the tyme, or quhill he be promouit to benefice of j^{cli.} or abone . . .; with command to the said Thesaurar to pay the samyn, and to the audituris of chekker to allow it . . . At Edinbrugh, the xxvj day of August, the yere forsaid [anno regni Regis xxiij, 1510]."

This letter contains the same condition as to a benefice as that granted in 1500—differing, however, in the amount of income, the one being £4c, and the other £100. Whether Dunbar still continued to be as solicitous for a benefice after this second eik to his pension as he was before it, cannot be satisfactorily asserted. It appears to us that his numerous hints and addresses to the king on the subject of his neglected claims, were written before his pension was augmented to £80, as all of them, either expressly or by implication, refer to a state of poverty and destitution which he could not with propriety allege afterwards. If he could exist at all upon £10 a year, his position must have been vastly enhanced upon £80. We have therefore printed the whole of these appeals, as if

they had been written prior to the 26th August
1510.

THE QUEEN'S RECEPTION AT ABERDEEN.

Blithe Aberdeen, thou beriall* of all tounis,
   The lamp of beauty, bounty, and blitheness ;
Unto the heaven ascendit thy renoun is,
   Of virtue, wisdom, and of worthiness ;
   Hie noted is thy name of nobleness,
Into the coming of our lusty Queen,
   The wale of wealth, guid cheer, and merriness :
Be blithe and blissful, burgh of Aberdeen.

And first her met the burgess of the toun,
   Richly arrayit as become them to be,
Of whom they choysit four men of renoun,
   In gouns of velvet, young, able, and lustie,
   To bear the pall of velvet cramasie
Aboon her head, as the custom has been ;
   Great was the sound of the artillerie : †
Be blithe and blissful, burgh of Aberdeen.

Ane fair procession met her at the Port,
   In a cap of gold and silk, full pleasantlie,
Syne at her entry, with many fair disport,
   Receivit her on streets lustilie ;

------

* Brightest, from *beryl*, a precious stone.

† The practice in artillery was brought to considerable perfec-
tion in the reign of James IV., although, at the battle of Flodden, probably from the excess of chivalric feeling on his part, the
artillery which accompanied his army was not brought into play.

Where first the salutation honourably
Of the sweet Virgin, guidly micht be seen ;
  The sound of minstrels blawing to the skies :
Be blithe and blissful, burgh of Aberdeen.

And syne thou gart the Orient Kings three,
  Offer to Christ, with benign reverence,
Gold, sence,* myrrh, with all humilitie,
  Shewing him King, with most magnificence ;
  Syne how the angel, with sword of violence,
Furth of the joy of Paradise put clean
  Adam and Eve for inobedience :
Be blithe and blissful, burgh of Aberdeen.

And syne the Bruce, that ever was bold in stour,
  Thou gart as Roy come riding under croun,
Richt awful, strong, and large of portratour,†
  As noble, dreadful, michty champion .
  The noble Stewarts syne, of great renown,
Thou gart upspring, with branches new and green,
  Sae gloriously, while gladed‡ all the toun :
Be blithe and blissful, burgh of Aberdeen.

Syne came there four-and-twenty maidens ying,§
  All clad in green, of marvellous beautie,
With hair detressit,‖ as threads of gold did hing,
  With white hats all broident richt bravelie,
  Playing on timbrels, and singing richt sweetlie ;
That seemly sort, in order weel beseen,
  Did meet the Queen, her saluand¶ reverentlie :
Be blithe and blissful, burgh of Aberdeen.

---

* Incense.   † Visage.   ‡ Delighted.
§ Young.   ‖ Hanging in tresses.   ¶ Saluting.

The streets were all hung with tapestrie,*
　　Great was the press of people dwelt about,
And pleasant padyheanes† playit prethlie ;
　　The lieges all did to their lady lout,‡
　　Wha was convoyed with ane royal rout
Of great baroness' and lusty ladies sheen ;
　　Welcome, our Queen ! the commons gave ane shout :
Be blithe and blissful, burgh of Aberdeen.

At her coming great was the mirth and joy,
　　For at their Cross abundantly ran wine ;
Until her lodging the toun did her convoy ;
　　Her for to treat they set their whole ingine,§
　　Ane rich present they did to her propine ;
Ane costly cup that large thing wald contene,
　　Coverit and full of cunyeit‖ gold richt fine :
Be blithe and blissful, burgh of Aberdeen.

O potent Princess ! pleasant, and preclair,¶
　　Great cause thou has to thank this noble toun,
That for to do thee honour, did not spare
　　Their geir, riches, substance, and persoun,

---

* This practice was fashionable ; but it must not be presumed
that the streets were wholly decorated.   It was merely the stairs
of the principal street—which jutted out as in other old towns—
that were so decorated.   The magistrates enacted that the inhabitants were "to furnys and graith the staris of the forgait with
arress werk daily, as efferis, for the ressauing of our Souerane
Lady the Quene."

† Pageants.　　　　　　　‡ Bow.　　　　　§ Ingenuity.
‖ Coined.　　　　　　　　　　　　　　　　¶ Supereminent.

> Thee to receive on maist fair fashoun ;
> Thee for to please they sought all way and mean ;
>   Therefore, sae lang as queen thou bearis croun,
> Be thankful to this burgh of Aberdeen.

The visit of the queen to Aberdeen occurred in May 1511. Dunbar was no doubt in her suit, for the very minute, though poetical, and interesting account which he gives of her reception, could hardly have been penned by any one save an eye-witness. She was met by a procession, well conceived and executed, while pageants, music, and wine, kept the dense crowd in a joyous state of excitement. From Kennedy's " Annals of Aberdeen," we learn that great preparations had been made in April for the queen's coming, and that the " rich present they did to her propine," consisted of £200.

A GENERAL SATIRE.

> Devourit with dream, devising in my slum'er,
> How that this realm, with nobles out of num'er,
>   Guidit, providit, sae mony years has been ;
> And now sic hunger, sic cowarts, and sic cummer,
>   Within this land was never heard nor seen.
>
> Sic pride with prelates, so few till preach and pray,*
> Sic haunt of harlots with them, baith nicht and day,†

---

* In explanation, Hailes refers to the preface to Archbishop Hamilton's Catechism.

† Numerous illustrations of this could be given from the ecclesiastical history of the times.

That sould have aye God before their e'en,
So nice array, so strange to their abbey,
 Within this land was never heard nor seen.

So mony priests clad up in secular weed,
With blazing breasts casting their claiths on breed,*
 It is no need to tell of whom I mean,
So when the Psalms and Testament to read,
 Within this land was never heard nor seen.

So mony maisters, so mony gukkit clerks,†
So mony wasters, to God and all his werks,
 So fiery sparks of despite fro the spleen,‡
Sic losin sarkis§ so mony glengoir merks,
 Within this land was never heard nor seen.

Sae mony lordis, sae mony natural fules,
That better accordis to play them at the trules||

---

* Breadth.

† So many masters of arts, yet so many foolish clerks.

‡ From the heart, so overbearing.

§ Lord Hailes made out this to mean "so many lost shirts," but he was not satisfied with the explanation ; and Mr Laing contented himself with referring to an unexplained quotation from the Aberdeen Register, in Jamieson's Scottish Dictionary : "ane new sark *losin* with blak velvet." *Losin*, we apprehend, signifies *lozenged*—after the manner of glass windows in old times. "Sic losin sarks" would therefore mean "such *lozenged* shirts," (lozenged with black velvet, or otherwise,) which seems to have been the top of the fashion at the time—a fashion in some measure revived in our own day, for we have now shirts printed and wrought into various patterns, checked, *lozenged*, and flowered.

|| Jamieson says *trulis* is a kind of game. No doubt it is ; but of what kind? Hailes guessed it to be *Te-totum*, or the *cappy-*

Nor sees the dules* that commons does sustene,
New ta'en frae scules, sae mony anis and mules,†
Within this land was never heard nor seen.

Sae meikle treason, sae mony partial saws,‡
Sae little reason, to help the common cause,
   That all the laws are not set by ane prein ;
Sic fenyeit flaws,§ sae mony wastit waws,
   Within this land was never heard nor seen.

Sae mony thieves and murderers weel kend,
Sae great relevis of lords them to defend,
   Because they spend the pelf them between,
Sae few till wend ‖ this mischief, till amend,
   Within this land was never heard nor seen.

This to correct, they schoir ¶ with mony cracks,**
But little effect of spear or battle-ax,
   When courage lacks the corpse†† that sould mak
      keen ;
Sae mony jacks and brats on beggar's backs,
   Within this land was never heard nor seen.

Sic vaunt of woustours ‡‡ with hearts in sinful statures,
Sic brawlers, boasters, degenerate frae their natures,

---

hole ; and Jamieson thought it might be a game of the nature of
bowls. But may it not mean the pastime of *trindle-hoop*, so
much in use amongst boys, and even girls, of juvenile years ?

  * Sorrows.   † Asses and mules.
  ‡ Partial decisions, perhaps, as Hailes suggests.
  § Sic feigned objections.   ‖ Ward.   ¶ Threaten.
** Big words.   †† Body.   ‡‡ Boasters.

And sic segratours,* the puir men to prevene ;
Sae mony traitours, sae mony sebeatours,†
    Within this land was never heard nor seen.

Sae mony judges and lords now made of late,‡
Sae small refuges§ the puir man to debate ;
    Sae mony estate, for common weel sae quhene‖
Oure all the gait, sae mony theaves sae tait,¶
    Within this land was never heard nor seen.

Sae mony ane sentence retreitit,** for to win
Geir and acquaintance, or kindness of their kin ;
    They think no sin, where profit comes between ;
Sae mony ane gin,†† to haste them to the pin,‡‡
    Within this land was never heard nor seen.

Sic knaves and crakkars,§§ to play at carts and dice,
Sic halland-schekkars,‖‖ whilk at Cokkilbeis gryce,¶¶
    Are halden of price, when limmers* does convene;
Sic store of vice, sae mony wits unwise,
    Within this land were never heard nor seen.

Sae mony merchants, sae mony are mensworn,
Sic puir tenants, sic coursing even and morn,

---

* Forestallers.   † Abaters.
‡ The Lords of Daily Council, if this refers to such lords at
all, were instituted in 1503.
§ Hailes explains this, "such little quirks to lay the poor man
low. *Refuge*, in Cotgrave, is said to be *demurrer*."
‖ So few.   ¶ Active.   ** Reversed.
†† Device.   ‡‡ Point.   §§ Boasters.
‖‖ Hallanshakers, sturdy beggars.
¶¶ The feast of Cockelby's pig.
* Worthless persons.

Whilk slays the corn, and fruit that growis green ;
Sic skaith and scorn, sae mony paitlatts* worn,
　　Within this land was never heard nor seen.

Sae mony rakketts,† sae mony ketche-pillars,‡
Sic balls, sic knacketts,§ and sic tutivillars,‖
　　And sic evil-willars to speak of king and queen ;
Sic pudding-fillars, descending doun from millars,
　　Within this land was never heard nor seen.

Sic fartingaills¶ on flaggs** as fat as whals,
Facit like fules with hats that little avails ;††
　　And sic foul tails‡‡ to sweep the causey clean ;
The dust upskails, mony fillok§§ with fuk sails,
　　Within this land was never heard nor seen.

Sae mony ane Kittie, drest up with golden chenyie,
Sae few witty, that weel can fables fenyie,
　　With apill renieis‖‖ aye shawing her golden chain,
Of Satan's seinyie, sure sic an unsall menyie¶¶
　　Within this land was never heard nor seen.

---

* A woman's ruff.

† *Racket*, the bat which strikes the ball at tennis.

‡ Pillars in the game of *ketche* or *caiche*. This game is often mentioned in the Treasurer's Accounts.

§ From *nacquet*, in French, a lad who marks at tennis.

‖ Fiends.　　　　　　　¶ Farthingales, hoop-petticoats.

** Flanks.　　　　　　†† Hats of censurable form.

‡‡ Long trains. Acts of parliament were made to regulate these and sundry other sumptuary matters.

§§ A giddy young woman.

‖‖ "*Apill renye* is a rein, string, or necklace of beads."—*Hailes*.

¶¶ Of Satan's synod, or company, such an unhallowed number.

In the Bannatyne MS. this poem is ascribed to Dunbar, and in the Maitland, to Sir James Inglis. There was a person of this name, abbot of Culross. Of his fame as a poet, nothing more is known than what is conveyed in the following lines by Lyndsay—

> " Quha can say mair than Schir James Inglis sayis
> In ballatis, farsis, and in plesand playis ?
> Bot Culross haith his pen maid impotent."

That is, the benefice of Culross had cooled his pursuit of the Muse. The abbot, for some cause not mentioned, was slain on the 1st of March 1531, by the Baron of Tulialane and his followers. We have no doubt whatever that the Bannatyne MS. is correct. The verses bear all the characteristics of Dunbar's muse. From the line,

> " Sae mony judges and lordis *now made of late*,"

it is supposed that the poet must either refer to 1503, when the Lords of Daily Council were appointed, or 1532, when the College of Justice was instituted. If the latter, the verses could be written by neither Dunbar nor Inglis; and if to the former, they must have been written by Dunbar, it is said, soon after 1503. But this could hardly have been the case. Such a satire he would not be inclined to write, even although such national corruption had prevailed, so immediately after inditing the " Thistle and the Rose," and when the hopes and feelings of the people were in agreeable buoyancy. And because he speaks of evil-willers to " king and queen," it has been held that the poem was composed prior to the death of James IV. at Flodden, in 1513. It certainly would have been improper in Dunbar to have used that phrase, after the death of James, even figuratively. We are inclined, therefore, to think that the " general satire " was written in the lifetime of James—perhaps between 1510 and 1513. The expression, " now made of late," in reference to " so many judges and lords," would as obviously be improper, if the institution of the Lords of Council in 1503 was meant; but this can hardly be the true interpretation of " judges and lords," because the Lords of Council were *all lords* and *all judges*. The poet, on the contrary, seems to allude to some late addition to the judges, probably provincial; and the creation of a new batch of barons, or lords, all of whom would have jurisdiction in their own baronies. The only thing certain is, that the poem must have been written before the death of James, in 1513.

TO THE QUEEN-DOWAGER.

O lusty flow'r of youth, benign and sweet,
    Fresh bloom of beauty, blitheful, bricht, and sheen ;
Fair, lovesome lady, gentle, and discreet,
    Young breaking blosom, yet on the stalks green,

Delightsome lily, lusty for to be seen,
Be glad in heart, and expel heaviness ;
    Though bare of bliss, that ever so blithe has been,
Devoid languor, and live in lustiness.

Bricht sterne* at morrow that does the nicht hyn† chase,
    Of love's lightsome day the life and guide,
Let no dark cloud absent from us thy face,
    Nor let no sable from us thy beauty hide,
    That has no comfort where that we go or ride
But to behold the beam of thy brichtness ;
    Banish all baill,‡ and into bliss abide ;
Devoid languor, and live in lustiness.

Art thou pleasant, lusty, yourg and fair ;
    Full of all virtue and guid condition,
Richt noble of blood, richt wise and debonair,§
    Honourable, gentle, and faithful of renoun,
    Liberal, lovesome, and lusty persoun,
Why sould thou than let sadness thee oppress ?
    In heart be blithe and lay all dolour doun ;
Devoid languor, and leif in lustiness.

I me commend with all humilitie
    Unto thy beauty, blissful and benign,
To whom I am, and sall aye servant be,
    With steadfast heart, and faithful true meaning,
    Unto the death, without ere departing ;
For whose sake I sall my pen address,
    Sangis to mak for thy recomforting,
That thou may live in joy and lustiness

---

* Star.   † Back.   ‡ Sorrow.   § Gentle, easy.

O fair, sweet blossom, now in beauty's flow'r,
    Unfadit baith of colour and virtue,
Thy noble lord that died has done devoir,
    Fade not with weeping thy visage fair of hue ;
    O lovesome, lusty lady, wise and true,
Cast out all care, and comfort do incress,
    Exile all sighing, on thy servant rew !*
Devoid all languor, and live in lustiness.

This poem, in Bannatyne's MS., has no title, nor is the author mentioned. But there can be no doubt that the verses are by Dunbar, and Mr Laing did right in addressing them to the queen-dowager, who was only twenty-five years of age when the king was slain at Flodden, 9th September 1513.

ANE ORISON WHEN THE GOVERNOUR PAST INTO FRANCE.

Thou that in heaven, for our salvation,
    Made justice, mercy, and piety to agree ;
And Gabriel sent with salutation
    On to the Maid of maist humilitie ;
    And made Thy Son to tak humanitie,
For our demerits to be of Mary born ;
    Have of us pity, and our protector be !
For, but † Thy help, this Kynrick ‡ is forlorn.

---

* Banish all sorrow, and on thy servant have pity.
† Without.   ‡ Kingdom.

O hie supernal Father of sapience,
  Whilk of Thy virtue does every folly chase,
Ane spark of Thy hie excellent prudence,
  Give us, that nouther wit nor reason has !
  In whase hearts no prudence can tak place,
Example, nor experience of beforn ;*
  To us, sinners, ane drop send of Thy grace !
For, but Thy help, our Kynrick is forlorn.

We are so beastly, dull, and ignorant,
  Our rudeness may not lichtly be correctit ;
But Thou, that art of mercy militant,
  Thy vengeance seize on us to sin subjectit,
  And gar Thy justice be with reuth† connectit ;
For quite away so wild frae us is worn,
  And in folly we are so far infectit,
That, but Thy help, this Kynrick is forlorn.

Thou, that on rude‡ us ransomit and redeemit,
  Rew§ on our sin, before your sicht decidit ;
Spare our trespass, whilk may not be expreemit,‖
  For breif¶ of justice, for we may not abide it,
  Help this puir realm, in parties all dividit !
Us succour send, that wore the crown of thorn,
  That with the gift of grace it may be guidit !
For, but thy help, this Kynrick is forlorn.

Lord ! hold Thy hand, that strucken has so sore ;
  Have of us pity, after our punition ;**

---

* Before.	† Pity.	‡ The cross.
§ Pity.		‖ Expressed.
¶ Writ.		** Punishing.

And,give us grace Thee for to grieve no more,
    And gar us mend with penance and contrition ;
    And to Thy vengeance mak non addition,
As Thou that of michtis may to morn,*
    Fra care to comfort Thou mak restitution :
For, but Thy help, this Kynrick is forlorn.

There is little difficulty in fixing the date of this poem. The queen acted as regent for some time after the death of the king, but the country was dissatisfied, and John, Duke of Albany, who resided chiefly in France, on his estates there, was chosen as regent. He arrived in Scotland on the 15th of May 1515, and was gladly welcomed by the people. Party divisions, however, ran so high, that Angus—who married the widowed queen, at the head of the English influence, in opposition to the governor and the national cause—even although his policy had been carried out with a stronger hand, could hardly have expected success. But he bent so far to the storm that he three times abandoned his trust, and retired to France, in the hope, perhaps, that his absence would shew the necessity of greater union. His first return to France occurred in 1517 ; and that the poet's " Orison " was composed on this occasion there can be no doubt. Dunbar must have been deeply affected by the death of the king, and the distracted state into which the country was thrown by its party dissen-

* To-morrow.

sions; and his anguish must have been heightened by the manner in which his patroness, the dowager queen, whom he had so often celebrated for her beauty and virtues, joined in these cabals, and degraded herself by her conduct otherwise. At the time he wrote his " Orison," no one could see how the kingdom was to be kept from falling to pieces by its own dissensions, even although there had been no danger of invasion from England.

How long Dunbar survived this period there is no means of ascertaining. On the 14th May 1513, the Treasurer's Accounts shew that he was paid lvjs. to account of his pension. From August 8 1513, to June 1515, these accounts have not been preserved, and his name does not occur in them at a subsequent date. But that he was living in 1517, is proved by the foregoing poem; and it has been surmised that his pension may have been transferred to some other department of the public revenue, or on the breaking up of the court, consequent on the death of James, the queen may have conferred a benefice upon him. All this is probable, although it is curious that there is no trace of such a thing; but it is to be hoped he was not neglected. His address " To the Queen-Dowager" shews that he had no misgivings on the score of provision for old age—

" To whom I am, and sall aye servant be,
    With steadfast heart, and faithful true meaning."

In such circumstances, it is not improbable that the
following verses—conveying a fine moral—were
amongst the last of his productions.   At all events
they come in very appropriately here.

———

OF LOVE, ERDLY* AND DIVINE.

Now coolit is Dame Venus' brand ;
True love's fire is aye kindiland,
And I begin to understand,
In fenyet† love what folly been ;
    Now comis age where youth has been,
    And true love rises fro the spleen.‡

While§ Venus' fire be dead and cauld,
True love's fire never burnis bauld ;
So as the tae love waxes auld,
The other does increase mair keen :
    Now comis age where youth has been,
    And true love rises fro the spleen.

No man has courage for to write,
What pleasance is in love perfite,
That has in fenyet love delight :
Their kindness is so contrar clean :
    Now comis age where youth has been,
    And true love rises fro the spleen.

Full weel is him that may imprent,
Or ony ways his heart consent,

———

* Earthly.   † Feigned.   ‡ From the heart.   § Until

To turn to true love his intent,
And still the quarrel to sustein :
  Now comis age where youth has been,
  And true love rises fro the spleen.

I have experience by mysell ;
In love's court anis did I dwell ;
But where I of a joy could tell,
I could of trouble tell fifteen :
  Now comis age where youth has been,
  And true love rises fro the spleen.

Before, where that I was in dread,
Now have I comfort for to speed ;
Where I had maugré to my meed,*
I trust reward and thanks between :
  Now comis age where youth has been,
  And true love rises fro the spleen.

Where love was wont me to displease,
Now find I into love great ease ;
Where I had danger and disease,
My breast all comfort does contein :
  Now comis age where youth has been,
  And true love rises fro the spleen.

Where I was hurt with jealousy,
And wald no lover were but I ;
Now where I love I wald all wy†
As weel as I lovit I ween :

---

* " Where, instead of being rewarded, I met with discourage-
ment."—*Hailes.*
† Every person.

Now comis age where youth has been,
And true love rises fro the spleen.

Before where I durst not for shame
My love descrive,* nor tell her name,
Now think I worship were and fame,
To all the warld that it were seen :
    Now comis age where youth has been,
    And true love rises fro the spleen.

Before no wicht I did complein,
So did her danger me derene ;†
And now I set not by a bean
Her beauty, nor her twa fair e'en :
    Now comis age where youth has been,
    And true love rises fro the spleen.

I have a love fairer of face,
Whom in no danger may have place,
Whilk will me guerdon give and grace,
And mercy aye when I me mein :‡
    Now comis age where youth has been,
    And true love rises fro the spleen.

Unquiet I do no thing nor sane,§
Nor wares a lovis thought in vain ;
I sall be as weel lovit again,
There may no jangler me prevene :||
    Now comis age where youth has been,
    And true love rises fro the spleen.

---

* Describe.   † Disorder.   ‡ Lament.
§ Say. || Prevent.

Anc love so fair, so gude, so sweet,
So rich, so rewthful* and discrect,
And for the kind of man so meet,
Never more sall be, nor yet has been :
   Now comis age where youth has been,
   And true love riscs fro the spleen.

Is none so true a love as He,
That for true love of us did die ;
He sould be lovit again, think me,
That wald so fain our love obtein :
   Now comis age where youth has been,
   And true love riscs fro the spleen.

Is none but† the grace of God I wis.
That can in youth consider this ;
This false, deceiving warld's bliss,
So guides man in flouris grecn :
   Now comis age where youth has becn,
   And true love rises fro thc spleen.

That Dunbar was well advanced in life when
this contrast between "love earthly and divine"
was written, can hardly be doubted. Almost all
his productions were prompted by some reality of
circumstance or circumstances which communicated
a corresponding reality of influence on his feelings.
And here we have him exponing the salutary change
which age had effected upon himself, in withdraw-
ing his affections from the things of the world to
those of heaven.

   * So full of pity.   † Without.

Dunbar differed from most of his contemporaries of whose works we have any knowledge, in this, that his muse laid hold of the things around him, rather than soar, as others did, upon abstract or mere sentimental flights. No doubt he so far yielded to the prevailing taste for allegory, and in so doing shewed that his fancy was fully equal to whatever task he undertook. His "Golden Targe," the most purely ideal of all his writings, will ever remain a golden proof of the power with which his genius could revel in the regions of fancy. But the great body of his writings—at least what portion of them has been preserved—hold him up as a man of the times—one who, though a poet, had an eye to what was going on around him—ready to applaud what he deemed right, or denounce, satirise, and ridicule what he conceived to be wrong. Nor did he spare the high more than the low. Even the king, his patron, did not escape his censure—

> " I say nocht, sir, you to reprcif!
> *But doubtless I gae richt near hand it*"—

while the barons, the judges, the clergy, all came in for a share of his keen and cutting reproof. In this way he has left a living picture of the domestic state of Scotland, and especially of its courtly habits and pastimes during the reign of James IV., with which no historian of the times should be unacquainted. In this respect he may well be styled

the Burns of his day. His didactic powers are
great, and his humour and sarcasm, notwithstanding
the antiquated idiom in which his thoughts are
conceived and expressed, are of the highest description, while his sense of the ridiculous is beyond
that of any poet we are acquainted with. As Burns
has done in later times, Dunbar mixed himself
up, in numerous and amusing instances, with his
subject, as in "The Visitation of St Francis," the
"Dance in the Queen's Chalmer," the "Petition
of the Auld Grey Horse, Dunbar," &c. Nor did
he refrain from those admissions of his own delin-
quency which have given to Burns a peculiar
position amongst modern poets. Much might
be said as to the character of both the author
and his poems, for there can be no doubt that his
writings had no small influence on the times.
Though himself in holy orders, no one could be
more effective in exposing and denouncing the
foul hypocrisy of the priesthood, the effect of which
upon public opinion must have been thoroughly
awakening. It is remarkable that he should have
escaped censure; but this may to some extent be
accounted for by his position at court.

It is deeply to be regretted that so little, or
rather nothing, is known of the latter days of
one whose writings reflect so much lustre on the
early literature of his country. His death is guessed
by Mr Laing to have occurred about 1520, and
this only by inference. In a poem by Lynd-

say of the mount, written in 1530, the author
says :—

> " Or *quha can now* the warkis counterfait
>   Off *Kennedie* with termes aureait ?
>   Or off *Dunbar*, quha language had at large,
>   As may be seen intill his 'Golden Targe.'"

" From these words," says Mr Laing, " and from
the manner in which Lyndsay laments Bishop
Douglas, who died in 1522, it may be inferred that
our author's decease was previous to that of the
prelate; wherefore we cannot greatly err in sup-
posing that he died about the year 1520, when he
had attained at least sixty years of age." The
probability is, if we may judge from the strain of
various of his poems, that he was considerably
older.

There is an address by " The Lords of Scotland
to the Governor in France," urging his speedy
return in consequence of the distracted state of
the country. It also says—

> " Grit weir and wandrecht * hes bene us amang,
>   Sen thy departing, and yit approchis mair;
>   Thy tardatioun caussis us to think lang,
>   For of thy cuming we haif richt grit dispair."

This refers to the inroads of the English, and shews
that the verses could not have been written before

* Misfortune.

1519 or 1520. They have been attributed to Dunbar, and are printed in Mr Laing's edition; upon the strength of which, apparently, the writer of the article "Dunbar," in the last issue of the "Encyclopædia Britannica," comes to the conclusion that nothing is certain as to the poet's death, but that he died before 1530. This may be true; but if the assertion rests upon the idea that Dunbar wrote the address referred to in 1519 or 1520, it seems utterly fallacious, for it must be obvious that there is nothing of Dunbar in the verses except a very weak and prosaic imitation of his style.

Amongst the pieces known to be truly Dunbar's, besides "The Tua Maryit Wemen and the Wedo," of which some account is given at the commencement of this volume, we have found it necessary to exclude "The Tod and the Lamb," a poem composed upon some intrigue, now unknown, of his royal patron. It has no claim to particular merit, and is exceptional both in point of subject and language. Also an address "To the Quene," beginning—

> " Madame, your men said thai wald ryd,
> And latt this Fastrennis evin ower slyd."

It is meant as a joke, but the wit of the thing is lost to modern readers, because of the obscurity of the allusions. Enough, however, is obvious to shew that ladies, including queens, in the poet's time, were much less squeamish than in our day; other-

wise such verses could not have been presented,
even by way of amusement, to any lady whatever.
Nor was Queen Margaret alone in this respect.
Her contemporaries of England, from whence she
came, were equally free from restraint. It may be
said, and truly enough, no doubt, as the statistics
of Scotland and the Divorce Courts of England
shew, that since Dunbar's day we have only made
a reformation in *words*, not *deeds*; still even that
little is a step towards accomplishing more solid
results.

Amongst the poems attributed to Dunbar, we
can only admit of "A General Satyre," which,
endorsed by the authority of Bannatyne, as well as
from its own internal evidence, cannot be questioned; and his address "To the Quene-Dowager,"
which also plainly proclaims its author. "The
Droichis Part of the Play: an Interlude," may or
may not be Dunbar's. We have his own authority
for saying that he did write plays as well as ballads,
but there is nothing to guide us in attributing this
particular piece to the poet, and it may have
undergone many emendations by others, as was the
case with all such pieces, every performer eking or
paring as he thought proper. Besides, it is extremely indelicate. "A Brash of Wowing" bears
the unquestionable stamp of Dunbar's genius, but
it is inadmissible. "The Freiris of Berwik," though
a well-told story, does not at all bear the same
stamp, albeit Pinkerton thought so.

Such anonymous pieces, of acknowledged merit, might be collected into a volume or volumes by themselves, with suggestions as to the probable authors, but conjectures of this kind ought not to be carried further.

THE FLYTING OF DUNBAR AND KENNEDY.

DUNBAR TO SIR JOHN THE ROSS.

Sir John the Ross, ane thing there is compilit
  In general be *Kennedy* and *Quinting*,*
Whilk has them self above the sternis stylit;
  But had they made of menace any minting
  In special, sic strife sould rise but † stinting;
Howbeit with boast their breasts were as bendit
As Lucifer, that frae the heaven descendit,
  Hell sould not hide their harnes frae harmis hinting.‡

The erd sould trem'le, the firmament sould shake,
  And all the air in venomous sudden stink,
And all the devils in hell for redour§ quake,
  To hear what J sould write, with pen and ink;
  For and I flyte some sege‖ for shame sould sink,
The sea sould brim, the moon sould thole eclippis,

---

* What this compilation, in common between Kennedy and
Quintine, was, is not known. For *Quintine Schaw*, see " La-
ment for the Makars," p. 248.   † Without.
  ‡ Being laid hold of.   § Terror.   ‖ Men.

Rockis sould rive, the warld sould hald no grippis,
    Sae loud of care the common bell sould clink.

But wonder laith were I to be ane bard,
    Flyting to use, for greatly I eschame ;*
For it is nowther winning nor reward,
    But tinsal baith of honour and of fame,
    Increase sorrow, slander, and evil name;
Yet micht they be sae bald, in their backbiting,
To gar me rhyme, and raise the fiend with Flyting,
    And through all countries, and kinriks † them pro-
       claim.

KENNEDY TO DUNBAR.

Dirtin Dunbar, whom on blawis thou thy boast ?
    Pretending thee to write sic scaldit skrowis ;‡
Ramowd rebald,§ thou fall doun at the roast,
    My laureat‖ letters at thee and I lowis ;
    Mandrag,¶ mymmerkin,** made maister but in
       mowis,††
Thrice-shield trumpir,‡‡ with ane thread-bare gown,
Say, "Deo mercy," or I cry thee down,
    And leave thy rhyming, rebald, and thy rowis.§§

---

* I would be ashamed.
† Kingdoms.
‡ Disconnected scrolls.
§ Raw-mouthed vagabond.
‖ Laurelled.
¶ Mandrake.
** Expressive of diminutive stature. As already shewn, Dunbar probably was of low stature.
†† Made master of arts but in jest.
‡‡ Thrice-hidden deceiver.   §§ Rolls, or writings.

Dreid, dirtfast dearch,* that thou has disobeyit
  My cousin Quintin and my Commissar ;
Fantastic fule, trust weel thou sall be fleyit,†
  Ignorant elf, ape, owl irregular,
  Skaldit skaitbird,‡ and common skamelar,§
Wanthriven funling, that Nature made ane yrle,‖
Baith John the Ross and thou sall squeel and skirl,
  And ever I hear ocht of your making mair.

Here I put silence to thee in all partis,
  Obey, and cease the play that thou pretendis ;
Weak walidrag,¶ and varlot of the cartis,**
  See soon thou mak my Commissar amendis,
  And let him lay six leeches on thy lendis,††
Meekly in recompensing of thy scorn,
Or thou sall ban the time that thou was born,
  For Kennedy to thee this schedule sendis.

DUNBAR TO KENNEDY.

Ersche brybour‡‡ bard, vile beggar with thy brattis,§§
Carrybald crawdoun‖‖ Kennedy, coward of kind,

---

* Dwarf.
† Put to flight.
‡ Arctic gull.
§ Frequenter of the shambles.
‖ Dwarf.
¶ Useless person.
** Cards.
†† Loins.
‡‡ Irish thief.
§§ Children. This is another evidence of what we adduced as to this poetic encounter having taken place after Kennedy had acquired Glentig, and settled down in marriage as a small proprietor.
‖‖ Scurvy coward.

Evil farit and dryit, as Danesmen on the rattis,[*]
   Like as the gleds had on thy gule[†] snout dined;
   Mismade monster, ilk moon out of thy mind,
Renounce, rebald, thy rhyming, thou but royis,[‡]
   Thy trechour [§] tongue has tane ane Hieland
     strynd;[||]
Ane Lawland —— wald mak a better noise.

Raven, raggit rook, and full of ribaldrie,
   Scarth [¶] frae scorpion, scaldit [**] in scurrilitie,
I see thee halting in thy harlotrie,
   And in to other science no thing slie,
   Of every virtue void, as men may sie;
Quitclaim clergy, and cleek to thee ane club,[††]
   Ane bard blasphemer, in bribery aye to be;
For wit and wisdom ane wisp frae thee may rub.

Thou speiris, dastard, gif I daur with thee fecht?
   Ye dagone [‡‡] dowbart,[§§] thereof have thou no
     doubt!.
Whenever we meet thereto, my hand I hecht[||||]
   To red thy ribald rhyming with a rout:
   Through all Britain it sall be blawin out,
How that thou, poisonit pelour,[¶¶] gat thy paiks;

---

[*] Supposed to allude to the practice, in Denmark, of exposing the dead bodies of criminals upon wheels raised above the ground.

[†] Red, a term in heraldry.   [‡] Raves.
[§] Deceitful.   [||] Strain.   [¶] Puny creature.
[**] Scalded.   [††] Take a staff and go a-begging.
[‡‡] A minced oath still in use, especially among boys.
[§§] Dull fellow.   [||||] Promise.   [¶¶] Thief

With ane dog leech I shape to 'gar thee shout,
And nouthir to thee tak knife, sword, nor aix.

Thou crop and root of traitors treasonable,
  The father and mother of murder and mischief,
Deceitful tyrant, with serpent's tongue, unstable ;
  Cuckold, crawdoun* cowart, and common thief ;
  Thou purpos't for to undo our Lordis chief
In Paisley, with ane poison that was fell,†
  For whilk, bribour, yet sall thou thole a brief ;‡
Pelour, on thee I sall it prove mysell.

Though I wald lie, thy frawart§ phisnomy
  Does manifest thy malice to all men ;
Fy ! traitor thief ; fy ! glengoir loun, fy ! fy !
  Fy ! fiendly front, far fouler than ane fen,
  My friendis thou reprovit with thy pen ?
Thou leis, traitor ! whilk 1 sall on thee preif,
  Suppose thy heid were armit times ten,
Thou sall recryat,‖ or thy croun sall cleif.

Or thou durst move thy mind malicious,
  Thou saw the sail above my heid up draw ;

---

* Base.

† This refers to some attempt upon the king's life, prior, perhaps, to his accession to the throne. It is not likely that
Kennedy was personally concerned in this affair, otherwise
Dunbar would not have wounded his feelings by alluding to it ;
but the Kennedies were on the side of James III., and the party
with whom they coalesced may have made some unrecorded
effort to destroy the heir to the throne, who was associated with
the disaffected party.   ‡ Undergo a legal charge.

§ Contrary.   ‖ Retract.

But Eolus' full wud, and Neptunus,
 Mirk and moonless, was wet with wind and waw,[*]
 And mony hundred mile hyne cowd[†] us blaw
By Holland, Zeland, Zetland, and Northway coast,
 In desert place where we were famist aw ;[‡]
Yet come I hame, false bard, to lay thy boast.

Thou calls thee Rethory, with thy golden lips :
 Na, glouring, gaping fule, thou art beguiled,
Thou art but Glunscoch,[§] with thy gilten hips,
 That for thy lounry mony a leech has filed ;
 Wan-visaged widdiefu', out of thy wit gane wild,
Laithly and lousy, as lathand[||] as ane leek,
 Sen thou with worship wald sae fain be stiled,
Hail, sovereign senior ! thy —— hangs through thy
  breck.

Forworthin [¶] fule, of all the warld refuse,
 What ferly is though thou rejoice to flyte,
Sic eloquence as they in Erschery use,
 In sic is set thy thrawart appetite ;
 Thou has full little feile[**] of fair indite :
I tak on me ane pair of Lothian hips
 Sall fairer English mak, and mair perfite,
Than thou can blabber with thy Carrick lips.

Better thou gangs to lead ane dog to skomer,[††]
 Pynit[‡‡] pyk-purse pelour,[§§] than with thy maister
  pingle.[||||]

---

[*] Wave.   [†] Hence begoud. [‡] All famished.
[§] Glunscoch, a sour-looking person. [||] Thin.
[¶] Execrable. [**] Knowledge. [††] Vomit.
[‡‡] Shrivelled. [§§] Pick-purse thief. [||||] Contend.

Thou lay full prideless in the pease this somer,
    And fain at even for to bring hame ane single,*
    Syne rub it at ane other auld wife's ingle ;
But now, in winter, for puirtith thou art traikit ;†
    Thou has nae breek to let thy —— gingle ;
    Beg thee ane cloak, for, Bard, thou sall go nakit.

Lean larber,‡ lounger, baith lousy in lisk and lunyie ;§
    Fy ! skoldert ‖ skin, thou art but skyre¶ and
        skrumple ; **
For he that roasted Lawrence had thy grunyie,††
    And he that hid St John's e'en with ane wimple,‡‡
    And he that dang St Augustine with ane rumple,§§
Thy foul front had, and he that Bartilmo‖‖ flaid ;¶¶
    The gallows gapes after thy graceless gruntle,*
As thou wald for ane haggis, hungry gled.

Commerwald craudoun,† nae man counts thee ane
    kerse,‡
    Sweer, swappit swanky,§ swine-keeper aye for swaits ;‖

---

* Handful of gleaned corn.   † Fatigued.
‡ Ghost, or worn-out person.   § Loin.
‖ Scorched.   ¶ Indurated skin.   ** Wrinkle.
†† Countenance.   ‡‡ Fold.   §§ Tail.
‖‖ Bartholomew.   ¶¶ Skinned.   * Snout.
† Henpecked coward.
‡ It is difficult to guess the poet's meaning. *Kerses* means
cresses, but we can hardly fancy such an expression as "na man
counts thee ane *cress.*" He might be too barren to be esteemed
a *carse*, a rich, level piece of land. Or it may be ane *curse*. It
is, perhaps, but too common an expression to say, "I do not
give, or care, a *curse* for thee !"
§ An unwilling, drawn-together, lean person.   ‖ Small beer.

Thy Commissar, Quintine, bids thee cum kiss his ——,
   He loves not sic ane forlane loun of laits ;*
   He says, Thou scaffs† and begs mair beir and aits
Nor ony cripple in Carrick land about ;
   Other puir beggars and thou are at debates,
Decrepit carlings on Kennedy cries out.

Matter enough I have, I bid not fenyie,‡
   Though thou, foul trumpour,§ thus upon me leid ;
Corrupt carrion, hie sall 1 cry thy senyie ; ||
   Thinks thou not how thou come in great need,
   Greeting in Galloway, like to ane gallow breed,¶
Raming and rolping,** begging ky and ox ;
   I saw thee there, in to thy watheman's weed,††
Whilk was not worth ane pair of auld grey fox.

Ersche cateran, with thy polk, breek and rilling,‡‡
   Thou and thy queen, as greedy gleds, ye gang
With polks to mill, and begs baith meal and shilling ;
   There is but lice and lang nails you amang :
   Foul haggerbald,§§ for hens thus will ye hang,
Thou has ane perilous face to play with lambs ;
   Ane thousand kids, were they in faulds full strang,
Thy limmerful|||| look wald fley¶¶ them and their dams.

---

* Importunate loun, without manners.
† Collects.   ‡ Feign.   § Deceiver.
|| Progeny.   ¶ Race.
** Incessant repetition, and crying with a hoarse voice.
†† Wanderer's weed.
‡‡ Shoes made of undressed hides.
§§ Coarse feeder. |||| Scoundrelly.   ¶¶ Frighten.

In till ane glen thou has, out of repair,
  Ane laithly* lodge that was the lipper men's ;
With thee ane soutar's wife, of bliss as bare,
  And like twa stalkers steals in cocks and hens,
  Thou plucks the poultry, and she pulls off the pens ;
All Carrick cries, God gif this dowsy† was drown'd ;
  And when thou hears ane goose cry in the glens,
Thou thinks it sweeter than sacred bell of sound.

Thou Lazarus, thou laithly, lean tramort,‡
  To all the world thou may example be ;
To look upon thy grizzly, piteous port,
  For hideous, howe, and houkit is thine e'e ;
  Thy cheek bane bare, and blackenit is thy blee ;§
Thy chop, thy choll,‖ gars men for to live chaste ;
  Thy gane¶ it gars us think that we maun die :
I conjure thee, thou hungert Hieland ghaist.

The larbar** looks of thy lang, lean crag,
  Thy puir pynit†† throat, peelit and out of ply,‡‡
Thy skolderit§§ skin, hued like ane saffron bag,
  Gars men despite‖‖ their flesh, thou spirit of Gy :
  Fy ! flendly front ; fy ! tyke's face, fy ! fy !
Aye lounging, like ane loikman¶¶ on ane ledder ;
  Thy ghaistly look fleys folk that pass thee by,
Like to ane stark thief glouring in ane tedder.

---

* Loathsome.   † Dull, stupid person.
‡ Dead body.   § Complexion.   ‖ Jowls, or jaws.
¶ Face.   ** Ghastly.   †† Wasted.
‡‡ Condition.   §§ Scorched.   ‖‖ Dislike.
¶¶ Public executioner.

X

Nyse nagus,* nipcaik,† with thy shoulders narrow,
　　Thou lookis lousy, loun of lounis aw ;
Hard hurcheon,‡ hirpling, hippit as ane harrow,
　　Thy rigbane§ rattles, and thy ribs on raw,‖
　　Thy haunches hurkles,¶ with hukebanes harth and
　　　　haw,**
Thy laithly limbs are lean as ony trees ;
　　Obey, thief bard, or I sall break thy gaw,
Foul carrybald, cry mercy on thy knees.

Thou puir, hippit,†† ugly averill,‡‡
　　With hurkling banes, houking through thy hide,
Reistit and crynit§§ as hangit man on hill,
　　And oft beswakkit‖‖ with ane oure hie tide,
　　Whilk brewis meikle barret¶¶ to thy bride ;
Her care is all to cleanse thy cabroch hows,*
　　Where thou lies saucy in saffron, back and side,
Powderit with primrose, savouring all with clows.†

Forworthin wirling,‡ I warn thee it is wittin,§
　　How, skittering skarth,‖ thou has the hurl behind ;

---

* This epithet is difficult to explain. *Nyse* means to pommel,
or beat down; and nagus may be from *Neccus*, Old Nick. Nyse
nagus would thus signify *fighting Devil*.
　† One who eats small portions of a cake stealthily.
　‡ Hedgehog.　　　　　　　　§ Backbone.
　‖ Row.　　　　　　　　　　¶ Hurkles, draw together.
　** With haunchbones sharp and hollow.
　†† Pained in the back or loins.
　‡‡ The diminutive of *aver*, a horse of burden.
　§§ Dried and shrunk.　　　‖‖ Immersed.
　¶¶ Contention.　　　　　　* Lean, meagre limbs.
　† Cloves.　　　　　　　　‡ Unworthy, rickety person.
　§ Known.　　　　　　　　‖ Cormorant.

Wan, wraigling* wasp, mae worms has thow beshittin,
　Nor there is gers on grund, or leave on lind ;†
　Though thou did first sic folly to me find,
Thou sall again with mae witness than I ;
　Thy gulsoch gane‡ does on thy back it bind,
Thy hosting hips lets never thy hose gang dry.

Thou held the burgh lang with ane borrowit goun,
　And ane caprowsy§ barkit all with sweat,
And when the lads saw thee sae like a loun,
　They bickerit thee with mony a bae and bleet :‖
　Now up-a-land thou lives on rubbit wheat,
Oft for ane cause thy buirdclaith ¶ needs no spreading,
　For thou has nowther for to drink nor eat,
But like ane beardless bard that had no bedding.

Strait Gibbon's air,** that never ourestred†† ane horse,
　Blae, barefoot bairn, in bare time was thou born ;
Thou brings the Carrick clay to Edinburgh corse,
　Upon thy botings,‡‡ hobbling, hard as horn ;
　Strae wisps hings out, where that the watts§§ are worn :
Come thou again to scar us with thy straes,

---

　* Unsteady in motion.　　　† Lime-tree.
　‡ Jaundiced face.　　　　　§ Short cloak with a hood.
　‖ The cry of a calf and sheep.　¶ Tablecloth.
　** Strait Gibbon occurs in the Treasurer's accounts. He has,
6th July 1503, 14s. given him by the king's command. Nothing
is known of him; but he was probably some odd character about
the Court.　　　　　　†† Rode.　　　　　　‡‡ Buskins.
　§§ *Wattis*, or *wats*. No explanation of this word has been
given by any of the annotators, nor is it to be found in Jamieson;
but, from the context, it probably means that protection between

We sall gar scail our scules, all thee to scorn,
And stane thee up the causey where thou gaes.

Of Edinburgh, the boys as bees out thrawis,*
   And cries out aye, Here comes our ain queer clerk !
Than flees thou, like ane howlet chased with crawis,
   While all the bitches at thy botings bark :
   Than carlings cries, Keep curches in the merk,†
Our gallows gapes ; lo ! where ane graceless gaes.‡
   Ane other says, I see him want ane sark,
I red you, cummer, tak in your linen claes.

Than rins thou down the gait, with gild§ of boys,
   And all the toun tykes hinging on thy heels ;
Of lads and louns there rises sic ane noise,
   While runsys‖ rins away with cart and wheels,
   And cadger avers¶ casts baith coals and creels,
For rerd** of thee, and rattling of thy buits ;
   Fishwives cries, Fy ! and casts down skillis and skeils :††
Some clashes thee, some clods thee on the cuits.

Loun-like Mahoun, be boun me to obey,
   Thief, or in grief mischief sall thee betide ;

---

the back and the burden which porters in our own day sometimes wear. Kennedy is represented, very grotesquely, as bringing his Carrick clay to Edinburgh, hobbling in his half-boots,
hard as horn, and straw wisps hanging out where the *wattis*
should be, namely, below his back-load of clay. In other words,
his *wats*, so called because they kept the body dry, were made
of straw, in place of the usual material, whatever that might be.

  * Out-thrangs.   † Pay attention to your head-dress.
  ‡ One without grace.   § Clamour.   ‖ Cart-horses.
  ¶ Horses.   ** Noise.
  †† Baskets and scales.

Cry grace, tyke's face, or I thee chase and slay ;
   Owl, rair and yowl, I sall defoul thy pride ;
   Peilit gled, baith fed and bred of bitch's side,
And like ane tyke, purspyk, what man sets by thee !
   Forflittin,* bittin, beshittin, barkit hide,
Climb ledder, file tedder, foul edder, I defy thee !

Mauch mutton,† byle buttoun,‡ peelit glutton, heir to
   Hilhouse,§
   Rank beggar, oyster-dregar, foul fleggar,‖ in the flet ;¶
Chittir-lilling,** ruch-rilling,†† lick-shilling in the mill-
   house ;
   Bard rehator,‡‡ thief of nature, false traitor, fiend's get ;
   Filling of tauch,§§ rak sauch,‖‖ cry crauch,¶¶ thou
   art oure set ;
Mutton-driver, girnall-river,* yad swyvar,† foul fell thee ;
   Heretic, lunatic, purspyk, carling's pet,
Rotten crok,‡ dirtin cok, cry cok,§ or 1 sall quell thee.

---

  * Severely scolded.   † Full of maggots.
  ‡ This phrase is not understood. Byle, in old Swedish, sig-
nifies a habitation.   § See Kennedy's reply, p. 338.
  ‖ A proclaimer of falsehoods.
  ¶ Flet, one story of a house, a mat of straw.
  ** Jamieson supposes this opprobrious term to be the same as
chitterlin, signifying, in English, the intestines.
  †† Shoes made of undressed hides.
  ‡‡ Uncertain.   §§ Tallow.
  ‖‖ Rak sauch, a willow or stick for twisting ropes.
  ¶¶ *Cry crauch*, acknowledge you are beat.
   * Granary reaver.   † An old horse-driver.
  ‡ Crok, an old ewe.
  § Cry cok, admit you are vanquished.

KENNEDY TO DUNBAR.

Dachan* devil's son, and dragon dispiteous,
   Abiromis birth, and bred with Belial ;
Wud war wolf, worm, and scorpion venomous,
   Lucifer's lad, foul fiend's face infernal ;
   Saracen, syphareit,† fra sancts celestial,
Put I not silence to thee, shepherd knave,
And thou of new begins to rhyme and rave,
   Thou sall be made blate, blear e'et, bestial.

How thy forbears come, I have a feil,‡
   At Cockburnspath,§ the writ maks me war,
Generate betuix ane she bear and a deil ;
   Sae was he call't Dewlbear, and not Dunbar :
   This Dewlbear, generate of a mare of Mar,
Was Corspatrick, Earl of March ; and, be illusion,
The first that ever put Scotland to confusion,
   Was that false traitor, hardly say I daur.

When Bruce and Baliol differed for the croun,
   Scots lords could not obey the English laws ;
This Corspatrick betrayit Berwick toun,
   And slew seven thousand Scotsmen within thae waws ;
   The battle syne of Spottismuir he gart cause,
And come with Edward Langshanks to the field,
Where twelve thousand true Scottismen were killed,
   And Wallace chased, as the Chronicle shaws.

---

  * A dwarfish creature.   † Pertaining to a cipher.
  ‡ Knowledge.
  § An ancient fortress belonging to the Dunbars, which com-
manded the ravine where the Peese-Bridge is now built.

Scottish lords, chieftains, he gart hald and chessone,*
  In firmance † fast, while ‡ all the field was done,
Within Dunbar, that auld spelunk § of treason;
  Sae English tykes in Scotland was abone.
  Than spulyeit ‖ they the Haly Stane of Scone,
The Cross of Halyrudhouse, and other jowells.
He burns in hell, body, banes, and bowels,
  This Corspatrick that Scotland has undone.

Wallace gart cry ane counsel in to Perth,
  And callit Corspatrick, traitor, be his style;
That damnit dragon drew him in diserth, ¶
  And said, he kenned but Wallace, King in Kyle: **
  Out of Dunbar that thief he made exile
Unto Edward, and English ground again:
Tigers, serpents, and taids will remain
  In Dunbar walls, tods, wolfs, and beasts vile.

Nae fowls of effect amangis thae binks ††
  Bigs, nor abides, for no thing that may be;
Thae stanes of treason, as the brunstane stinks.
  Dewlbear's mother, casten in be the sea,
  The wariet ‡‡ apple of the forbidden tree,
That Adam eat, when he tint Paradise,

---

* *Chessoun*, accuse.   † Prison.   ‡ Until.
§ Den.   ‖ Carried off.
¶ Desertion; he deserted the national cause or opposed it.
** The fact that the Earl of Dunbar refused to attend the summons, contemptuously saying he owed no fealty to " Wallace, King of Kyle," is borne out by the Tower Records. Patrick, Earl of Dunbar, was Edward's captain, " citra mare Scotiæ," on the south side of the Forth, in November 1297.
†† Benches or seats, or hives.   ‡‡ Accursed.

She eat, invenomit, like a cockatrice,
  Syne married with the Devil for dignitie.

Yet of new treason I can tell thee tales,
  That comes on nicht in vision in my sleep ;
Archibald Dunbar betrayed the house of Hailes,*
  Because the young lord had Dunbar to keep ;
  Pretending through that to their rowms to creep,†
Richt cruelly his castle he pursuit,
Brocht him furth bounden, and the place rescuit,‡
  Set him in fetters in ane dungeon deep.

It were against baith nature and guid reason,
  That Dewlbear's bairns were true to God or man ;
Whilks were baith gotten, born, and bred with treason,
  Belzebub's oys, and curst Corspatrick's clan :
  Thou was priestit and ordaint be Sathan
For to be born to do thy kin defame,
And gar me shaw thy antecessors' shame ;
  Thy kin that lives may wary§ thee and ban.

Sen thou on me thus, limmer, leis an trattles,‖
  And finds sentence foundit of envy,
Thy elders' banes ilk nicht rises and rattles,
  And on thy corpse, Vengeance, vengeance ! they cry.

---

* Pitscottie relates that, about 1446, Archibald Dunbar sur-
prised in the night, and took the castle of Hailes, in Hadding-
tonshire, putting all to the sword. He was afterwards taken by
James Douglas, into whose will he put himself and estates.
  † To get possession of Hailes's property.
  ‡ Rather captured the place.
  § Be aware.   ‖ Tells tales.

Thou art the cause they may not rest nor lie;
Thou says for them few psalters, psalms, or creeds,
But gars me tell their trentals* and misdeeds,
   And their auld sin with new shame certify.

Insensuate sow, cease false Eustace Air!
   And knaw, keen scald, I hald of Alathia,
And cause me not the cause lang to declare
   Of thy curst kin, Dewlbear and his Allia:
   Come to the Cross, on knees, and mak a cria;
Confess thy crime, hald Kennedy thy King,
And with ane hawthorn scourge thyself and ding;
   Thus dree thy penance with " Deliquisti quia."

Pass to thy Commissar, and be confest,
 .Cour before him on knees, and come in will;
And syne gar Stobo† for thy life protest;
   Renounce thy rhymes, baith ban and burn thy bill;
   Heave to the heaven thy hands, and hald thee still:
Do thou not thus, brigand, thou sall be brint,
With pike, fire, tar, gun powder, and lint,
   On Arthur's Seat, or on ane higher hill.

I perambulate of Parnasso the mountain,
   Inspirit with Mercury frae his golden sphere;
And dulcely‡ drank of eloquence the fountain,
   When it was purifit with frost, and flowit clear:
   And thou come, fule! in March or Februeir,
There till ane pool, and drank the puddock rude,§

---

* Service of thirty masses for the dead.
† See " Lament for the Makars," p. 248.
‡ Sweetly.   § Spawn.

That gars thee rhyme in to thy terms glude, *
　　And blabbers that noyis † men's ears to hear.

Thou loves nane Erische, elf, I understand,
　　But it sould be all true Scottish men's leid;
It was the guid language of this land,
　　And Scota it caust to multiply and spread,
　　While Corspatrick, that we of treason read,
Thy forefather, made Ersche and Erschemen thin;
Through his treason brocht English rumples ‡ in,
　　So wald thy self, micht thou to him succeed.

Ignorant fule! in to thy mows and mocks, §
　　It may be verifit thy wit is thin;
Where thou writes Danesmen driet on the racks,
　　Danesmen of Denmark are of the King's kin.
　　The wit thou sould have had was casten in
Even at thine ——, backward, with ane staff flung.
Herefore, false harlot, hurcheon, hald thy tongue:
　　Dewlbear! thou deaves the Devil, thy eme, with din.

Where as thou said, I stole hens and lambs,
　　I let thee wit, I have lands, store, and stacks,
Thou wald be fain to gnaw, lad, with thy gams,
　　Under my buird, smoch ‖ banes behind dogs' backs;
　　Thou has ane toom purse, I have steeds and tacks,
Thou tint culter, I have culter and pleuch;
For substance and geir thou has a widdy teuch
　　On Mont Falcon, ¶ about thy craig to rax.

---

* Dirty, or miry.　　　　　　　　　　† Annoys.
‡ Ungainly, disorderly persons.
§ Jests and jeers.　　　　　　　　　‖ Smoked, or broken.
¶ Montfauçon, in the suburbs of Paris, where criminals were

And yet Mont Falcon gallows is oure fair,
  For to be filit with sic ane fruitless face;
Come hame, and hing on our gallows of Air,
  To erd thee under it I sall purchase grace;
  To eat thy flesh the dogs sall have no space,
The ravens sall rive nàe thing but thy tongue ruits,
For thou sic malice of thy maister moots,*
  It is weel set that thou sic barret† brace.

Small finance amang thy friends thou beggit,
  To staunch thy storne,‡ with haly mulds§ thou lost;
Thou salliet to get a douker‖ for to dreg it,
  It lies closit in ane clout on Norway coast:
  Sic rewll¶ gars thee be servit with cauld roast,
And sit onsoupit** oft beyond the sea,††
Crying at doors, "Caritas amore Dei,"
  Barefoot, breekless, and all in duds updost.‡‡

Dewlbear has nocht ado with ane Dunbar,
  The Earl of Murray§§ bore that surname richt,

---

executed. Dunbar was in Paris, it is to be presumed, at the time.   * Indicates.   † Trouble.
  ‡ Store.   § Relics.   ‖ Diver.
  ¶ Mishaps.   ** Without soup.
†† This corroborates the statement of Dunbar, that he had frequently been abroad on the King's errands.
‡‡ Dressed.
§§ "Lady Agnes Randolph, the heroic daughter of the noble Regent, having married Patrick, ninth Earl of Dunbar and March, on the death of her brother, 1347, assumed the title of Countess of Moray, and her husband, in her right, that of Earl, and entered into possession of the extensive property of the family, the Earldom of Murray."—*Wood's Peerage.* The Earl died

That ever true and constant to the King's grace war,
   And of that kin cam Dunbar of Westfield knicht;*
   That succession is hardy, wise, and wicht,
And hes nae thing ado now with thee, deil:
But Dewlbear is thy kin, and kens thee weel,
   And has in hell for thee anè chalmer dicht.

Curst croapand† craw, I sall gar crop thy tongue,
   And thou sall cry "Cor mundum," on thy knees;
Duerch,‡ I sall ding thee, while thou baith —— and ——,
   And thou sall lick thy lips, and swear thou leis:
   I sall degrade thee, graceless, of thy 'grees;
Scale§ thee for scorn, and scar thee of the scule,
Gar round thy head transform thee as a fule,
   And syne with treason trone‖ thee on the trees.

Raw mowit rebald, rannegald rehatour,¶
   My lineage and forbears were aye leal:
It comes thee of kind to be ane traitor,
   To ride on nicht, to rug, to reif, to steal.
   When thou puts poison to me, I appeal
Thee in that part, and prove it on thy person;
Claim not to clergy, for I defy thee, garson,
   Thou sall buy it dear, with me, duerch, and thou deal.

---

about 1369, leaving two sons, *George*, tenth Earl of Dunbar, and *John*, Earl of Murray. The latter title became extinct during the fifteenth century.

  * Sir Alexander Dunbar, Sheriff of Murray, son of James Earl of Murray, by Isabel, daughter of Sir William Innes, was the founder of this branch of the Dunbar family.

  † Croaking.   ‡ Dwarf.
  § Leave the place.   ‖ Put thyself in the pillory.
  ¶ Raw-mouthed, worthless, impudent, faithless fellow.

In England, owl, sould be thy habitation,
  Homage to Edward Langshanks made thy kin,
In Dunbar received him thy false nation,*
  They sould be exiled Scotland mair and myn.†
  Ane stark gallows, ane widdy, and ane pin,
The head point of thy elders' arms ane;
Written in poesie abone "Hang Dunbar,
  Quarter and draw, and mak that surname thin."

I am the King's bluid,‡ his true special clerk,§
  That never yet imagin't his offence,
Constant in mind, in thocht, word and werk,
  Only dependent upon his excellence;
  Trusting to have of his magnificence
Guerdon, reward, and benefice bedene;
When that the ravens sall rive out baith thy een,
  And on the racks sall be thy residence.

Frae Ettrick Forrest furthward to Dumfries,
  Thou beggit with ane pardon in all kirks,
Collops, cruds, meal, groats, gryce,‖ and geese,
  And under nicht whiles thou stole staigs and stirks.
  Because that Scotland of thy begging irks,
Thou shapes in France to be a knicht of the field;

---

* Or race.
† Great and small.
‡ His claim to "the King's bluid" was well-founded—his grandfather, James, son of "Sir Gilbert Kennedy of Dunure and Agnes Maxwell his wife," having married the Princess Mary Stewart, daughter of Robert III.
§ He was Depute-Baillie of Carrick.　　　　‖ Pigs.

Thou has thy clamschells,* and thy burdoun† keild,‡
   Unhonest ways all, wolroun,§ that thou wirks.

Thou may not pass Mont Bernard for wild beasts,
   Nor win through Mont Savoy for the snaw;
Mont Nicholas, Mont Godard thee arreists,
   Sic bees of brigand blinds them with ane blaw.
   In Paris with thy maister, Burreau,‖
Abide, and be his 'prentice near the bank,
And help to hang, the piece for half ane frank,
   And, at the last, thy self maun thole the law.

Halting harlot, the devil a guid thou hes!
   For fault of puissance, pelour, thou maun pack thee;
Thou drank thy thrift,¶ and als** wadset thy claes,
   There is nae lord in service wald tak thee.
   Ane pack of flea-skins, finance for to mak thee,
Thou sall receive, in Danskyn,†† of my tailyie;‡‡
With " De profundis" set thee, and that felyie,§§
   And I sall send the black Devil for to back thee.

Into the Katherine‖‖ thou made ane foul kahute,¶¶
   For thou —— her, doun frae stem to steir;*

---

* Scallop shells worn by pilgrims.
† Burdoun, pilgrim's staff.
‡ Chalked with ruddle—"cauk and keil."
§ Useless fellow.   ‖ The hangman.
¶ Savings.   ** Also.   †† Denmark.
‡‡ *Tailyie* here evidently means *tailor*. A pack of flea-skins
he would receive from Kennedy's tailor, by way of raising money.
The humour is excellent.   §§ Fail.
‖‖ The vessel in which Dunbar is supposed to have sailed
in 1491.   ¶¶ A ship
  * From the bow to the helm.

Upon her sides was seen that thou could shoot,
  The dirt cleaves till her tows this twenty year:
  The firmament nor firth was never clear,
While thou, devil's birth, Dewlbear, was on the sea;
The sauls had sunken through the sin of thee,
  Were not the people made sic great prayeir.

When that the ship was saynit,* and under sail,
  Foul brow,† in hole thou purpost for to pass,
Thou shot, and was not sicker of thy tail,
  Be —— the steir, the compass, and the glass ;
  The skipper bad, gar land thee at the Bass :
Thou spewit, and cast out mony a laithly lump,
Faster nor all the mariners could pump ;
  And yet thy wame is waur nor ever it was.

Had they been so providit of shot of gun,
  Be men of weir but‡ peril they had past ;
As thou was lous, and ready of thy bun,
  They micht hae ta'en nac tollum§ at the last ;
  For thou wald cook ane cartful at the cast ;
There is no ship that thee will now receive ;
Thou filit faster nor fifteensum micht lave,
  And mirit them with thy muck to the midmast.

Through England, thief, and tak thee to thy foot,
  And boun to have with thee ane false botwand ;||
Ane horse merchell ¶ thou call thee at the mute,**

* Blessed.   † Synonymous with "ill-brow."   ‡ Without.
§ Toll, or impost. || Baton, or rod of power.
¶ The groom in charge of horses. The "Ingliss hors Mars-
chael" often occurs in the Treasurer's Accounts : 1498, April 22,
"Item, giffin be the Kingis command to the Ingliss hors Mer-
chael, to hele the broun geldin, 18s."   ** The meeting.

And with that craft convoy thee through the land :
Be nae thing arch, tak ferely on hand,*
Happen thou to be hangit in Northumber,
Than all thy kin are weel quit of thy cumber,
    For that maun be thy doom, I understand.

Hie sovereign Lord ! let never this sinful sot
    Do shame, frae hame, unto your nation !
That never nane, sic ane, be callit Scot,
    Ane rotten crok, lous of the dock, there doun.
    Frae honest folk devoid this laithly loun :
On some desert, where there is no repair,
For filing and infecting of the air,
    Cause carry this cankert, corruptit carrioun.

Thou was conceivit in the great ecclips,
    Ane maister made be great Mercurius ;
Na, hald again, nor poo† is at thy hips,
    Infortunate, foul, false, and furious,
    Evil shriven, wanthriven, not clean nor curious ;
Ane myting,‡ fule of flyting, the flirdom maist like,
Ane crabbit, scabbit, evil-faced messan tike ;
    Ane ――――, but wit, skirvit and injurious.

Great in the glaiks, guid Maister William guks,§
    Oure imperfite in poetry or in prose,
All close under clud of nicht thou cuks.
    Rhymes thou of me, of Rethory the Rose,

---

* Be not waggish, but take truly on hand.
† Coupling.   ‡ Mittane, probably a hawk.
§ Great in self-conceited folly, guid Maister William exults.

Lunatic. limmer, luschbald,* louse thy hose,
That I may twitch thy tone with tribulation,
In recompensing of thy conspiration,
  Or turs thee out of Scotland : tak thy choice.

Ane benefice wha wald give sic ane beast,
  But gif† it were to jingle Judas' bells ;
Tak thee ane fiddle, or a flute, to jeist,
  Undocht,‡ thou art ordanit to nocht else !
  Thy cloutit cloak, thy scrip, and thy clamshells,
Cleek on thy cross, and fair on into France,
And come thou never again but ane mischance ;
  The fiend fare with thee, forward oure the fells.§

---

  * Lazy fellow.   † Unless.   ‡ Puny creature.

§ Mr Laing is of opinion that this and the previous verse belonged to Kennedy's first reply, and that they have been transposed. His reason for thinking so is, that the "epithet" of "Rethory the Rose," noticed by Dunbar as having been assumed by Kennedy, occurs in them, and that he speaks of *tursing* Dunbar out of Scotland, that he may fare on into France, although the poet is understood to have been in Paris at the time. There is some appearance of reason in this; yet the first reply of Kennedy will not admit of these two verses. It is complete in itself. Besides, "The Flyting," be it observed, begins with "Dunbar to Sir John the Ross," in which he speaks of "ane thing" compiled by Kennedy and Quintin. We have not that "ane thing" in the correspondence, and the probability is, that in it Kennedy first assumed the epithet of "Rethory the Rose," and his allusion to it again in his second epistle comes in naturally enough; and this is rendered still more probable by the words of Dunbar —"Thou callis thee Rethory the Rose *with thy goldin lippis*." Now, Kennedy says nothing about his "goldin lippis" in his second reply, whatever he may have done in that "ane thing" which we have not seen. Nor is it inconsistent to speak of tursing Dunbar out of Scotland that he might sojourn in France,

Canker't Cain, tryit trowane,* tutevillous,†
   Marmadin,‡ mymmerkin,§ monster of all men,
I sall gar bak thee to the Laird of Hilhouse,||
   To swallow thee in stead of a pullit hen.¶
   Foumart, fazart,** foster't in filth and fen,
Foul felon, flend†† fule, upon thy phisnom fy!
Thy dok aye drips of dirt, and will not dry,
   To toom thy tone it wald tire carlings ten.

Conspirator, cursit cockatrice, hell's ka,
   Turk, trumpour, traitor, tyrant intemperat ;

---

because his absence in Paris was only temporary. But whether the verses are transposed or not, there is assuredly no room for them in the first reply of Kennedy.

  * Perhaps *truant ;* but *trow*, in Orkney, signifies a *devil*.

  † Fiend.   ‡ Myrmidon.

  § Apparently from *mim*, demure, affected, conveying the idea of diminutiveness.

  || From the allusion of Dunbar to this personage, "peelit glutton, heir to Hilhouse," and Kennedy's backing the poet to the same party, that he might be devoured like a chicken, it would appear that "the Laird of Hilhouse" was famous as a gourmand. Like *Dugald Dalgetty*, he seems to have been a campaigner, and knew how to store provender. At all events, a party styled "the Laird of Hilhouss," frequently occurs in the Treasurer's Accounts. In 1494, he receives cloth for a gown, and doublet and hose. In 1496, September 11—"Item, giffin to the Lard of Hilhouss, to remane upon the artailyery, [artillery,] and to helpe to gyde it, L.3." Again, in 1497, July 31, —"Item, to the Lard of Hilhouss, for his expenss cummand hame for Mons, 9s." This alludes to the celebrated piece of ordnance, *Mons Meg*. His name is mentioned for the last time in 1501, December 8—"Item, to the Lard of Hilhouss, that com furth of Ingland from the Lordis, be the Kingis command, 28s." That this was the party meant in "The Flyting," there can be little doubt.   ¶ Chicken.   ** Dastard.   †† Fled.

Thou ireful atter-cap, Pilot apostata,
  Judas, Jow,* juggler, Lollard laureat ;
  Saracen, Symonite, proud Pagan pronunceat,
Mahomet, mansworn, rebald abominable,
Devil, damnit dog, in evil unsatiable,
  With Gog and Magog great glorificat.

Nero thy nevoy, Golias thy grandsire,
  Pharaoh thy father, Egipya thy dame,
Dewlbear, thir are the causes that I conspire,
  Termigantis temptis and Vespasius thy eme ;
  Belzebub, thy full brother, will claim
To be thy heir, and Cayphas thy fector ;
Pluto the head of thy kin, and protector,
  To lead thee to hell, of licht day and leme.†

Herod thy other eme, and great Ægeus,
  Marcian, Mahomet, and Maxentius,
Thy true kinsmen, Antenor and Æneas.
  Throp thy near niece, and austere Olibrius,‡
  Puttidew, Baal, and Eyobulus ;
Thir friends are the flow'r of thy four branches,
Steering the pots of hell, and never stenches,
  Doubt not, Dewlbear, Tu es Diabolus.

Dewlbear, thy spear of weir, but fear, thou yield,
  Hangit, mangit, eddir stangit, stryndit stultorum,
To me, maist hie KENNEDIE, and flee the field,
  Pickit, wickit, stickit, convickit, lamp Lollardorum.

---

* Jew.   † Shining.
‡ *Austerne Olibrius* figures in the metrical legend of St Margaret, preserved in the Auchinleck library.

Defamit, shamit, blamit, Primus Paganorum.
Out ! out ! I shout, upon thut snout that snivels,—
Tale-teller, rebeller, indweller with the devils,
Spink, sink with stink ad Tartara Termagorum.

As "The Flyting" is a joint production, we print it apart from the body of Dunbar's poems. It was certainly a curious conceit to fall foul of each other in so scurrilous a manner; yet it may have been suggested not only by the invectives of certain ancient writers, and the practice of the Athenian women, but of the Edinburgh fish-wives—who retain the reputation of having been capital scolds in former times. The Highland bards used to indulge in similar sarcasms; and it would appear to have been a pretty general as well as early mode of exercising the intellectual powers. It is wonderful that any one could have conceived that the two poets were in earnest; yet such is the fact, for Mr Laing gravely gives Lord Hailes the credit of having been the first to *conjecture* that such was not the fact; and Dr Irving thought his opinion was "rendered *somewhat plausible* by the correspondent history of the altercation which subsisted between Luigi Pulci and Matteo Franco. Although, for the amusement of their readers, those authors loaded each other with 'the grossest abuse, yet the intimacy of their friendship is said to have continued without interruption." It is evident that Dunbar and Kennedy were on

the best terms. His affectionate reference to him in
the "Lament for the Makars" is a proof of this:—

> " Gud Maister Walter Kennedy,
>   In poynt of dede lyis veraly,
>   Gret reuth it were that so suld be:
>   Timor mortis conturbat me."

The object seems wholly to have been who should
excel in banter or scurrility, and they are so
well matched that it is difficult to say which
carries away the palm. The scolding—and its
coarseness must be overlooked, as in no way out-
raging the jocular freedom of the times—is interesting, as furnishing not only certain incidents in
the history of both poets, that might otherwise
have been overlooked, but individual pictures of
each other. Making due allowance for exaggera-
tion, it would seem that Kennedy was tall and
gaunt, and the portrait of him coming to Edinburgh with his Carrick clay for sale, hobbling in
buskins, hard as horn, with straw wisps dang-
ling from under his load, is extremely picturesque.
Nor is Kennedy less humorous with his dwarf of
an opponent. His liberality in offering to supply
the little man, after he had " drank his thrift "
with " ane pak of flea-skynis," which he would
receive from his tailor in Danskyn, is extremely
good; and if all failed—

> " I sall gar bak thee to the Laird of Hilhouss,
>   To swelly thee in steid of ane pullit hen."

Had Dunbar not been really of small stature, this eminently sarcastic allusion would have passed without effect.

"The Flyting" affords a graphic specimen of the range of the Scottish language for broad humour and scurrility. Indeed, the meaning of many of the terms can now be only guessed at; and we look in vain for them in any glossary or dictionary of the Scottish language. We have endeavoured to supply this deficiency in as far as possible; still there are a few terms which may be inadequately explained, and perhaps one or two not at all. "The Flyting" was printed in 1508, in the lifetime of Dunbar, and no doubt became very popular. It has had many imitators, the most successful of whom were Alexander Montgomerie, author of "The Cherrie and the Slae," and·Sir Patrick Hume of Polwart.

Of Walter Kennedy, some particulars will be found at p. 259.

The End.